The

Truthful

Story

The
Truthful
Story

HELEN STINE

Text copyright © 2016 Helen Stine

Published by Cardinal Press
www.truthfulstory.com
www.helenstine.com

ISBN: 978-0-9978530-0-1 (hardcover)
ISBN: 978-0-9978530-1-8 (paperback)
ISBN: 978-0-9978530-2-5 (eBook)
ISBN: 978-0-9978530-3-2 (audiobook)
Library of Congress Control Number: 2016911823

Cover design by Rebecca Lown
Cover illustration by Debra Lill
Map illustration by Elisabeth Alba
Interior design and page composition by Kevin Callahan/ BNGO Books
Printed in the United States of America

*To Nannie, who believed anything is possible,
and to Mama and Daddy,
who proved the enduring power of second chances.*

Here is my secret. It is very simple:
It is only with the heart one can see rightly;
what is essential is invisible to the eye.

—Antoine de Saint-Exupéry, *The Little Prince*

Chapter One

October 31, 1965

THE LADY IN THE FLOWERY DRESS said they found Nannie in the oyster bed just around the first bend in the Toogoodoo River, not far from the wharf on Gibson Island. I strained to hear more of what they were saying out on the porch, holding my breath, flattening myself against the heavy, opened door so they wouldn't see me, its big crystal doorknob digging into my back. Swirls of their cigarette smoke crept through the tiny holes in the screen, like little ghosts trying to get in. The wispy spirits lingered in the sunrays that hit hard on the wooden floors this time of day.

Daduh said afternoons were best for cleaning the front of the house because that's when all the dust showed up good. "It's cheatin' to clean there in the mornin'," she'd say. The morning was for the kitchen, where she'd open all the windows first thing when she arrived every Saturday, which was cleaning day at Nannie's house. Daduh would peer out the window over the deep

1

porcelain sink while she worked and make low chuckling noises as she watched Nannie out on the wharf. Up early in her fishing clothes and green-striped hat, Nannie would dart back and forth between the fishing rod sticking up in the air on one end of the wharf and the net full of chicken necks dangling off the other.

Nannie kept the chicken necks and other strange bait in a freezer that sat on a wooden plank in the little smokehouse next to the wharf. She said once upon a time the smokehouse used to be for hanging meat to cure, but now that it had electricity, it was used for other things like storing bait and fishing poles and different kinds of nets. It had a mostly dirt floor and giant hooks hanging from the ceiling, and it smelled like something was rotten. It was dark, too, despite the one grimy lightbulb sticking out of the wall by the door. Every time Nannie pulled the string, the light would flicker twice, and several mice who lived under the wooden planks would race out of sight. I was afraid of the smokehouse, but Nannie wasn't.

She'd get excited preparing for what she called her "dual expedition" — fishing and crabbing at the same time. She could do both, bragging, "Not everyone has the patience or the know-how." She showed me how to fix the fishing rod with her good-luck silver feather tied to the tip and how to arrange the chicken necks in the crabbing net so when you dropped it in the water, it would fan out perfect. She was right — you could catch a lot of crabs that way, and the silver feather all but guaranteed a full string of speckled sea trout. On those lucky mornings, she and Daduh could clean fish and cook and pick crabs faster than anybody, laughing the whole time. I never knew why they were laughing exactly, but I liked listening to them, absorbed in their secret, happy world.

Now at the screen door, I heard the funeral people shushing each other out on the porch. I jumped as Daduh touched me on the shoulder. "Genevieve! You come on with me to the kitchen right now and leave those grown-ups be." Daduh had a voice like a man, and when she whispered, it sounded like she was growling— but not in a mean way.

I sat on the kitchen stool, tucking my feet around the chrome legs and picking at a triangle-shaped tear in the green vinyl seat that had been there as long as I could remember. Daduh rolled the dough for cheese biscuits and handed me the little drinking glass we used to cut them out. When Nannie made these for supper, my job was to tear out the circles carefully and lay them out for baking. Now it was Daduh making the biscuits.

"When will they leave?" I was hoping Daduh could answer my question because I didn't like all these people here in Nannie's house talking about her and whispering on the porch. I watched Daduh's hands, brown on one side and white on the other, move through another ball of dough in the bowl. They reminded me of the doll I had that kind of looked like Daduh with her black hair tied in a checkered handkerchief, wearing her cleaning day dress and apron. When you turned her upside down, she was a white girl with blond hair tied up in satin ribbons and wearing a long, beautiful gown. Daduh wiped her hands on her apron, which was not her usual one. This one was purple and frilly and didn't really suit her at all, but it was her favorite color and the one Nannie had given her for her birthday.

I was getting angrier by the minute. No one seemed to be in charge. Mama was upstairs with her two sisters. She couldn't stop crying. Her mother was dead, and there was nothing I could do to help. Tipping the stool on its front legs, I leaned forward against the kitchen counter, raising myself up to the window that over- looked the driveway. My brothers were out by the tractor shed, shuffling their feet in the dirt with their heads down, trying to figure out what to do next and halfheartedly playing with Aunt

Alicia's four dogs. The dogs seemed confused, sensing this was not like our regular Sunday visit to Gibson Island. James, who was now eight, knelt down to nestle his face into the neck of the big, gentle German shepherd, Lady, who followed him everywhere. Markie and Dodi, the smart-as-a-whip poodles, danced around and nipped at the hem of six-year-old Ryan's blue jeans as he ran in figure eights to taunt them; and Teddy, the black, skinny terrier with no hair and a long, tan nose, paced nervously on his tiny toenails, glancing back at the house every few seconds. Then, with a burst of energy, like they often got, James and Ryan and the four dogs took off running down the long island road together, probably remembering Aunt Alicia had asked James to check the mail that had been sitting in the mailbox for the last two days.

Behind me, the back door of the kitchen opened to the river. I heard the motor of a small boat fading and the plopping sound of waves as they slapped against the wharf's wooden stilts. I could see my father standing on the wharf, wearing his brown dress pants with the pleats down the front and a short-sleeved white shirt. He tucked his Winston cigarettes back into his shirt pocket and then lit one, holding it between two fingers while at the same time clamping his thumb and little finger together to pick the loose flecks of tobacco off his lips and tongue. He looked lonely out there by himself, staring out at that bend in the river. There was nothing he could do to help, either.

Aunt Alicia was in her office, the biggest room in the house, and which used to be the Gibson family dining room. From the kitchen, Daduh and I could see her through the wide screen door at the end of the hallway, sitting at the head of the long black walnut table. I always thought it was odd to have screen doors on the inside of the house. Nannie said it helped keep mosquitoes and gnats out but allowed the river breezes to move through the rooms. Aunt Alicia had left the gathering of funeral people out on the porch, retreating to her office to rummage through papers stacked on top of the table, the sideboard, and the floor. You could barely see the top of her gray head behind the piles. Nannie said it was a shame the dining room had been turned into Alicia's "office" because, once upon a time, that room had been where all the family celebrations happened, and besides, Aunt Alicia wasn't a bookkeeper anymore and didn't even need an office. Aunt Alicia was Nannie's older sister, and they were as opposite as could be. Nannie would shake her head every time we walked past Aunt Alicia's bedroom. That's because there were hundreds of *Detective* and *National Geographic* magazines stacked in every corner of the room up to the windowsills. She'd whisper to me, "She's my sister, and maybe I shouldn't say this"—Nannie always said that part before she said what she needed to say—"but I can't, for the life of me, figure out how anyone in their right mind can collect such piles of papers and magazines for no good reason—taking up space meant for people. It's no wonder she forgets where she puts things all the time—everything's buried ten feet under!"

Although she called her sister a pack rat and acted like she was complaining, deep down, Nannie really didn't care one way or the other. She was too busy having a good time doing things like making cheese biscuits and fishing and crabbing and telling her "truthful stories." Truthful stories were special stories about things most people didn't believe in or weren't interested in, but Nannie worked them into lots of conversations, and I loved them.

Daduh stirred the okra soup simmering on the stove. It was strange to have Daduh there on a Sunday because that was a big church day for her and her family. We had driven by her house lots of times on Sunday mornings, and we'd see Daduh in her big white hat all dressed up, walking with her family trailing behind her to Hope Baptist Church in Meggett. That was a long walk for someone as old as Daduh, but they did it every Sunday, and if it got too hot, they'd sing "Down by the Riverside" to get their minds off themselves.

Daduh didn't have a husband, but that didn't stop her from bragging plenty about her big family. She had four children and two grandchildren who were all grown and lived close by. Nannie said Daduh had her youngest daughter kind of late in life and was partial to her over the others. People called her Lumpy, and she stayed right there in the same house with Daduh. Nannie said even though Lumpy was older than my mother, Lumpy couldn't live by herself because she had learning problems. Lumpy didn't make friends too easy, but Nannie said she must have made at least one or two friends because she managed to give Daduh her only two grandchildren, Gloria and Jackson.

There was big news for Daduh last year, when Gloria surprised everyone with her own baby, so now Daduh had a great-grand-son, too. Even though he was a surprise, Daduh said that baby boy was sure a miracle because he was born in her house on the day her own mama died years ago. "And the best part of all," Daduh would say proudly, "it was the Lord's birthday!" Daduh loved the Lord's birthday. At Christmastime, she would always go around saying, "Happy birthday, Jesus. Thank you, Lord!" instead of "merry Christmas" like everyone else.

This was probably the first Sunday Daduh had missed church ever. But this wasn't an ordinary day. We both watched through the kitchen window as the old Griffin sisters and the other funeral people stood around in the driveway, still talking in low voices.

"Just relax. They're gettin' ready to go," Daduh assured me. Her dark skin was glistening from the heat of the stove, and she looked more tired than usual. She had black raccoon circles under her eyes, and her hair looked like a mess of little gray wires. She tilted her head down to meet my eyes. "Look here at me." Her finger lifted my chin. "It's proper for people to come and pay their respects to the family after a funeral."

"But the funeral was yesterday, and they keep comin'."

"Your Nannie had a lot of friends, and your mama and Miss Marjorie and Miss Vivian has friends out here still, ever since a long time ago when they was little girls."

I wished they would hurry up and get in their cars and leave, but they kept running their mouths. I jumped down from the stool, startling Daduh. "Genevieve Donovan! Child, don't you . . . you get back here!" Daduh demanded in her growly whisper, but I was too fast. I ran down the warped floorboards of the dark hallway past Aunt Alicia in the dining room office, heading toward the front of the house and the long porch. But right before I burst through that screen door, I felt a wall of cold air, and as it swept through me, I stopped at the foot of the stairs, resting my hand on the wide curve of the banister. I could smell the sweet oiliness of the wood Daduh had shined up so carefully. The sad, muffled female voices of my mother and her sisters from a bedroom upstairs suddenly fell away.

And then I heard her. *"Genevieve."*

"Nannie?" I whispered, holding my breath tightly in my chest.

I turned to face the old hall tree leaning against the wall with its dull, brass hooks sticking out, waiting for a hat or a scarf, its oval mirror in the center, cloudy and dotted with age. Where was she? The air became heavy and wrapped around me like a soft blanket, and all I could hear was a whooshing, buzzing sound in my ears. I felt light-headed. I leaned close to the mirror and touched the tiny curlicue carvings in the wood. I studied the image and saw an almost ten-year-old girl with squinty, blue eyes and dark, curly hair, and even though I knew it was me in the mirror, I felt like something strange was happening to me and that I should look different. I touched the mirror with the palms of my hands, then brought them to my face. I could feel Nannie with me. I couldn't see her, but I had heard her call my name. Yet, it was still just me there in the mirror.

Slamming car doors told me they were finally leaving. I went outside and down the porch steps that led to the circular driveway. I sat on the last step at the foot of the huge, grouchy oak tree that guarded the house. Its thick, twisted roots, famous for trying to trip almost everyone who walked by, climbed angrily out of the ground, and I dug my bare toes underneath them. The crunching of gravel grew faint in the distance, the funeral people leaving their dingy clouds of dust and their whispers about Nannie in the air behind them.

"They found her body tangled up in the oyster bed at low tide."

"I heard there was nothing left of her face, and if it wasn't for the bright-yellow blouse she'd been wearing . . ."

I closed my eyes and shook their voices out of my head. You don't come to somebody's house, to *her* house, and say things like that. You don't *ever* say things like that.

I felt sick to my stomach and ran across the yard to the smokehouse. I shut the door and slammed the latch down. Long ribbons of light fought their way through the cracks in the walls. I bent over, wrapping my arms around my waist. I clamped one hand tightly over my mouth, smothering sounds I'd never made before—sounds that didn't belong to me. I closed my eyes and cried quietly—for my Nannie, for my mother, for me. My heart pounded like a thunderstorm exploding in my chest, and I thought I might die right there at that moment. I walked around in tight little circles in the middle of the dark smokehouse. Her crab nets and fishing rods hung on the wall, but the lucky rod with the little silver feather was missing. As I slid down the side of the bait freezer to the dirt floor, I tried to breathe slowly and deeply. One time, I asked Nannie why she didn't fish from the small green boat that always hung underneath the wharf.

"Is it because of those bumpy things growing all over the bottom? Or does it have a hole in it?" I asked.

"No," Nannie said. "The truthful story is I don't take much to being *in* the water itself, but that doesn't stop me from fishing and crabbin'. I'm damn good at it, and it's fun work." Even though she was a little bit afraid, she loved the river almost as much as she loved people, she would say. I knew what she meant. That was just how it was with Nannie and me. We could tell each other things that didn't make much sense to other people, but we understood it.

As I sat there in the smokehouse rocking back and forth, I wondered: How was it that I had heard her call my name so clearly in the hallway? And then the grimy lightbulb by the door flickered twice.

Chapter Two

October 17, 1965

Mama didn't know for sure she was pregnant with her fourth child when Nannie went missing. We had moved into our new house at Bailey's Place, just down the road from Gibson Island, where we'd been staying with Nannie and Aunt Alicia temporarily. Mama and Daddy thought we'd be there for only a few months, but it ended up being a lot longer. It was worth the wait, though, to get into our very own place. While our new house was no match for the one my great-great-grandfather Ellis Gibson had built with his own hands on the forty-acre island, it felt like a dream come true compared to where we'd lived before.

The last place we lived, before finally coming back home to the Lowcountry, as Nannie called it, was a tiny apartment in the middle of Los Angeles, California. It had a pool with no water and a yard so small you couldn't even hula-hoop in it without bumping into the chain link fence that surrounded the complex. Our parents both worked for a company that sold lawn mower equipment. Daddy was a salesman, and Mama was a secretary, and the company must've really liked them because they paid for all of us to move across the country. Before that, Mama and Daddy worked at other important jobs that took us all over the place for two years — from our home in Charleston to Miami, from Miami to Atlanta, and then from Atlanta to Los Angeles.

Mama and Daddy always missed home, though. Charleston was where their families lived, where they'd gotten married and planned to stay, and where James and Ryan and I were born. Mama's side was from out in the country, raised on the river, while Daddy's side was from the beach, raised on the ocean. Even though these places were only about thirty miles apart, Nannie was quick to point out somewhat proudly that beach people and river people were as different as night and day. Nannie was not one to stir up trouble, so she always added, "No matter the differences, we are all part of the Lowcountry." Nannie said the Lowcountry was the best part of South Carolina. "It's called the Lowcountry because it's tucked down far below the foothills and as close to sea level as you can get without fallin' into the Atlantic. It's like its own country with its own music and food and traditions, and Charleston — well, she's like the queen. She's adored by all her subjects — the rivers and marshlands, the beaches, the old oak trees and palmettos . . ." I loved hearing Nannie talk about the Lowcountry.

Moving around for those two years was hard on our family, and when we got to California, Mama sounded just like Nannie and talked about the Lowcountry more than she ever had before. That's because California was the worst place ever. Later, my mother would say it was like we were cursed there. I had to agree.

The day I was called a liar in front of the third-grade class at my new school had started out okay. Mama dropped James and me off at the front door, waved good-bye, and then left to take Ryan to his own school. I hated that we had to be separated, but Mama said that was how it had to be here in California now that James and I were in grade school and to be a big girl about it. I'd been there a week, and though neither my classmates nor my teacher were very friendly, I figured they'd all come around once they got to know me. I knew one thing: I was beginning to dread the arithmetic races Mrs. Powers made us do every morning. For some reason, she thought it was fun to see which kids could solve a problem the fastest on the blackboard in front of everyone, and the more I failed at this game, the more she called on me.

Lunchtime at school was boring and quick. We all had to bring our lunch and eat it in the classroom, and I got used to eating my bologna sandwich and Hydrox cookies at my desk in silence. Mama always bought Hydrox cookies because she thought they were like Oreos, only cheaper, but they really weren't very good.

One day after lunch, Mrs. Powers stood up suddenly, her heavy chair scraping across the tiled floor, and asked, "Class, do you know that there are starving children in the world?" Giving her the answer she wanted to hear, we automatically nodded. "In that case," she continued, "all of you will be punished with no recess until whoever has wasted this perfectly good food admits to it." She reached into the trash can and very slowly extended her hand out for all of us to see. "Someone has thrown away these Oreo cookies, and I would like for that person to speak up now." I breathed a sigh of relief, since I'd certainly not had any Oreos in my lunch.

Then, out of the blue, Myron, the boy next to me, pointed and said, "*She* did it. I saw her with Oreos." I couldn't believe my ears and quickly added I'd brought Hydrox cookies, not Oreos, and even showed the black remnants in my teeth to prove I'd eaten them. Mrs. Powers shook her head sadly as if I was the biggest disappointment the school had ever seen. She made me stand in front of the class and say I was sorry. I said it, but I didn't mean it.

"And you should never lie—like Genevieve did," she added. I felt like my face was on fire, and at that moment I knew I would never have a friend in California and I would never be happy there—ever. I couldn't understand why I was being blamed for something I didn't do. Maybe it was because I was new and not from California or because our family bought the cheaper cookies or just because some people are mean for no reason at all.

I decided not to talk anymore at school. This caused another problem because Mrs. Powers wrote a note to Mama and Daddy saying I was not participating in class or getting along with others. I begged them to take me to another school, but I knew that was not going to happen. It was around this time when I began to think Mama and Daddy had more important things on their minds than my feelings.

The curse continued. One day while we were on the playground, all the teachers started to cry, and they quickly started giving out little paper cups of vanilla ice cream with tiny, flat wooden spoons. We all stood around and ate our ice cream and watched the teachers cry until the loudspeakers on the playground said the President of the United States had been shot and killed. Then we were all crying, even though we didn't quite understand what was happening. I saw James by himself with no grown-ups around him, and I went to the fence and stood with him until they made us separate and leave the playground. It felt like the world was coming to an end. School closed early, and there was a lot of commotion with children and parents and teachers going out into the halls, crowding around at the front door, and leaving the building. I looked everywhere for James and finally found him leaning against the water fountain, his eyes wide with fear.

"It's okay. Mama will come to get us now," I told him and led him outside.

And then, just like that, we were the only ones left, except for the janitor who stood by his truck jangling his keys and acting mad because we were still there. So we sat on the front steps waiting, and I prayed every car I heard or saw was going to be Mama. I wondered who was in charge of the United States now and who would take care of the people—of all of us. Were we in danger? I absolutely did not feel safe in California. Finally, after what seemed like hours, Mama pulled up, and we jumped into the car.

"President Kennedy has been shot—I just can't believe it!" she said, tears streaming down her face. She was talking a mile a minute, not even noticing she'd left us waiting alone. "Everyone's going crazy, trying to get home and hear what's happening. The traffic is awful! God, what are we going to do? How could this happen?" She seemed scared as she gripped the steering wheel and leaned forward. Even though James was trying not to cry, I could hear whimpering noises from the backseat, but I don't think Mama even knew we were in the car. I'd never seen her like this before. Speeding out of the parking lot and down the narrow, winding road overlooking the deep valley, she took the curve of the road too fast, and as my body leaned to the right with the turn, the car door flew open. The black pavement was rushing beneath me, and in a flash, I saw my body tumbling out onto the highway and rolling over the side of the cliff, bouncing off the jagged rocks and dried-up tree limbs, landing in a circle of coyotes, never to be seen again.

As I braced for the impact and the end of my life, Mama slammed on the brakes and grabbed my arm, pulling me into the middle of the seat toward her. "Oh, Genny! Oh, Genny!" She cried hard and loudly and didn't let me go for the longest time.

It took awhile for Mama to forgive herself for the car door opening, but it wasn't her fault really. It was the curse of California. Even when we tried to have a good time, it wouldn't end up that way. Daddy would take us to places like the county fair or the movies, but the car would break down or Ryan would start throwing up or it would thunderstorm. On paydays, we got to buy lots of groceries, but our mean landlady, who didn't seem to like Daddy very much, wouldn't let him park his car in the front like the other people who lived there, and we always had to walk a long way with all our bags of groceries.

The final straw was after our Lake Arrowhead Christmas trip. That was the trip where I learned there was no Santa Claus, which was bad enough, but when we got back to Los Angeles, a terrible smell greeted us at our apartment door. Our icebox was gone, and all the food was out on the kitchen table—spoiled. The landlady had given the icebox away to another tenant who needed it. We watched my father's reaction as she told him this, not even stopping as she crossed the parking lot to leave. She was a wrinkled woman with very tanned skin, a long nose like a horse, and just a few strands of red hair, all different lengths. She continued to walk past my parents, slumping her shoulders and dragging her pocketbook on the ground, heading to her big car.

"We have three young children. This is not right, and you know it!" Daddy said as he followed behind her.

"You're late on your rent again, and the icebox is extra. You pay me fifty dollars today. That's how it works," she said, and the way I remember it, she started laughing like a witch. My father stood there with his hands open, not believing what he was hearing. Then she slammed the car door in his face and drove away.

That same week, Daddy announced the lawn mower company was going out of business, and Nannie told Mama we needed to leave California and not wait another minute. Sure enough, the day after they learned the news, Mama picked me up from school early and told the principal we were "gettin' the hell out of here." We were in such a hurry I left everything inside my desk in the classroom. This included my lunch (along with the Hydrox cookies) and my foot-long eraser with the writing on it that said, "If at first you don't succeed, try, try again." I hated that I'd left my new eraser but hoped Mrs. Powers would find those Hydrox cookies and realize what a bad mistake she'd made.

Knowing she was finally coming home to her mama, my mother sang songs with my father all the way across country. James and Ryan and I could feel how happy our parents were, and it had been a long time since we'd seen them that way. We especially liked to hear them sing "Sentimental Journey" and "Carolina in the Morning" and harmonize to "On Moonlight Bay." They wore sunglasses and smoked cigarettes while they drove, and we stopped at motels with pools so we could swim until dark. Even though we had to leave all our Christmas presents in California for the movers to pack, we didn't mind because we could feel something big was about to happen. Nannie and Aunt Alicia had said to just come on ahead and stay with them at Gibson Island until the lawn mower company sent all of our furniture and Christmas presents back home and until Daddy got another job.

On the long drive back, Daddy made sure we did educational things like visit the Alamo and look at cactus plants, but all I could think about was my Nannie. I knew she was excited—even more than me—that we were coming home. I could picture her in her Bermuda shorts and sleeveless cotton shirt waiting on the porch, waving her arms in the air as we drove up the long driveway. She would run down the steps and clap her hands together until we all climbed out of the car. She would hug my mother first—and she would hug me last. I was always last—that was the way it was supposed to be. I got the longest, deepest hug, the one that said, "This is where you belong. We're together again, and I'm never letting you go."

What started out to be a few weeks living with Nannie and Aunt Alicia turned into a year and a half because the moving company stole everything my parents owned, including our Christmas presents. California was a curse.

So, it was a very happy day in early October when we moved into the house we'd be renting from the Baileys on their property. The Baileys were longtime friends of the Gibson family, and this was just the perfect house—that big thing my brothers and I were waiting for. It sat on another branch of the Toogoodoo River and had a porch that wrapped around it like a big hug. Mama and Daddy had found jobs, so everything was finally going our way, and the best part of all was that Nannie agreed to live with us at Bailey's Place during the weekdays while Mama and Daddy went to work, and then she would go back over to Gibson Island on the weekends.

Mama's job was a couple of miles away at the bank in Hollywood, named just like the movie town. Daddy had to drive out to a fertilizer plant where he would be in an important position as the site manager. One Saturday after Daddy started working there, he took the boys and me to the plant with him. It had huge warehouses filled with mountains of multicolored fertilizer, and while he went inside to get some paperwork, James and Ryan and I raced up those mounds with lightning speed, taking large leaps so we wouldn't sink in, the smell burning the inside of our noses. Suddenly, out of nowhere, it seemed, a man came running into the warehouse.

"Get outta here, you brats, or you'll be sorry!" he yelled. He was shaking his fists wildly and stumbled as he ran toward us, falling face first into a small pile of pink fertilizer and showing us a perfect bald circle surrounded by strings of dark hair. He sputtered and looked up at us, pink speckles stuck in the deep pits and creases of his forehead and cheeks. Scared to death, we ran to the car and hid in the back until Daddy came out. I told James and Ryan to keep their heads down, and as I peered over the backseat, all I could see was the parking lot with a bulldozer parked off to the side, an empty guard shack, and a shiny black truck.

When we got back home that day, Mama, Daddy, Nannie, and the boys and I sat on the porch and looked out over our piece of the river. James and Ryan were planning their first campout, which meant a card table with a sheet over it. We watched Ryan drag out pillows and blankets while James set up two flashlights, a stack of comic books, and some late-night snacks, which included some Red Hots and a pack of Target candy cigarettes. Even though Mama and Daddy and Nannie knew my brothers wouldn't last long out on the porch at night by themselves, they got excited right along with them, and Daddy even surprised them with walkie-talkies. He told them they needed to have them in case of emergencies or if anything strange happened. Daddy reminded us about Nicodemus, the man from Goat Island whose goats were all found dead up in the trees. Nobody knew what to make of it, but after that Nicodemus was never heard from again. Now, according to Daddy, he roamed through the Lowcountry late at night. When he told us that, my mind went straight to Robby, who worked for the Baileys, because I'd seen him around the property talking to no one in particular, and he didn't seem right. Then, James brought up the wild man who'd chased us down at the fertilizer plant earlier that day.

"He was sure mad," James said, describing what had happened. "And we weren't even doing anything!"

"What if he followed us and comes here tonight?" Ryan asked, holding his pillow against him tightly.

"Well, you better keep that flashlight and walkie-talkie handy just in case," Daddy said and then caught Mama's eye. "Listen, boys, you don't have to worry about him. That was only Landry.

He works at the plant and just has a big mouth, that's all. He's not worth thinkin' twice about."

"Well, it's real good you have that job, now," Nannie said to Daddy as Mama handed her a drink, "but that Landry fellow does have a bad reputation. You know his family's been trying to buy up waterfront property like crazy lately, including Gibson Island." She paused. "And everyone around here knows Gibson Island will *never* be for sale."

"I know, but I don't think it's the old man who's pushin' that," Daddy said as James and Ryan ran to opposite sides of the porch to test the walkie-talkies. "Actually, from what I can tell so far, Mr. Landry seems like a pretty decent boss, and all he really cares about is his fertilizer business. Jeffrey—now, that's another story. He's always braggin' about how much money his family has, and now he claims he's on the verge of becoming a genuine millionaire. People say he's all talk and nothin' good ever comes from what he does. No one pays him much attention—not even his own father."

"Seems kind of sad that his father pays him no attention. Maybe that's part of his problem," Mama commented.

"Well, I'm payin' close attention, and if I have anything to do with it, Gibson Island won't be eaten up in one of those ventures of his. I don't want to rain on your parade, but I wouldn't trust him if I were you," Nannie warned.

"Okay, let's change the subject, please," Mama interrupted. "Jim hasn't had the job long enough to be worrying about it."

"The walkie-talkies are working good, Daddy," James yelled from the far side of the porch, "but just in case, for extra protection . . ." He called out to Fella, and we all laughed as our new yellow dog bounded up the steps and dived under the card table tent, saving barely enough room for the two boys.

Sometimes during those first few weeks in our house, right before the nighttime crept in, I would sit outside at the end of our sidewalk. Pulling at the little clumps of weeds that had grown through the cracks over time, my back to the narrow dirt road and the pecan orchards, I'd watch our house come to life, the river behind it breathing in and out. The house seemed grateful and alive with activity—the lights wildly bright in every room, Daddy hammering noisily to get the pictures hung, pots and pans banging together as Mama and Nannie set up the kitchen cabinets, James and Ryan thundering across the hardwood floors, their voices, happy and hopeful, bouncing off walls and floating out to me. This was our house now, and it needed us as much as we needed it.

One evening while they were putting up new curtains that were made special for the living room, I overheard Nannie asking Mama, "Louisa, don't you know about birth control?"

"Mama, please!" she whispered loudly. "Of course I do." She made a big sighing noise.

With the door slightly open to my bedroom, there was just enough space where the door hinges met the wall for me to peek through. "Well, we don't admit to it, but even Catholics use birth control," Nannie said. She paused and waited for my mother's reaction and then whispered back to her, "I have a feeling you're pregnant, Louisa."

My mother turned to her quickly. "No. I'm not," she snapped and climbed higher on the foot ladder, the curtains flowing from her arms to the floor below like a ballroom gown. Since neither Nannie nor Mama could sew anything at all, I thought it was real nice that our neighbor, Cynthia Cook, who also worked with Mama at the bank, offered to make the curtains as a housewarming present. Cynthia Cook was kind of famous because she'd been crowned Miss Hollywood last year, and I even had a newspaper picture of her waving from a convertible in the Fourth of July parade. Mama turned away from Nannie and held the curtains up in front of the window, admiring them, then added, "We're good with the three we have, believe me. And stop with those funny feelings of yours."

But Nannie would have none of it. "Trust me. As hard as you try, you can't control everything. Anyway, I'm here to help," she added, grinding Mama's lit cigarette into the ashtray on the end table. And that was that—end of discussion.

My mother ignored this last comment, as she often did when Nannie pushed a subject. Actually, everyone tended to ignore Nannie when she pushed a subject, but I'd seen her do this many times and be right, and suddenly at that very moment, I, too, knew my mother was going to have a baby. Mama said she was going to bed early with a headache, so Nannie made her famous saltine cracker milk, which was guaranteed to help you relax and sleep through the night. As she heated milk in the saucepan, I crushed up the saltine crackers into three big cups. She poured the hot milk over the crackers until they practically overflowed. After taking some to Mama, we brought ours with us outside and settled on the porch. Nannie and I watched the river calm itself under the moonlight as we stirred up the last bit of soggy crackers from the bottom of our cups. Even though it was the same river, it looked much smaller than it did from Gibson Island. After a few minutes, she laughed softly and said, "Before long, your mama will be sleeping like a baby." I laughed, too, and started to hope for a sister.

Chapter Three

July 15, 1965

CHARLESTON WAS ONLY A HALF-HOUR DRIVE from Gibson Island and our new house at Bailey's Place, but it always felt like we were in some faraway city that belonged to just Nannie and me. The summer before Nannie went missing, we took our last trip to Charleston together. It was mid-July, and we moved through the city's gauzy heat a little more slowly but with a mission. Nannie's oldest daughter Marjorie and her family were coming down from New York for a visit, and we needed to buy some Southern specialties like stone-ground grits and plantation gold rice. Nannie, always practical, wore a sleeveless, peach-colored shirt, tan slacks, and plaid Keds. We had so much to do.

We started on Market Street and took our time going through the old open market, where people sold everything under the sun — pottery, jewelry, hand-embroidered baby clothes, seashells, toys, even antique furniture. We bought little brown bags of boiled peanuts and watched the Gullah women as they sat on blankets or stools, their fingers expertly weaving and tying the long strands of sweet grass, creating beautiful bowls and baskets. Like magnets, we were drawn to a shady corner of the market where we got lost in a sea of used books stacked dangerously high on tables. We ended up with a bagful for ourselves, and feeling a little guilty, we added a true-crime book for Aunt Alicia and some comic books for James and Ryan.

Nannie loved to surprise me with these day trips to downtown Charleston—just the two of us. We'd start out on our drive early, going through Meggett and Hollywood and passing by my new school, R. B. Stover Elementary. Nannie told me it still made her furious how I was treated at the school in California, but I told her not to worry anymore about it because it was much better here. We didn't have arithmetic races, the teachers were a lot friendlier, and all the boys and girls were together on one playground. There was even a cafeteria where you could buy milk and lunch if you wanted to. Nannie and I would then drive into Rantowles, going slowly around Dead Man's Curve, past the meat-packing plant and crowded Durant's Truck Stop (with more motorcycles than trucks), then finally up Savannah Highway. As soon as we crossed the bridge over the Ashley River, we were there.

Nannie liked to tell stories about her family, and our day trips brought out a lot of those stories. She'd take me by her old house on Smith Street where she raised her three girls—Aunt Marjorie, Aunt Vivian, and the youngest, my mother, Louisa. She and my grandfather, Owen Cooper, had divorced when their girls were in high school. She never talked about that part much, but I knew he'd left Charleston, moved to Miami after their divorce, and married again, and that my mother and her sisters didn't get to see him much during their teenage years.

When one of Daddy's jobs took us to Miami for a little while, Mama got to spend more time with her father, and he seemed like a nice grandfather from what I could tell. He took us to his favorite restaurant, and we had so much food he had to ask the waiter to box up the leftovers for his dog, Buster, and we got to pick suckers off a big, colorful sucker tree in the lobby before we left. He also showed us how to crack open a coconut he'd gotten off the tree in his yard, and we tasted the white pulp inside, which we pretended to like since he'd gone to all that trouble. He died of cancer soon after we moved there, but before he died, Mama took my brothers and me into his room one by one, and he gave us each a gift. I got a red rose, James got a tape measure, and Ryan got his hospital wristband. That's all I remember. Then we moved away from Miami because Daddy got a better job.

Some say Nannie and my grandfather Owen never stopped loving each other. She never remarried, so maybe that was true. She did stay close friends with his sister, though—Old Aunt Vivian, who lived in Charleston down a bumpy cobblestone alley off Broad Street. We all called her Old Aunt Vivian behind her back so as not to confuse her with Nannie's daughter, Young Aunt Vivian. If we had time to kill, Nannie and I would go to Old Aunt Vivian's for a little visit. I liked that Nannie took me there so I could hear more about my grandfather and his side of the family.

Old Aunt Vivian lived in a carriage house, which is where horse carriages used to be kept a long time ago, and it was surrounded by wild flowers. Everything inside was so small—the furniture, the dishes, even the lamps—it seemed like it should be a dollhouse. Nannie and I could always count on having delicious little squares of homemade fruit cocktail cake, which she served on glass plates covered with paper doilies. The cake would sweat through the doilies, leaving wet, sugary outlines, and I always wanted a second piece but never asked for it. We sipped hot tea with lots of milk in thin china cups, and when it cooled down, I had to hold mine with two hands because my fingers were too fat to fit through the skinny handle. Sometimes when we were there, Nannie would walk around and look at books on the shelf or old photographs on the side table, and it seemed she was remembering back to when my grandfather was her husband.

Nannie was born the fourth of five children—four girls and one boy. They were all raised on Gibson Island, but most of them had worked or lived downtown at some point over the years. The oldest was Aunt Alicia, who never married but was known to be a hard worker like her father and grandfather and now ran Gibson Island with Nannie's help. Next came Aunt Sis (whose real name was Agatha). She was a nun and lived in a convent with other nuns on James Island near Charleston. Aunt Sis was the smartest person in our family, taught history at the College of Charleston, and had been to Rome twice to see the Pope. Now she was a mother superior, which was like the boss of all the nuns. After Aunt Sis came Uncle Donald, who was the oddest one and lived west of the Ashley River. He used to work at the old Majestic Theater on King Street doing Vaudeville acts, which Nannie said was pretty crude entertainment in her opinion, and he was always laughing at things no one else laughed at.

Aunt Theresa was the youngest of the five Gibson children, and she was married to Uncle Martin. They lived downtown in half of a house near Hampton Park, which had two front doors and two families living in it. Uncle Martin was a big man with broad shoulders, and he had one fake eye that stayed still while the other one moved around. Nannie said he let Aunt Theresa do whatever she wanted, which was the key to their successful marriage. I loved hearing Aunt Theresa talk about the days when she was a debutante and had lots of dates with young men from The Citadel, Charleston's military college. "But looked who she picked!" Uncle

Martin would say, grinning. Aunt Theresa always seemed to have lots of busywork to do, and on one visit, Aunt Theresa told Nannie she should get a meaningful hobby. That same day, Nannie took me to a special knitting store on George Street. This hobby was a big surprise to anyone who knew Nannie. Afterward, we went over to Woolworths for grilled cheese sandwiches, and she looked at her bags of yarn as if she was sorry she'd bought them and said quietly, "I guess I'll make you a sweater, Genevieve." She never did make a sweater, but a week later she gave me all the yarn, and I used it to tie bows in my hair and to help me lace together handmade books of poetry for Christmas presents. Mostly, though, when we went downtown, we took walks and visited folks and talked about the old days. We went to Colonial Lake and fed the ducks. We went to the fancy shops on King Street, like The Bandbox and Elza's, and sometimes visited Uncle Martin at Condon's, where he was in charge of the shoe department.

In the afternoons, we'd walk along the Battery, and even though we were surrounded by history—with Fort Sumter off in the distance, the Civil War cannons, the statues like soldiers guarding the park, the beautiful homes lined up gracefully along the waterfront with their plantation shutters and brass plates of famous family names, we didn't talk or care about any of that. Instead, we talked a lot about the hurricanes and storms that had come through Charleston and about the marshes, the high and low tides, and where to find certain types of fish.

Once while we sat on the bench at the Battery overlooking the harbor, Nannie told me about the time she caught, by mistake, a shovelnose shark the size of a large dog. It was the summer Mama got kicked out of the all-girls school in Asheville. It had been a rough time after the divorce, Nannie said, so the four of them took a weekend down at Edisto Beach, and while the girls were shell hunting early in the morning, she set her line. "Well, no sooner had I cast into the waves when it took my line down like a rocket and just about dragged me into the ocean behind it. I fought that thing like it was the devil himself—and it pulled me along the shoreline like a puppet. I kept yellin' for the girls to come back, but they were too far ahead to hear me. I ran back and forth, back and forth, tugging and letting go, tugging and letting go. When I saw it rear its ugly shark head, it scared the living daylights out of me. I was so shocked, I stumbled back and fell, and then the line popped, and he was gone!" We were both so tired out by the time she finished telling her story we had to sit on the bench for a while longer to catch our breath.

Even though Nannie liked talking about her daughters and the old days living in Charleston, I could tell that spending time with me in the city was one of her very favorite things to do. The most fun I ever saw Nannie have was on that last day trip when we were at the Battery watching a huge sailboat regatta. She could barely keep in her excitement as the harbor filled up with different colors, some sails bouncing and eager, some nervous and shy, some confident and brave, all dancing around in preparation for a thrilling race. "Look at that one," she said, pointing to a particular sailboat decorated with yellow and red swirls and gliding fearlessly through the big white waves peaking around her. We leaned far over the railing, our hair damp and curly from the salty spray of the water slamming up against the Battery's seawall. "Genevieve, she will be the winner! You can just tell by how comfortable she is—she knows just what to do. We'll check the Sunday paper and see that she was the winner—mark my words." And, of course, I always did mark her words, and she was always right.

Before going home, Nannie and I walked by the Farmers' and Exchange Bank on East Bay Street where years ago she worked as a secretary. It had giant, dark wood double doors with gold handles and thick, etched glass.

"Did you like working here, Nannie?" I asked as we peeked through the glass.

"Yes, it was a busy time, and I made a lot of good friends." I smiled picturing Nannie dressed up for work every day, walking downtown, and going to lunch with her friends. "I was lucky to work here because there had been a bad depression, which is when lots of people couldn't find any work at all. My daddy and Grandfather Ellis knew practically everyone in Charleston, so they helped me get that job, and I ended up staying there over twenty years." Nannie's father was Michael Gibson, a successful farmer and the only child of Ellis and Genevieve Gibson. He'd married Emily Walton, his childhood sweetheart, and they'd lived with his parents at Gibson Island for the rest of their marriage, going on to have five children of their own.

"That must've been a real busy house with all those people!" I exclaimed, thinking how crowded it could get with just us three kids. "Did your mama like fishin' and crabbin' like you do?"

"Not really," she said in a disappointing voice. "She never had much time for me, and we were pretty different from each other. For one thing, I was quite the tomboy, so I was always outside. My mama liked dressing up in nice clothes and being proper, and I was not like that at all."

"Maybe she just had too many children and couldn't get to everyone," I offered up, but I was thinking it would be sad to feel different from your own mother, especially if she didn't have any time for you.

"It's not that we didn't love each other," Nannie said. "Of course we did. But it's true — my mother seemed overwhelmed with her five children. Plus, she couldn't tolerate all my stories and said I exaggerated too much. She said that made me different from the other children, and she was probably right about that."

"But that's the best part about you, Nannie." Nannie stopped and looked at me and touched my cheek with the palm of her hand like she always did when she was paying close attention to what I was saying.

Her voice got happier. "Well, it was my grandmother Genevieve who understood me best, and she knew me like no one else. We had a special bond—just like us." She winked at me and smiled.

At the end of the day, Nannie took me to see the new Hayley Mills movie playing at the Riviera Theatre. I remember getting our tickets at the box office outside, then handing them to the attendant at the door, who paused and looked at me with soft eyes as if to say, "I wish I had a Nannie like that." We settled into the deep, cushioned chairs in the cool, dark theater, the back of my shirt and shorts damp and sticking to my skin after a long, summer day in our city. The heavy red velvet curtains opened, and we watched the cartoons, anxiously waiting for the movie to begin. I remember us holding hands like we did so easily, and then Nannie started snoring so loud she woke herself up. I think she was embarrassed, but I just acted like I didn't notice.

As we headed back to Gibson Island late that afternoon, I shifted the heavy bags of grits and rice off my lap. I was beginning to get more and more excited about my cousin Ellie coming down from New York that Saturday. I hadn't seen her since last summer when she'd come down with Aunt Marjorie and Uncle Peter and her little brother, Sam. Ellie was short for Ellison, the name Aunt Marjorie created to remember Ellis, our great-great-grandfather. Ellie and I were the same age, and even though she lived all the way up North, we wrote long letters to each other every week. Except for the time when our family was in California, we hadn't missed a summer together yet. I was anxious to tell her about my idea for a magazine project we could start on right away.

"Genevieve, you and Ellie are a lot like your mama and Aunt Marjorie when they were growing up — always reading and singing and making big plans for the future."

"Seems like we're practically sisters, just like them," I said, "and we sure do have plans, all right. We're going to go to the same college together; we're going to be in each other's weddings and have children the exact same age; and we're going to live right here for the rest of our lives," I said, believing every word. Nannie nodded in agreement.

Nannie was always saying Aunt Marjorie should get out of New York and move back to the Lowcountry to be closer to her two sisters. Aunt Viv and her family lived in Orangeburg, not far from Charleston, and since we were back from California, Nannie just needed her oldest daughter down here, and she would have all three of her girls together again. That made good sense to me, too.

"It's not for me, mind you," Nannie said as we turned down the road to Gibson Island. "It's for Marjorie and Ellie and Sam's sake. They'd all be happier here. Every time they come down for vacation, they cry a river when they leave. It breaks my heart." Nannie never talked a whole lot about Uncle Peter, but I could tell she wasn't looking forward to him coming, and sometimes something would just slip out of her. "Of course, it would be easier on them if their daddy didn't insist on livin' up North and if he didn't have such an ill temper."

Nannie knew what she was talking about because two days later Uncle Peter tried to kill her.

That Saturday morning, Ellie's arrival couldn't come fast enough for me. We all went over to Gibson Island to help get things ready. Daddy and the boys helped Aunt Alicia clean up the yard while Mama and Nannie put clean sheets on the beds upstairs. In the kitchen, Daduh was finishing up the deviled eggs and pork chops, and she shared a taste of Nannie's famous bean salad with me.

"That's some good eatin' there!" Daduh shook her head from side to side and smacked her lips three times. She'd always do that after taking a delicious bite of something, then I would do the same to make fun of her, and we'd both laugh out loud. "They're goin' to never want to leave Gibson Island again once they remind themselves of this good Southern cookin'. I don't know what they eat up there in New York, but it sure ain't nothin' like this." She covered the bowl and put it in the icebox.

"Ellie says they eat steaks and potatoes a lot," I said, and Daduh mumbled something.

I took the broom Daduh handed me and swept some crumbs out the back door. "Maybe we can talk 'em into staying here for good this time." I paused on purpose. "If only Aunt Marjorie and Ellie and Sam could stay, that is."

"What are you talkin' about that for?" Daduh said, frowning and taking the broom from me.

"Well, it seems no one likes Uncle Peter very much," I said, thinking Daduh might want to add some more information.

"Huh! You need keep to your own self about things you don't know about," Daduh said sternly. "What gets into you? You're not grown enough for that kinda talk."

"Yes, I am. Nannie tells me stuff all the time," I argued.

"Well, that's her." Daduh sighed. "You don't have to repeat everything you hear then." Daduh pointed. "There they are now comin' in the driveway. Go on." I raced down the steps, and Ellie jumped out of the car before it even stopped moving.

Nannie gave Ellie and me her bedroom so we could stay up late talking and planning our magazine. The next morning, we spent time with Nannie while she fished on the wharf and then set up our magazine office on the small screened-in porch next to the red breakfast room. From there, we had a good view of the river and could watch her and talk back and forth. We called it the red breakfast room because the table and chairs wore thick, bubbly coats of bright-red paint, and the short curtains were white with red cardinals across the top. The red cardinal was Nannie's favorite bird, so we always saw a lot of them around the house—on the coffee cups and breakfast dishes—even the salt and pepper shakers were little red cardinals.

Daddy took Sam and my brothers on a hike to find old bottles and treasure, and I think Mama and Aunt Marjorie must have stayed up all night because they got up late and were looking pretty tired when they sat down in the breakfast room with their coffee.

"I just hope he gets out of this rotten mood of his," Aunt Marjorie was whispering. "The whole trip down was miserable. He criticizes the kids about every little thing—I know that's why Sam stutters like he does."

Then, I heard Mama say, "Shh." I thought they must have realized Ellie and I were on the porch, so we kept our heads down, cutting and pasting sections for our magazine and pretending we didn't hear anything. But that wasn't it. The reason they stopped talking was because Uncle Peter walked in.

"*Now* what are you saying about me?" he asked, his voice booming angrily across the breakfast room and screened porch, clear out to the wharf. Ellie looked out at Nannie, who had turned toward us, her fishing rod in her hand. Ellie lowered her head, avoiding my eyes, and somehow I knew this was not an unusual situation for her. Uncle Peter continued, "I waited for you to come to bed all night. Do you think I'm so stupid I don't know what gets discussed behind my back? And you ask why I hate coming here?" We heard him kick one of the red chairs across the room, and Ellie tucked her head down close to her chest and

32

closed her eyes tightly. I reached out for her hand, but she pulled it away.

"Peter—don't start!" Aunt Marjorie yelled back.

"What's happening?" Nannie asked, entering the breakfast room out of breath. "We can't have this!" She then leaned her head out to the porch where we were sitting. "Ellie, you and Genevieve better go on outside."

"No! You don't tell my daughter what to do," Uncle Peter interrupted.

"Peter, stop it right now," Aunt Marjorie said. "Mama, it's okay. Peter and I will go upstairs."

"We're going upstairs all right," Uncle Peter said. "We're going up to get our suitcases, and we're leaving. This trip is over." Uncle Peter stormed out of the room, and we could hear his heavy footsteps moving up the stairs and across the floor above our heads. Ellie jumped up from our table covered with strips of colored paper and drawings and ran past her mother through the breakfast room and out the back door.

"What is his problem, Marjorie? You just can't go on like this!" Mama said.

Aunt Marjorie left the room, and Nannie and Mama went after her, pausing at the base of the stairs. I should have gone outside after Ellie, but instead, I waited in the foyer to see what was coming next. I could see Nannie's face looking upward, and I could hear Uncle Peter screaming at Aunt Marjorie. I couldn't see him, but I know he came to the top of the stairs and looked down at Nannie directly because I saw her face change. According to her, it was the most evil look on anybody's face she had ever seen.

I saw Mama reach for Nannie, and before she could pull her away, Uncle Peter grabbed the huge crystal ashtray from the table on the landing upstairs and hurled it, aiming for her head. She ducked, so it just grazed her ear and then slammed against the doorframe, splintering the wood and shattering into a thousand little pieces. Mama said Uncle Peter looked like he wanted to kill her, and with no remorse, he turned around and went back into the bedroom to get the suitcases.

Mama told me to get ice and a washcloth for Nannie, and they went out on the front porch and sat down, still in shock. Aunt Marjorie came fast down the stairs and ran to her mother, hugging her and saying how sorry she was. Nannie held her daughter until she stopped crying, then said, "Marjorie, listen to me carefully. Peter has to leave now, or I will call the police. He will never be welcomed back to Gibson Island again." What she didn't know, or understand, was that when Uncle Peter left an hour later, Marjorie and Ellie and Sam would be going with him.

Nannie and Mama begged her not to go, but Aunt Marjorie said it was best for them all to go back to New York now and deal with this as a family. Even though Aunt Marjorie's words said she was horrified by what had happened, she didn't act surprised by it, which Mama said was "very telling." I barely had time to say good-bye to Ellie. She hung her head and mumbled, "Hurry up and write me so we can finish our magazine." When Sam walked up the driveway with Daddy and the boys, he didn't even have time to go into the house because Uncle Peter made him get in their car right away. Daddy and the boys just stood in the yard confused, while Uncle Peter drove off with his family.

Soon after that terrible day, I got a letter from Ellie.

> Dear Genny,
>
> How are you? I still think the idea for us to have a magazine is good. We can sell it and make some good money. Mama says I draw pretty good so here are some pictures we can use. One is a ballet dancer. You can write a

story about her to go with it. I am taking ballet lessons now. You can write a story about a
girl who is first the worst one in the class and
the mean girls tease her. Then at the dance
show the girl is the star and the mean girls
are sorry. Another picture is a girl's face with
bangs. She is crying and the story you can
write is she can't find her mother and father.
I have bangs now like that. I like all the stories you write. The story you wrote one time
about a big storm is a good idea. That was
real scary!

Sam is being a brat now so I have to go. It
must be hard to have two brothers. Let's be
sisters and tell everyone we are sisters! Ok?
Write the answer fast. I think next time I
come to Gibson Island will be better. I was
sad last time because I had to leave so soon.

OOOXXXX

Your cousin, I mean sister,

Ellie

As soon as I finished reading her letter, I sent mine along with
the first stories for our magazine.

Dear Ellie,
Yes we can be sisters! I'm going to tell
everyone when I start back at school. Hurry
and come back down to Gibson Island!

Nannie says there will be lots of crabs next summer. She will make us crab cakes. Bring your dance clothes so we can put on a show. Here is a page for the magazine. You can read in it the story I wrote about the crying girl you drew who couldn't find her parents. They are in a big city and the girl gets lost and has to live by herself in the city. She thinks she is going to be an orphan but at last her mother finds her! Her mother says you never have to live in the big city again and be afraid. She says we will move away to the country where it is safe. Then the girl lives happily ever after! It's your turn to write on the page and send it back with more pictures.

Aunt Alicia got a new camera and the picture pops out of it after you take it! She said we can use it when y'all come down. Promise next time you will stay for the whole summer. Write soon!

Your sister, XXXOOO,

Genny

P.S. There is a chili stain in the corner of the magazine page. I circled it and wrote about it so people will think it is a real story instead of that I spilled something.

It seemed Ellie wrote me almost every day. Most of her letters talked about new story ideas, and most of the stories sounded lonely, which didn't seem like Ellie. For months, we took turns writing and drawing pictures so that once summer came again, we would put it all together and finish our magazine.

When Ellie left that July day, I was feeling sad and so was Nannie, but not for long. That's because Nannie always knew how to make me feel better. In her room, just like she'd done so many other nights before, Nannie told me how pretty I was and brushed my hair until it shined. I hated my hair because it was so curly and thick, but she told me one day I would be thankful and to be patient.

The truthful story is Nannie loved my brothers and my cousins with all her heart, but she loved me the most. That's not meant to hurt anyone's feelings; it was just the way things were. She said I was unique and was named Genevieve after her grandmother, who was my great-great-grandmother, and who was known to be kind and beautiful and also very unique. She added that her grandmother Genevieve had special God-given talents.

"Tell me about her God-given talents, Nannie," I said, and even though I'd heard about it hundreds of times, she would always add something new to the family story.

"Well, she helped a lot of people. For example, she'd tell the farmers at planting time when it was going to rain, and she'd say it was because her knees ached so bad. If people really knew it was because of the dreams she had, they wouldn't have believed her. Most of all, she helped the fishermen. She could predict the tides without a tide chart. She'd have dreams that told her when the bad storms were coming. Whenever she had a dream about the water and a big white wave cresting, that meant something was about to happen. My grandfather's fishermen friends would say, 'Mr. Ellis, how's Miss Genevieve been feelin'? Does she have any aches and pains? What does she think about our big shrimpin' trip next week?' And my grandfather would pass on the information to them. He got plenty of thanks for it, too. When they went to buy produce and fish down at the market in Charleston, the farmers and fishermen would give my grandmother a special discount, and some wouldn't take any money from her at all."

Nannie paused. "One time, though, a well-known sea captain who'd come to Charleston from Boston for trading business refused to believe the local fishermen when they told him and his crew that a hurricane was whipping up the coast from the Florida Keys and headin' straight this way. He said he would never rely on some backward Southern folklore to predict the weather or dictate his business, and that caused some hard feelings around town. The way I understand it, my grandmother had had this dream about an unexpected, wild storm with huge white waves, and it was coming here faster than anyone could track. My grandfather didn't want her telling people all about this dream, of course, so instead, they both told everyone who would listen that her joints were aching and hurting all over so bad she could hardly walk. That way, folks were able to put two and two together and figured we were definitely in for some dangerous weather. The locals prepared as they always did, but the sad ending is the sea captain paid no attention, headed out that day, and those poor souls were lost at sea." Nannie let that story sink in with me for a minute. Then she said, "Some say the sea captain still wanders along the Charleston Battery on stormy nights looking for his crew and shipmates."

"She sure was unique," I said, thinking about what it must have felt like to have those dreams and to try and help people when they most likely wouldn't believe you. "Did my great-great-grandfather really believe her dreams?" I asked.

"Oh. He did, all right. He was the one who had to calm her down at night when she woke up from them. Sometimes she'd wake up crying because she knew the dreams meant something bad was going to happen, and she had just a little bit of time to try and warn people. Grandpa Ellis had to protect her from skeptics, though — so they wouldn't think she was crazy or some kind of witch. That's why the two of them had this agreement — to pretend to have a few aches and pains every now and again that served as the warning for folks — instead of talkin' about the dreams. My grandfather bragged his Genevieve was better than a lighthouse because she gave them the warning *before* they went out to sea." For a second, Nannie looked like she was in a faraway place.

I loved that my name was Genevieve, and I knew what was coming next. As I sat on the stool at her dresser, she continued to brush my hair, my scalp tingling and my heart beating fast. Locking her eyes on mine in the mirror, Nannie leaned down and whispered in my ear. "Do you know what your name means?"

And as always, I whispered back, "What?"

She said, "It means 'white wave.'" And I would feel the hairs on my arms stand up and a lucky chill go through my body from head to toe.

Nannie told me I had God-given talents, too, and I believed her. She appreciated everything I did. When I wrote a poem or a story, she'd stop what she was doing and read it out loud immediately and then hold it to her chest, smiling. When I sang a song, she closed her eyes as if she was listening to an angel. That night she said, "Pay attention to the gifts you have, Genevieve. You're meant to do special things with them. You'll see."

We talked late into the night, and before I finally went to bed, she said, "I have a surprise for you," and she went over to her nightstand, opened up the Sunday paper, and showed me a beautiful photograph that took up almost half the page. "Look who won the regatta!"

Chapter Four

October 23, 1965

ONCE WE GOT ALL SETTLED IN our new house at Bailey's Place, Mama woke up crying three nights in a row. It was the third night that was the worst, the night before Nannie disappeared. The late October air was starting to turn cool, but I still kept my bedroom windows open. Better than any lullaby, the river would breathe in and out, its sighs lifting the thin, sheer curtain panel back and forth gently against the top of my hair until I fell asleep. When I heard Mama cry out, I sat up startled, just as I'd done the last couple of nights, and pulled the curtains aside. The moon was larger than I'd ever seen and lit up the river, beaming an unnatural spotlight across the sleepy water. This same light spilled into the hallway outside my door, and I followed it past my brothers' room, where they were both asleep in the double bed they shared. I stopped outside my parents' bedroom, and I could hear the familiar, panicky voice from inside.

"Mama was driving our car, and I was sitting next to her," my mother was saying. She was describing her dream. They were driving over the long, very narrow Cooper River Bridge, and rather than looking ahead, Nannie could not take her eyes off the regatta in the harbor. "I told her to stop looking and to keep her eyes on the road," Mama continued, "but she kept smiling and pointing at the sailboats out on the water, and the water was sparkling so brightly, blinding me. I begged her to look where she was going, but it was too late. And then . . ." She paused. "Waves splashed up over our windshield, and I reached for her. 'Mama, Mama!'" My mother made choking sounds — as if she was in the water herself. And she was crying now. "There was only water. I tried to find her, but there was only water and foamy, white waves rolling over and over. She was gone. Oh God!" I knew my father was holding her because her sobs became muffled as if pressed against his chest. And then, there was a change in her voice that I had not heard the nights before. It got stronger. "Jim, this dream was different than last night. Someone else was there this time."

"What do you mean? Who was it?" he asked quietly. I imagined he was stroking her hair.

"I don't know. The next thing I remember I had made it to shallow water near the riverbank. I was shivering, and I was searching for her head, her arms, any sign that she was fighting those waves. But she was gone. And then I realized there was someone behind me on the bank just watching, not helping at all. I yelled, 'My mother's in the water — she can't swim. Please go in and get her!' It was as if, all this time, this person could've helped but just wanted to watch her die."

My father stopped her, and like the nights before, he told her it was just a dream. He said it over and over again. It took a long time before their voices faded, and the house went back to being silent. After that, Mama never spoke of those dreams to anyone. It was like they never happened.

Even though Nannie came back to our house each Sunday evening to take care of us for the week, we kept to our ritual of stopping by Gibson Island on Sunday mornings after Mass for coffee. St. Anne's was not even a mile from the turnoff to the island and was the church that my mother's side of the family had been attending for years. Nannie told me that her grandmother, Genevieve, used to sit in the same spot every Sunday—on the front pew beneath the stained glass window of Mary and Joseph. After Mass, Genevieve would leave a dime in the crack of the windowsill, and the following Sunday she would discover, with great satisfaction, that the dime was gone. I liked St. Anne's, got to sing in the choir at Christmas, and made my First Communion there when we got back from California. That was on Mother's Day of 1964, and I was the oldest one getting First Communion because, according to Nannie, Mama and Daddy had been a little neglectful in that department. I wore a lace chapel cap that looked like a handkerchief held on with bobby pins and a white dress with a pale-blue satin ribbon around the waist.

Nannie bought my Communion dress for me at Kerrison's, west of the Ashley. It cost fifty dollars, and I saved the price tag (pasting it later in my scrapbook next to the picture of Miss Hollywood). Nannie said that Kerrison's was the best department store in Charleston, but she pointed out many times that it was very expensive. There was a big black-and-white cow that rotated on top of the Coburg Milk sign at the entrance of the shopping center. The center had a hat shop that Nannie said never had customers, a Laundromat, and a drugstore that carried everything from transistor radios and huge boxes of Whitman's candy to nail polish and blue eye shadow. It also had Lowell's Cafeteria, where we ate fried shrimp, hush puppies, and banana pudding with vanilla wafers to celebrate our purchase. Nannie said, "I swear, Lowell's has the best sweet tea I've ever tasted, but don't tell your mama because she thinks she is the queen of sweet tea." When we brought my dress back to the house hanging in a dark plastic bag with Kerrison's name across it, Mama knew it was going to be a good one. She lifted the bag carefully from the bottom, and when she saw it, she threw her arms around Nannie, thanking her for giving me the most wonderful First Communion dress that any girl could ever want.

Unfortunately, her mood turned later that day, after my father took me along for a ride with him to Fox's Barbershop in Hollywood. While Mr. Fox cut Daddy's hair, Daddy bragged that I had gotten a new dress and was going to make my First Communion. Mr. Fox said that the occasion called for me to get a special hair trimming. So, I climbed up into the barber's chair, which swiveled around and gave me a good view of all the lotions and combs and scissors laid out in front of a huge mirror. When he was done, Mr. Fox and Daddy stood next to me, grinning with pride at the results.

"Angel Baby," my daddy said, "wait till your mama sees you. She's going to be so surprised!" I could barely contain my excitement driving back to Gibson Island. My father thought it would be a much better surprise if I put a paper bag over my head when Mama came to the door. When she saw me, she screamed and shook her head in disbelief. "What have you done to Genny's beautiful hair?" She acted like she was looking at a monster. I was so ashamed I pulled the paper bag back over my head. I felt bad for Daddy because he'd been pretty proud of himself. Mama worked on my hair all that night to get it to look the way she wanted, and the next day, she took me to Ouida's Beauty Shop, which was in the back of Miss Ouida's house in Ravenel. She and my mother tsked and tutted the whole time Ouida tried to work her beauty magic. I couldn't understand how I could feel so happy and beautiful one minute and so sad and ugly the next. But I still made my First Communion that next Sunday, tugging on the little lace chapel cap and wishing it would cover my whole head, barely able to concentrate on the Holy Eucharist.

Over a year later, on Sunday, October 24, 1965, the morning after Mama's bad dream, we went to Mass at St. Anne's. Right after Communion, we kept walking past our pew toward the back of the church rather than staying for the last blessing and hymn. Aunt Sis said good Catholics don't skip out after Communion, but Nannie said she had to say that because she was a nun and it was okay as long as you don't do it every time. On the way out, Marylou Griffin, with her twisted facial expressions, watched us from her place on the pew, and it seemed like she was trying to smile at me with a look that said, "I know you're sneaking out of Mass early."

It was hard to tell how old Marylou was, but she was a lot older than me and a lot younger than Mama. She had very short coal-black hair, was thin as a rail, and held her wrists intertwined and hands locked together close to her chest as if they would fly out from her if she let them go. She could barely walk and was brought in and out in a wheelchair by her mother every Sunday. She never missed Mass, and each Sunday, Father Cuddihy would go down the aisle to where she was seated and give her Communion so she wouldn't have to come up to the altar. Nannie said she was crippled from birth with a muscle disease and couldn't talk right either, but that she was brilliant.

Marylou's mama and aunt were the Griffin sisters, old friends of Nannie and Aunt Alicia's. They had all grown up together out in the country but sometimes didn't see eye to eye. Nannie said the reason was that the Griffin sisters were busybodies and spent too much time minding other people's business when they had more than enough of their own to mind. "I try not to be too hard on them, though, because of Marylou and her situation," Nannie said.

Nannie liked Marylou a lot and took her a new book on her birthday each year. She said Marylou read all kinds of books about geography and countries around the world and about science and medicine, but her favorite was reading about the planets and stars. Nannie told me about a special table Marylou had where a book could be propped up without falling over, and Marylou could move the pages with a long stick in her mouth. There were books all over the house, and Marylou's mama couldn't keep up with how fast Marylou read them and the number of trips to the Charleston Library they needed to make each month. When the bookmobile started coming around, Nannie said it was a big relief. Miss Pratt, the librarian, even put a special wooden plank on the outside of the van so they could wheel Marylou's chair right inside. Until then, I never heard of anyone, except Nannie, who loved books as much as I did.

After I learned more about Marylou Griffin and how Nannie took to her so much, I looked forward to seeing her on Sunday mornings. I wondered what books she'd just read and if she paid much attention to Father Cuddihy. I thought that probably during Mass, her mind wandered off like mine did. She might travel in her imagination to other countries she'd read about or swim in the ocean or climb mountains and sleep under the stars. She might have conversations with scientists and solve mysteries that no one else could. I wondered what she did with all those things she'd learned that had to stay inside her head and what she would say if she could talk. On our way out of church that Sunday morning, as I walked past her, I saw that her mouth was definitely trying to make a smile at me, and I smiled back.

We were always really hungry after Mass. One reason was because Mama said the Church rules said we weren't supposed to eat before Communion. That makes you appreciate God more. But the skinny Communion wafer Father gave us didn't last long, so we'd hurry over to Gibson Island each week. As we drove over the rickety old bridge on Gibson Island Road that morning, I held my breath out of habit. It seemed our car could barely squeeze onto it, and in the few seconds it took to cross that piece of rotting wood over the little stretch of the river, I always pictured us, clear as day, crashing through and sinking into the marsh. But we bumped along over it and down the winding dirt road leading to the house where we'd spent the last year and a half recovering from our cursed adventure out west. Even though we loved our new house at Bailey's Place, this was always going to be home. Gibson Island had rescued our family.

Coffee and our favorite, shrimp and grits, were waiting for us in the red breakfast room next to the kitchen. This was the only time I was allowed to have coffee, and I loaded it up with sugar and milk. Aunt Alicia handed me the section of the newspaper that listed horses for sale. I loved horses, and even though I'd never ridden, I fantasized about owning one just like the girl in *Golden Sovereign*, my favorite book that month. The bookmobile came around the first Saturday of every month, and we were allowed to check out up to six books each time. Miss Pratt told me I'd already checked out every horse book she had, so I'd better move on to another subject.

As we settled at the table with our newspapers and coffee, James and Ryan went out on the screened porch attached to the breakfast room. I could see the wharf stretching across the river, pointing to the marsh in the distance, and the old green boat underneath it rocked, its rusty chains creaking and complaining from the weight. It was almost high tide; I knew this because Nannie kept a tide chart taped on the icebox. It was taped next to her most recent hurricane chart, which had her handwritten drawings and notes. The October morning sun was unusually warm, and the Spanish moss swayed lazily in the trees. It was as if they were all talking to each other that morning—the wharf, the boat, the river, the trees—all joined in a private conversation.

"I dreamed last night I died," Nannie announced casually as she walked into the breakfast room that morning. We all turned to face her as she stood in the doorway sipping her coffee, wearing a bright-yellow blouse and her green-striped fishing hat.

"Do, Fannie—that's enough!" Aunt Alicia dismissed her quickly. Aunt Alicia always said, "Do, Fannie" when she really meant "be quiet—we don't want to hear another one of your stupid stories." Fannie was what most people called her and was a nickname for Frances. I didn't like that nickname at all since that was another name for a person's bottom. Nannie started to describe her dream, but no one was listening. James and Ryan were teasing the dogs. Lady just rolled over on the floor at Aunt Alicia's feet, but Markie and Teddy and Dodie responded together with their annoying little dog yelps. Mama scolded my brothers and told them to go outside and play, and Daddy held the newspaper up higher in front of him.

"Hey—look at this," Daddy said, folding the newspaper in half, pointing to an article and reading aloud. "'The Oyster Industry: Progress or Pollution? Powerful partnerships are forming to rebuild the local oyster business, starting with the once-productive but now-defunct oyster factory on the Toogoodoo River adjacent to a privately held property,'" he read. Daddy looked at Nannie and said, "They must mean Gibson Island. We made the news."

"Read the rest of it, Jim," Nannie said, setting her coffee down on the table.

He went on. "'A local businessman, in conjunction with a group of investors, believes reopening the factory could provide gainful employment for over one hundred individuals and become a major supplier for restaurants across the Lowcountry. However, local landowners and community representatives are raising their voices to express concerns that, if permitted to reopen, the factory will poison the surrounding oyster beds.'"

"You bet it will," Nannie chimed in. "Go ahead. Keep reading, Jim."

"'Under its previous ownership, the factory faced considerable fines for labor violations and sanitation issues. Despite these penalties, the factory's owners attributed the ultimate failure of their business to a lack of access to more efficient distribution routes. The owners long desired but never acquired an overland route from the factory to the mainland.'"

"Distribution routes, my fanny!" Nannie said. "There was a big typhoid outbreak in New York City because the oyster beds were all fouled up. People thought the same thing would happen here."

Daddy finished up the article. "'At a town hall meeting held Friday night'" — Daddy looked up at Nannie — "'a small but vocal minority urged supporters of the factory redevelopment plan to reconsider. They insisted that more research should be conducted to assess the impact on the Toogoodoo River before any decision is made.'"

We all smiled at the end, and Nannie exhaled slowly. Mama said to Nannie, "I have a feeling it wasn't a coincidence that a newspaper reporter was at the meeting you went to on Friday."

"Okay, so, I did ask Graham Pierce from the *News and Courier* if he could stop by. You know, his daddy and I worked at the Exchange Bank together for years, so —"

"Well done, Fannie!" Daddy exclaimed.

"Well, we weren't getting very far. Those rich businessmen aren't too inclined to listen to us small-town folk. We needed some help."

Mama took the article from Daddy. "I should have known you were behind this," she said. "Maybe this will make all the difference, Mama."

"You should have seen Nannie talk at the town hall meeting. She was the leader, and there was a petition!" I added, showing how much I knew about everything. Nannie had let me go with her on Friday. It was the first time I'd ever gone to a town hall meeting, and I didn't understand what they were for exactly. That night when we walked into the Meggett Town Hall, she explained it was a meeting where people can go and speak their mind about things and stand up for what's right, and it was time for me to learn what that meant. That sounded good to me, especially since Nannie said this was about protecting Gibson Island.

At the meeting, Nannie headed straight for the swarm of people gathered around a big table, signing their names on a petition. She said, "A petition is a way for people to say what they want or what they don't want. In this case, we don't want that oyster factory next to Gibson Island to open up again. If we gather enough names, important people like the mayor might listen to us. We got almost fifty names last month at the town hall in Hollywood, so let's see if we can get more than that at this one." When I got up to the table, I saw there were already four pages filled with names.

I'd never seen Nannie so riled up, and while she was talking at the meeting, some people shouted out and clapped. She really knew how to get their attention, and I sat up straight in my chair in the front row, feeling proud and almost grown up.

"And on top of everything else," Nannie was saying to the audience, "no one even talks about protecting the river life we've known and worked for all our lives. Our oysters need natural, clean rivers and deep tidal creeks to grow in, and the baby oysters need the shells to attach themselves to, so they can survive. In the past, we know garbage has been dumped in our river, and shells have been tossed away in heaps or sold so they can be crushed up to make roads.

"I'm sure many of you have gotten the same calls and letters from lawyers that Alicia and I've gotten—probably ten since the last town hall meeting. Frank Mercer, Jean McConnell—you got them, didn't you?"

Mr. Mercer and Mrs. McConnell were sitting next to me and nodded. Nannie continued, "Well, the letters started out nice sounding, then they started offering bribes, and now the tone is downright demanding. They tell Alicia and me we need to sell Gibson Island to give them a better distribution route and help the economy and move forward into the future—all that kind of stuff. Well, we're not that stupid, and we're not going to sell." A loud cheer came from the crowd. "If they haven't already, they'll come to you, too. But without your property, without Gibson Island, and without your support as a community, this factory cannot open," she said. "So, before you leave tonight, make sure you sign the petition."

A couple of others got up and spoke, and the petition got a lot more signatures. The meeting ended early, though. Later Nannie said it was because someone involved in rebuilding the oyster factory was supposed to come and give a talk, but he never showed up. When the meeting let out, Daddy was waiting for me out front. Nannie waved at us on the way to her car to head back to Gibson Island for the weekend. Daddy started to drive away but stopped as he noticed a man approaching Nannie in the parking lot. The man was pacing back and forth as he talked and pointed at her. Something about him looked familiar, but it was dark and hard to tell for sure. Nannie shook her head, then got in her car and left, and the man climbed into a black truck.

"Well, I think we know who the new owner of the oyster factory is," Daddy said.

"Who?" I asked, as the black truck pulled in front of us, and the man looked right at Daddy without waving. It was the same man who had chased after James and Ryan and me at the fertilizer plant.

"Jeffrey Landry," Daddy answered. He rubbed his chin like he did when he was thinking hard about something, and we drove back to Bailey's Place.

In the red breakfast room, the river sparkled behind us, reminding Nannie to get up and head for the wharf. "Fannie," Daddy said before she left the room. "I saw you and Jeffrey Landry talking after the meeting on Friday night. What was that about?"

"Nothin' much," she answered. "He said he'd been prepared to speak at the meeting, but my talk stirred up such a reaction, he changed his mind. He's the new owner, and he wants to come over and have a talk with Alicia and me, but I said no thanks. It was a good thing he didn't talk at the meeting; his breath smelled like booze — saved himself a little face."

"Well, let's hope this article slows things down for a while," Mama said.

I turned back to look at Nannie, but she had already walked out of the room, heading for the smokehouse to get her fishing gear ready. I watched her from the screened porch, carrying her tackle box and fishing rod, the silver feather glittering at its tip, as she hurried down onto the wharf. When it came to fishing, Nannie looked like and had the energy of someone much younger. She got right to work, her tanned arms and legs moving quickly to set up.

"Genevieve! Come on down," she called, and I went down to join her while Ryan and James were busy digging up old bottles to add to their collection, and Mama and Daddy and Aunt Alicia finished up their coffee in the breakfast room. Once the nets and poles were set, Nannie and I took a walk along the river that led to the farthest point of Gibson Island.

"When you look around you, Genevieve, you can see why that town hall meeting was so important. All this land is surrounded by rich marshes and oyster beds, and even a long time ago, there were people always trying to buy it from my father and my grandfather, but they held on strong. The most pressure of all, though, is coming from that oyster factory right down the river there." She pointed at the broken-down-looking building with boarded-up doors and windows, hiding beyond the largest section of the marsh. Our path on Gibson Island ended at the oyster bed and the narrow strip of shallow marshland that separated us from the factory, but if you wanted to, you could easily walk across at low tide. I'd never come this far before, so it was like a whole other world over there, and I was curious about it.

We sat down under an old, skinny oak tree along the path that was missing most of its bark, and Nannie must have been reading my mind because I had questions about how things used to be. "They say bringing this factory back would bring jobs. When I was a little girl, the oyster factory gave people jobs, but the jobs were really hard on people. Men, women, and even children worked there all hours of the day and night, and most times they didn't get paid what they should. Plus, the factory was real dirty, so a lot of people got sick. Daduh's father worked there, you know. During the fall, he and all the men would go out in flat-bottomed boats and use these long-handled tongs to grab the oysters from their beds. I used to love watchin' the boats movin' through our creeks—in and out—in search of food. Daduh said her father used to brag that he'd bring back the most of any man—over a hundred bushels a day. And the women and children would help shuck and can them once they got to the factory." For a minute, I felt like I was going back with Nannie in her memory, and I could see Daduh's father working in the creeks, and I could hear the people's voices from the factory.

"Why'd it change?" I asked, leaning my head back against the tree and staring at that old factory.

"Just like everything does, I guess. People want more money, so they add more modern machinery so things can happen faster and more money can come in. But then those machines hurt people, too—kids your age, even—and they forget about what's important. This here. This is what's important." Nannie stood up to stretch. She raised her arms high and took a deep breath of the river air, and I did the same. She put her arm around my shoulders. "I'm glad you went with me to the town hall meeting. Gibson Island is yours, too. It's more than just land—it's who we are. Once it gets in your blood, you can't get it out—no matter how hard you try."

"Do you think something bad will happen? I mean, could we lose Gibson Island?" I asked.

"No, you mark my words on that. Never. My daddy and his daddy would roll over in their graves." I didn't like picturing that, but I got the message. She picked up the pace heading back to the wharf. It was time to check her nets and the lines. I scooped up a couple of oyster shells and tossed them back in the river, wondering if it might be too late for the baby oysters to attach themselves. I saw that Nannie was way ahead of me. "Wait up, Nannie! I'm coming with you!"

She turned around with her big smile and crinkly eyes and gestured for me to hurry, and we walked as fast as we could along our path toward the wharf so we could see what was waiting for us.

I wanted to stay longer at Gibson Island that day, but Mama and Daddy had lots of work to do around the house, and I'd promised Rachel Robertson, who was our next-door neighbor and maybe my new best friend, that we would practice singing some new songs together. I had big hopes for her being my best friend because I hadn't had too much luck finding one. There was Lenora Day, whose mother was a teacher at the school, but she just seemed too smart to have much fun with. Then there was Penny Dixon, who was funny and went to catechism classes with me at St. Anne's, but right when she was turning into my closest friend, she went and pointed out after Mass in front of everyone that my new brown sandals were made of plastic instead of leather.

So now there was Rachel, who was one of seven kids in the Robertson family. She was the same age as me; she had a really good singing voice; she liked to make up stories and have adventures; and she wasn't stuck up. The only thing I noticed about Rachel was she could be so happy one day, and the next day she'd be mad for no reason. I couldn't figure that part out, but Nannie said some people are moody, and you just have to stay out of their way until they change back to their regular selves. That Sunday, though, Rachel and I practiced songs together for hours until we were hoarse and couldn't sing anymore.

Late in the afternoon, before it was time to pick up Nannie and bring her back over to our house for the week, Aunt Alicia called from Gibson Island and said Nannie was missing.

"What do you mean *missing?*" my mother shouted into the phone, standing in our kitchen. Aunt Alicia said she'd looked everywhere for her all over the island. My parents raced out of the house, and Rachel's big sister Karen, who was in the twelfth grade and the oldest of all the Robertson children, came to babysit us. After a while, Karen told Rachel to go on back home, and she made supper for us and helped the boys get ready for baths and bed.

I knew the boys wouldn't go right to sleep, and they were worried, so I climbed in between them for a little while. "Genny, where's Nannie?" Ryan asked. He was always first to greet her when she arrived back each Sunday. Sometimes Daddy went to pick Nannie up from Gibson Island, and sometimes she drove her own car over, depending on if Aunt Alicia needed it or not. Last week, when she drove herself, Nannie stood waiting outside for Ryan to run to her excitedly like he always did, but he didn't come. We called out to him, and James even checked a couple of trees because it would be typical Ryan to get stuck in one of them. Finally, Nannie remembered Ryan was probably expecting her to come in Daddy's car, so she went to check, and sure enough, he was sound asleep on the floor of the backseat. He had planned to go with Daddy and surprise her. She helped him out of the car and then sat in the yard with him in the cool evening breezes, rubbing his head as he leaned against her and slowly woke up. "There you are, Nannie!" he'd said in his usual excited way.

Now, I rubbed his head, too, until he fell asleep. "She'll be home soon," I said. James lay there with his eyes open, just watching me.

"I think we should say a prayer," he whispered.

"Like one from church?" I asked.

"No. A better one. One we make up," he answered.

"Okay, you start," I said to him, and he closed his eyes tightly.

"Dear God, we need our Nannie to come back, so Genny and me want to ask you to please, please find her. If she got lost in the dark, please make the stars really bright so she can find her way back. We need her because she watches us every day and rings the bell for us to come inside."

"And she fixes supper so Mama and Daddy don't have to when they get off work," I added. James was better at this than I was, so I let him continue.

"God, I know we aren't always good, but we promise to always be good from now on. Please give us another chance, and let Nannie come home to us. Amen."

"In the name of the Father, the Son, and the Holy Ghost," I said quickly, thinking it would be extra helpful to put that part in there.

Long after they went to sleep, I was still in our living room, lying on the new gray brushed-velvet sofa that faced the front door. We didn't have any chairs for the living room yet, so Karen sat on the floor next to me and kept me company, playing her guitar and singing "Down in the Valley" over and over. Much later, I remember my father saying softly as he carried me to my bed, "Angel Baby, we're still looking for Nannie. I think we'll find her very soon."

I got up as soon as he closed my door and opened my music box with the ballerina that popped up and twirled in circles. I took out the rolled-up piece of tissue tucked in the bottom of the box and unwrapped the thin gold band with the tiny diamond. Nannie's daughters had given her this ring after the divorce from their father, and even though my birthday wasn't until November, she'd decided to give it to me early. "I can't wait another minute!" she said, watching my face as I opened it. Nannie just couldn't keep a secret. She was the same way about Christmas presents. In fact, everyone knew she opened up all of her own presents under the tree, wrapped them back up again, and then acted surprised on Christmas morning. I found a finger the ring would fit on. As I climbed into bed and pulled up the covers, I left my hand out on top so I could see it, and I waited there till morning came.

I had to go to school the next day, even though we still didn't know where Nannie was. Karen Robertson came back over to help out because Mama and Daddy had left early in the morning. Karen told us practically the whole town had come out to search Gibson Island. As she walked us down to the bus stop, she held Ryan's hand, but when she reached out to James, he shook his head and kept walking ahead. "Try not to worry. Your Nannie could have fallen asleep under a tree or maybe was bitten by a possum or a raccoon and just needs a doctor," Karen said.

The bus ride home that afternoon was unusually noisy and bumpy. I looked over at James and Ryan in the seat across the aisle, and they held their Daniel Boone and Batman lunchboxes close on their laps, staring straight ahead quietly. I wanted to say something that would help. I wanted to be a comforting big sister and promise them that everything was okay, but I just couldn't. Sitting at the back of the bus, our bodies popped up off the seats as we took the sudden shift from pavement to dirt road, and the dust billowed in through the open windows. I struggled to raise my window by holding down the metal latches and pulling upward, but it wouldn't work, one side getting stuck halfway up. Curt, who was one of Rachel's brothers and a year older than me, turned around in his seat and pinched the clamp down on the side of the window closest to him, and together, we managed to raise it. He caught my eye, and just as quickly, glanced downward. "I bet everything's okay, Genny," he said, but I could tell he was worried about Nannie, too.

The bus grinded to a stop, and all nine of us who lived at Bailey's Place and attended R. B. Stover Elementary got off at the Wishing Well. The old brick well that served as our bus stop sat in front of the Robertsons' house, and although it was filled with dirt and weeds, everyone still made wishes there. All the kids disappeared quickly. The Butler girls, Tracy and Pat, ran to their house, which was the first one in the row at Bailey's Place. The four youngest Robertson kids, Curt, Rachel, and the twins — Susan and Sarah — headed into their yard just as the three oldest ones, Karen, Lis, and Bob, who attended St. Paul's High School, pulled up. Karen, who was driving, looked into my eyes briefly, then quickly led all of her brothers and sisters into the house. As soon as James and Ryan and I stepped down off the bus, I knew something was wrong because Mrs. Robertson was standing there with a glass of water. She reached into the pocket of her apron, and for some reason, she gave me two baby aspirin. Then she hugged me and told the three of us, "Go on home, now." James said he wanted to make a wish at the well, so I waited. That was just like James—to do something thoughtful, even prayerful. I looked down the road at our new house, our happy house. There were cars parked outside I didn't recognize. I took a deep breath and looked at my brothers, their faces confused and scared.

"Who's at our house, Genny?" Ryan asked me. He tugged at the sleeve of my sweater and wouldn't let go. I put my hand on the top of his head, his blond crew cut soft and bristly, framing his little-boy face that still had a few leftover summer freckles.

"Listen to me. When we get to the house, you find Daddy right away, you hear?" I looked them straight in the eyes. They nodded and understood that I had to go ahead of them. I had to do this separately from them. I ran, and when I went in the front door, Daddy's sisters, who lived way on the other side of Charleston, over on Sullivan's Island, were sitting on the gray velvet sofa. They reached out to me as I walked past them. There were others around, too, and I heard them whisper, "Poor Genevieve," but all I wanted was my mother. I knew Nannie was gone. No one had to tell me.

Mama was sitting on my bed. She opened her arms to me, and I went into them. I listened carefully as she told me it looked like Nannie had fallen off the wharf into the water while she was fishing, and she was in heaven now. They didn't know, but they thought maybe it had been her heart that gave out.

I remembered what Nannie had said—that she didn't take much to being in the water. I hoped maybe her heart gave out first so she didn't have to be afraid. Mama and I held on to each other for a long time. When I tried to pull away, she wouldn't let me, and I knew she didn't want to look in my eyes. Over her shoulder, I could see the wisteria tree leaning against my bedroom window, its thick vines naked now without the droopy purple flowers, but still hanging heavy and low, moving ever so slightly, scratching against the house and casting faint, calming shadows across my room. Beyond it, I saw the river, not breathing at all, but quiet and still.

Even though I was still in that room, in Mama's arms, I could feel myself leaving her, and I went back to earlier that summer, when we still lived at Gibson Island and Ellie was visiting from New York. It was early morning, and we were sitting on the little screened porch outside the red breakfast room drawing pictures for our magazine and watching Nannie fish off the wharf. All of a sudden, Nannie started yelling.

"Genevieve! Ellie! Come quick!" We ran as fast as we could down the back brick steps and onto the wharf. Nannie's voice shook with excitement, and she pointed to the river. "I just saw a white dolphin! I've never seen anything like it in my life!" She described it in great detail as maybe eight feet long and white as snow. It had risen gently out of the water, then headed out toward the mouth of the river, riding the crest of a single white wave—the kind of frothy white wave a river makes when something big stirs it up from underneath.

Of course, no one believed her when she told the story, not even Mama. But Ellie and I knew it was true. We were there and had just missed seeing that dolphin, but we had seen the crest of that single white wave as it folded over itself and returned to the smooth, glass-like river, and it had left us breathless.

Chapter Five

April 7, 1966

RACHEL AND I WERE CONVINCED THAT Crazy Robby wandered around Bailey's Place at night, but we weren't sure why. Robby worked for the Bailey family as the nut collector, bagging pecans that fell on the ground. The pecan orchard was a big part of the property, and Daddy said that it brought in a lot of money for the Baileys. Robby stored the burlap bags full of pecans in the Nuthouse, which was right next to our house, and trucks would come every now and then to pick them up. Once the pecans were picked and bagged, the families living in the four houses on the property could have all the remaining nuts that were left on the ground, which was more than we could handle. In fact, Mama and Rachel's mother had thought of every way under the sun to use pecans — in pies, cakes, casseroles, or just sprinkled with salt and baked in the oven — and we never tired of them.

For a while, we'd noticed that Robby acted strangely. He talked out loud to himself, pointing at nothing in the air, and dragged around heavy bags of something that didn't look like pecans.

"Doesn't it seem strange that there's a padlock on the door and only Robby has the key to open it?" Rachel asked one day when we were walking by the Nuthouse. "It's just a storage place for bags of pecans. What's he hiding in there?"

"And why would he need to go in there at night when the workday is over?" I asked.

"He's taking something else in that Nuthouse besides pecans, I can tell you that right now," Rachel said. "I think we need to investigate."

Certain there was something secretive that Robby was up to, we made a plan to keep watch on the Nuthouse at different times of the day and night. One evening, we got brave enough to go up to the one window in back of the Nuthouse, but it was too high for us to look through, so Rachel and I went up to the bolted door, put our ears up against it, and thought we heard crying sounds inside. Just then, Robby appeared behind us, dropping another sack of something at our feet. It landed with a heavy thud, and we yelled out and ran away.

It didn't stop us, though. "What if someone is being held prisoner in there?" Rachel asked. "When the coast is clear, let's write a note and slip it under the door."

So we did that the very next morning and then hid ourselves nearby. The note said, "Knock if you need help. We can bring food." We waited and even checked back a few times, but nothing happened. We decided to slide some cookies under the door in case the captive needed food, but we never heard any more sounds. Rachel said if a person was in there, they would have suffocated by now.

"He probably already came and removed the body while we were sleeping last night," I said. We knew this needed some more investigation, especially since I now had a brand-new little brother to protect.

"We can't have Crazy Robby coming around while we're asleep. What if he tries to steal Thomas?" Rachel asked after our latest failed attempt to get into the Nuthouse. That was something I hadn't thought of, but now that she said it, it was stuck in my brain. I had tried to warn Mama and Daddy about Crazy Robby, but they wouldn't listen. I wished Nannie was here because this was just the kind of thing she would want to know about, and she'd believe me.

Nannie had been gone since October, and a lot had happened since then. Mama had had a baby just like Nannie said she would—another boy. Mama told us in November that she was expecting, and we were all very excited, mainly because we figured she would finally be happy again after a long month of sadness. We got to work right away setting up the nursery area next to Mama and Daddy's room, and we all fussed over Mama when she was extra tired. Through all this preparation, I had strong feelings Nannie was around. I remember one day when Mama was napping, I sat on the floor of the nursery, lining up some books for the baby on the bookshelf. As I turned the worn pages of the little *Peter Rabbit* book Nannie had read to her daughters and to us, there was a cold burst of air in the room, followed by a familiar whooshing sound in my ears and the sense of a warm blanket wrapping around me. I saw no one, but I knew I wasn't alone. Nannie was here with me, and I believed she wanted to be here with us as we got ready for the new baby.

Over the months, we watched as Mama's tummy grew, and she let us feel the quick kicks and rolls of the baby inside of her. She said this baby was the most active of her four and determined to come out running, so no one was surprised when he arrived a couple weeks earlier than expected. I'd wished hard for a sister, but that early morning in March when I got to hold Thomas Patrick Donovan for the first time, I knew he was, as Daddy called him, "a keeper." I fell in love with him.

Mama let me help take care of Thomas from the very beginning. He was no trouble, and soon I was taking him out in his baby carriage on little walks on the short dirt road that ran between Rachel's house and mine. I remembered why I was afraid of Crazy Robby, though, on one of those afternoon walks. Heading toward Rachel's house, I wasn't paying much attention to what was behind me, but I noticed the sound of the Bailey's riding mower getting louder and louder, and I saw Rachel waving her arms in a panic from her porch. When I turned around, there was Crazy Robby on the mower, heading straight for us, and just as he was almost on top of Thomas and me, I jerked the carriage off the dirt road into the Robertsons' driveway in the nick of time. As Rachel waved her arms in the air at Robby, he turned around and waved back and just continued on.

"He tried to run you over!" Rachel yelled. I looked down at Thomas, who was awake from the noisy mower but didn't seem upset, and I hugged Rachel because she had saved both of us from Crazy Robby. Then Rachel's brother Curt came over and told us to calm down and that Robby always picks up a little speed on the dirt road before he gets back on the grass and it wasn't even a close call. But Rachel and I knew better. Later, when I told Mama about it, she said to just pay attention to what was going on around me and to keep Thomas away from all the cut grass and sticks and dirt blowing around the riding mower.

When Robby wasn't tending to the Nuthouse or mowing the grass, he helped keep up the gardens around the Baileys' house. Sylvia Bailey belonged to the Lowcountry Garden Club and held luncheons outside in the spring. Although she had many different flowers in her garden, she was known best for her prize camellias.

The other thing Miss Sylvia was known for was a good heart. Everyone knew Robby was "crazy as a loon"—those were Aunt Alicia's words. Aunt Alicia told us he'd been in an asylum when he was a teenager and was now living with his mother and father in a little house the Baileys owned on the narrow inlet that ran along the back of their property. Robby's mother was their housekeeper, and his father was in charge of all the outside help. Miss Sylvia gave them their old clothes and extra food when she could, and she wouldn't let anyone say bad things about Robby or his family. Whenever Mr. Bear, who ran Bear's Store at the end of Bailey's Road, called Robby that "lazy, crazy colored boy," Miss Sylvia would take offense, and she'd say right to his face in the store, "I take offense at each of those words, Mr. Bear."

After we moved to Bailey's Place, Aunt Alicia said, "I'll let you in on a little secret." Aunt Alicia had a lot of those. She told us that Miss Sylvia herself had had a nervous breakdown when she was a young woman and that was why she got so upset when people spoke mean about Robby. Mr. Bailey was more like a father figure who stepped in and took care of Miss Sylvia. He was a good bit older and had a lot of money and spoiled her rotten. Aunt Alicia knew Miss Sylvia from her childhood days, so this information seemed like it was on pretty good authority.

Before he retired and moved down South, Mr. Bailey had been a lawyer in New York, working with people in the movie business. Daddy said he was really a good old country boy down deep who just happened to be rich. They did lead interesting lives, though. Mama told us one afternoon we were to stay in our own yard and not go into the Orchard around the Baileys' house because they had big movie stars visiting them for the weekend. She said Cliff Robertson and Dina Merrill were staying there, and she got on the phone and invited everyone she knew over to our house for supper.

None of us saw the movie stars that night, and we ended up having a nice party, I guess. I spent considerable time, though, on the porch wondering how things were going at the Baileys' house. I imagined them in white robes over their swimsuits, Miss Merrill with red lipstick and long fingernails and a big straw hat, and Mr. Robertson with a dark tan, standing over her with a cigarette in one hand and a martini in the other. They were probably talking about the movies they were in, the vacation in Paris they took last summer, and their friends, like Bob Hope and Judy Garland and Sandra Dee.

The Baileys had a white, two-story main house with tall columns, a small guesthouse, a pool, and a separate garage that held three cars, and all this was surrounded by shrubs and hedges, perfectly trimmed by Robby's daddy. When Rachel and I walked by there at night, we could see the heavy drapes in the windows, the teardrop chandelier in the dining room, and the dark wood paneling in the drawing room. I learned they called it a drawing room when I went over there by myself, uninvited, late one afternoon after the riding mower incident. I don't know what got into me, but Rachel wasn't able to come outside for some reason, and ever since the movie stars visited, I'd gotten more and more curious, so I just rode my bike right up to their house and knocked on the door.

Mr. Bailey and Miss Sylvia seemed to be real happy to have me visit. We sat in a narrow little library off the drawing room that had two chairs and a footstool just right for Miss Sylvia's tiny feet, a small table with a lamp, and books that went up one whole wall from the floor to the ceiling. They let me look through their favorite books, like their Agatha Christie mystery collection, and Miss Sylvia showed me a row of framed photographs of her award-winning camellias. Then she brought out lemon cookies covered in powdered sugar and tall, frosted glasses of iced tea with mint leaves. It wasn't as sweet as Mama's tea, but it was still good and had a long silver spoon for stirring in extra sugar.

While I was feeling very grown up having tea and discussing odds and ends, I suddenly realized it was dark outside. I was not allowed out after dark, unless it was in our own yard, and I knew I was in big trouble. I didn't let on to the Baileys, but they could probably tell something was wrong by the way I tore out of there when they told me what time it was. As I raced back home along the winding dirt road, I felt like someone was watching me from the Orchard. I wondered if Crazy Robby was out there. I pedaled faster and faster toward our porch light way in the distance. Against my better judgment, but to save time, I decide to take the bumpy shortcut across the Orchard, and just as I left the dirt road, I hit a deep hole that sent me flying into the darkness. When I landed in between a couple of pecan trees, I knew I wasn't hurt, but I also realized I wasn't alone. With eyes from unknown creatures lighting up in the trees around me, and fearing that Crazy Robby was nearby, I jumped up and grabbed my bike.

It was then that I heard the whispering over and over, close to my ears, close to my face. *"You're okay. You're okay."* I froze for a second. There it was. It was her voice. Nannie was back. I closed my eyes, waiting to be touched by her. I needed to feel the softness of her hand against my cheek like she always used to do. Instead, I heard words that were either out loud or in my head—I couldn't be sure. *"Genevieve, remember things aren't always as they seem."*

Then, my mother called out, and I got back on my bike, wobbling my way through the remainder of the Orchard. Finally, I reached the porch, and Mama was standing there with her arms wrapped around the top of her body, as if they were holding her up. Her face was full of worry, and I stood in front of her ready for what I deserved. I tried to tell her what I had just heard in the Orchard because she needed to know. I pointed into the darkness behind me. "Mama! In the Orchard, I fell and then I heard her—"

"Your daddy and the boys are out looking for you. I thought you were kidnapped or dead!" she said, her voice shaking.

That night, Mama spanked me with a hairbrush. Unlike my brothers, I think that was the only time I ever got spanked, and I didn't mind. I took it bravely and refused to make a sound. I just kept thinking of Nannie brushing my hair at night while she told me the stories of my great-great-grandmother. I could hear Mama crying after she left my room. Daddy told me he was disappointed in me when he got home. His eyes were red, and I knew he was scared. That was the first time I saw how Mama and Daddy's love could look like something totally different—like anger and fear. It was also the last time I crossed the Orchard in the dark. More than anything, I wished that I could tell someone about what happened there—that I had heard Nannie—but no one was in the mood to hear what I had to say.

A few nights later, Crazy Robby scared the devil out of Mama when he showed up at our kitchen door with a knife the size of an ax. It was pouring rain, and the thunder was already to the count of three away. Nannie used to say, "Watch for the lightning. Then start counting slowly, and stop counting when the thunder claps. One, two, three, four . . . the higher you can count before the thunder comes, the farther away the storm is."

Daddy wasn't home that night. He had to travel more and more lately because there were two new plant sites that had opened in the state, and he had to help Mr. Landry out. He would sing "King of the Road" while he packed, which irritated Mama because she didn't like the idea of him being gone so much, and on top of that, she was anxious about returning to work at the bank so soon after having Thomas. Sometimes when Mama was holding him, she would just stare into space, and I knew she was thinking about Nannie. They had just hired a maid to help with the cleaning and to watch us during the weekdays. Her name was Ruby, and she came highly recommended by Daduh, not only because she was good but also because she was married to Daduh's grandson, Jackson.

Ruby didn't work for us at night, though, so on nights when Daddy was out of town, I was a big help to Mama and kept her company, too. If it was a Tuesday, she let me crawl under the covers with her in bed after the boys were down, and we'd watch *The Alfred Hitchcock Hour*. Every week, we looked forward to being scared to death by that TV show, and there was one episode that was the scariest of all. It was the story of an insane criminal who was killing nurses just for the fun of it. The main character was a nurse who was taking care of an invalid in an old house one stormy night, while this criminal was on the loose. What the main character didn't know was that the nurse she let in to relieve her on duty was really the killer in disguise. Those shows always ended up with something shocking we didn't expect, and on the night Robby showed up, I remembered that a knock at the door and a stormy night were not a good combination.

At the sound of loud banging on the back door in the kitchen, the first thing I thought was — between that and the thunderstorm — Thomas would surely wake up. Mama leaped to her feet from the kitchen table and automatically opened the door, thinking it was a neighbor. And it *was* a neighbor, kind of. It was Crazy Robby. One hand held the large knife, and the other was covered in blood. He was yelling, and the rain was blowing sideways against his face and clothes. Mama somehow seemed to move in slow motion and talk quietly as if that might help calm him down.

"Robby, what are you doing? Put the knife down." Mama wouldn't let him in and motioned wildly behind her back for me to get out of the kitchen. Without taking her eyes off of Robby, her right hand reached for the phone that hung on the wall by the door. "I'm going to call Miss Sylvia for help, so wait outside." Robby kept crying and crying, louder and louder, and wouldn't stop. He leaned hard into the back door as Mama tried to push it shut. He was so strong, and Mama couldn't close the door by herself. "Genevieve, go back there now with your brothers — get Thomas." Her tone remained strangely flat. I turned and ran to the back of the house. As I did, I heard the kitchen door slamming against the wall as it was forced open, and bodies hitting the floor, my mother's voice crying out, and thunder roaring at the count of one, following a bolt of lightning that lit up the entire house.

I picked Thomas up out of the cradle that had been my mother's when she was a baby and ordered James and Ryan to get under their bed. I tried to do the same but couldn't fit under the bed with Thomas in my arms, so I hid next to it behind the stuffed orange chair Aunt Alicia had given us. From my crouching position, I could see the seat of the chair sagged below its frame, and there was a perfectly round cigarette burn in the middle of its back. James and Ryan would not be quiet, their whispers louder than shouts, asking so many questions, but Thomas was calm despite my whole body shaking and my heart beating loudly in his ears.

After a few minutes of waiting, we tiptoed out of the bedroom slowly. We strained our necks forward as we listened for sounds of our mother, but the storm was too loud. James led the way as we inched along the hallway wall toward the kitchen. I could feel Ryan up against me, holding onto the tail of my shirt as I held Thomas close against my chest. We expected the worst — our mama killed by a crazy man just because Miss Sylvia had protected him and let him roam the property at night. The town was right about Crazy Robby. Rachel and I had been right about the Nuthouse, and now he was going to kill us, too.

What we saw was confusing. Our mama sat on the floor with Robby's head in her lap. She had a bloody dish towel wrapped around his hand, which she held up in the air. With her other hand, she rubbed Robby's head while he moaned pitifully like a hurt dog.

We weren't sure whether to go in or not. Mama nodded as if to say, "Everything is fine, now."

She spoke slowly. "Genny—go on and call Mr. Bailey. The phone number is on the pad by the phone. Tell him to come on over now."

James took Thomas, and the three of them stayed close to me as I dialed the number, barely taking my eyes off of Mama rubbing Robby's head.

"Hello, Mr. Bailey? This is Genevieve Donovan across the Orchard. My mama says to come on over to our house right away because Robby's here and needs you to come get him. He's crying and has blood all over him. He's lying in the middle of our kitchen floor, and Mama is holding onto him, so you better hurry."

Shocked by what was happening, my brothers and I just stood there, not saying a word. Robby cried like a baby in her arms, and Mama was saying over and over, "You're okay. You're okay." Those words. I'd just heard those same words the other night. I recognized what was happening. When I'd been afraid of Robby, falling off my bike in the Orchard, I'd heard Nannie say, *"You're okay. You're okay."* And then, *"Things aren't always as they seem."* And I knew now there was no reason to be afraid. There never was.

Miss Sylvia and Robby's mama said if it wasn't for our mother, Robby might have lost use of that hand, that cut was so bad. Robby had to go to the hospital and get a lot of stitches and wear a sling for a good month. It seems he was trying to get into the Nuthouse that rainy night and had lost the key to the lock, so he tried to use a knife out of Mr. Bailey's shed to cut the lock off the door. With the rain coming down so hard in the dark, Robby couldn't see very well, and the knife slipped and sliced up his hand. At first, we couldn't figure out what in the world Robby was doing there at night in the rain, but we learned there were leaks in the Nuthouse roof that Robby was worried about, so he had placed buckets inside to catch the rain coming through. He was going back to empty those buckets and check that the bags of pecans were staying dry.

About a week later, Robby's mama came by and brought us jars of crab apple jelly she'd made as a thank-you to our mama for helping her son. She was a big woman and took our front steps slowly, pausing on each one to catch her breath. She was shaking her head and talking almost to herself, like Robby sometimes did, saying how she didn't know how Robby thought he could get a big steel lock off a door with a knife, but she was glad he'd gone to the Donovans' house for help, even if he did scare the devil out of everybody with all his foolish carrying on.

Chapter Six

April 10, 1966

THE WORD GOT AROUND FAST THAT Mama had saved Crazy Robby's life, and we all just let the story go where people wanted to take it, which was in a lot of different directions. Daduh and Ruby both said all their folks at Hope Baptist Church were singing praise to Mama and Miss Sylvia, but Aunt Alicia scolded Mama, saying she had no business letting him in the house like she did.

"What got into you? Letting an idiot straight out of a loony bin into your home during a storm, and what with Jim out of town, and with a new baby!"

Mama had no intention of letting what Aunt Alicia said bother her. "That's just how Aunt Alicia is, saying her mind like that whenever she wants," she said. I never did really understand Aunt Alicia very well and couldn't talk to her the way I could to Nannie.

There were two reasons Aunt Alicia turned out differently from Nannie, Mama explained a while back. One was because as a young woman, Aunt Alicia had fallen madly in love with a man named Paul Watts. As the story goes, he was already married, and Alicia's father, Michael Gibson, got so angry that he chased Paul out of town and told him to never set foot in Charleston again. Aunt Alicia never married anyone and moved back to Gibson Island, where she stayed forever. The summer before Nannie went missing, Ellie and I found an old hatbox upstairs in the closet that was filled with love letters to Aunt Alicia from Paul Watts and another bundle of letters she wrote and never mailed.

The other reason she was different, Mama said, was because she'd been attacked when she had worked as an accountant downtown. A man robbed the place and hit her over the head with a gun and tied her up. She was able to identify the man, and he went to prison, but she was always very suspicious about everyone and everything after that. That was about when Aunt Alicia decided she didn't want to drive downtown anymore and turned the dining room at Gibson Island into her office, where she continued to work as a bookkeeper for her friend Dr. Meg. There was only one thing that made me nervous about Aunt Alicia. She always thought someone was on the verge of breaking into the house or hiding on the island somewhere. Daddy said James and Ryan and I were not to go near the hall closet next to her bedroom because that was where she kept her guns.

Aunt Alicia said proudly more than once, "If any strangers come near my property, I won't bother with any law that says you can't shoot 'em till they break into your house. I'll shoot 'em dead first and then drag their asses over the threshold." Daddy laughed at this, but I didn't think it was very funny because I believed she would do just that.

While Ruby and Daduh's church praised our mama, we could tell some of the people at our own church felt the same way Aunt

Alicia did. The Griffin sisters avoided all contact with us the Sunday after the Robby ordeal, and people gave Mama looks like she'd done something wrong. During Mass, Mama sat up nice and tall and told me to do the same. She stared straight ahead at Father Cuddihy, and when Marylou Griffin reached out from the pew behind us and clumsily touched the back of my mother's hair during the homily, Mama didn't turn around. But I did, because I knew what Marylou was doing.

Marylou looked me square in the eye, and her body was still and quiet for a second, like she was normal and there was nothing wrong with her. I think she was letting us know she was proud of what Mama did for Crazy Robby. Marylou seemed much better than she had a few weeks earlier when right in the middle of Mass, her body started shaking wildly, and her mama called out, "She's having a convulsion!" Father Cuddihy dropped the chalice on the altar table and ran to her praying. When they carried her out, I was afraid she'd die because she was so sick to begin with, but she was back at St. Anne's the very next Sunday, her body twitching and jerking as usual all through Mass. Today, I waved my fingers to Marylou from the bottom of my skirt as we sneaked out again after Communion.

As far as Robby was concerned, it wasn't a secret in our town he was different, and I have to admit I had my doubts about him, but according to Mama and Daddy, being different didn't give folks the right to judge. Sometimes people couldn't help it, or they just came on hard times. Daddy said, for example, he'd lost jobs in the past and we'd had trouble bouncing back, but we wouldn't want anyone judging us about that.

"I really don't appreciate getting the cold shoulder from those busybodies," Mama told Daddy as we climbed into the car after church. I leaned my head against the window and watched James and Ryan argue over who was going to get the other car window seat, which was a waste of time because James always won. As we turned onto Gibson Road like we still did each Sunday, Mama kept talking. Sometimes when she was worked up about something, her voice could sound exactly like Nannie's, so I closed my eyes tightly and listened. "They weren't there that night when that boy was so desperate for help and so scared. What kind of human being wouldn't help someone as pitiful as that and injured so badly? Jim, once I saw his eyes, I knew he wasn't going to hurt us—I just knew it. I can't explain it." Daddy placed his hand over hers on the front seat.

The fact is, most people thought Mama had practically invited Robby in that night when he came crying to the door. No one could understand how she could let him in because it was known all over town that he was crazy. But what they didn't know, and Mama said it was best to keep it that way, was that in Robby's panic about all the blood from his hand and the thunder and lightning, he'd forced the kitchen door open, falling to the floor on top of my mother. If people knew this, the idea that she was attacked would set off a worse reaction, and this would cause Robby and his family real problems. So, Mama purposefully left that part out. She just let folks believe she'd grown naïve about the way things were around here, probably from the influence of California and because she'd been so distracted by her mother's death. The truth was Mama had a way of knowing things and helping people in a quiet kind of way.

When the car stopped in front of the house, Mama turned around to Ryan and James and me, and she looked like she was going to cry. Daddy noticed it, too, but just as he reached over to her, she shook her head. Then she abruptly opened the car door, carrying Thomas and waving and smiling at Aunt Alicia, who was coming down the front steps with Lady, Dodi, Markie, and Teddy prancing around her. Mama knew how to change real fast from being sad or mad to happy, but I could tell it wasn't real. Mama missed her mother terribly.

It had been five months since the funeral. We were all trying to go on as usual, but it was hard, and I was noticing Mama and Aunt Alicia were having more and more trouble going about their regular lives like nothing had changed. Our family continued to go over to Gibson Island after Mass each Sunday, which was fine, but about once a month, Aunt Alicia still insisted on having Big Sunday Dinner Day. That's what Nannie used to call it because it included the rest of the Gibson side of the family from Charleston, as well as Father Cuddihy. This was one of those Sundays, and the whole crew would be coming over in an hour. Aunt Alicia and Mama seemed as if they were forcing themselves to go through with it, like they were tired of it all. I wanted them to be like Nannie used to be—happy that it was Big Sunday Dinner Day—as she ran around doing last-minute preparations, shaking out tablecloths, arranging chairs on the porch, setting out clean ashtrays, counting out the silverware and plates, stirring the hot sugar water into tall pitchers of freshly brewed tea, checking the cheese biscuits in the oven, and sneaking some for just the two of us. Instead, as they got ready today, their footsteps echoed heavily back and forth on the wooden floors, and the busy screen door to the front porch that used to open and shut cheerfully, as if clapping, now just slammed noisily each time someone went through it.

Today, a light April shower that lasted no more than a minute cleaned the yellow spring dust off the porch steps, just in time for Mama and Aunt Alicia to welcome folks to Gibson Island for Big Sunday Dinner. Daddy was arranging ice and bottles and glasses on the teacart and making sure everyone had something to drink. Father Cuddihy was pouring his Irish whiskey, but almost every-one else was sipping bourbon. Nannie always said that Southerners did not drink bourbon—they "sipped bourbon." The only one who didn't sip bourbon was Aunt Sis. That's because she was a nun, although she did sip a little sherry at Christmastime.

Since Aunt Sis, who always wore her nun's habit, was now a mother superior, she'd been traveling a lot and didn't have as much time as she used to for Big Sunday Dinner Days. But today she came and brought her nun friends, Sister Mary Ignatius and Sister Mary Clare, who had to be the funniest nuns any Catholics had ever seen. They called Aunt Sis "Mother" because of her new job. They were very talkative and friendly with our family, and I was particularly fascinated with Sister Mary Clare, the plump one with bright-red cheeks who was always humming. I asked her if she knew the Singing Nun or had ever met Debbie Reynolds, but she just laughed and said, "No, but I can sing 'Dominique,'" and we sang it together.

On her recent trip to Rome, Aunt Sis brought back a crystal rosary for me that had been blessed by the Pope, and I kept it in my ballerina music box. I used to go to the convent sometimes to visit her with Nannie. She had only a single bed and a dresser in her room with a small crucifix on the wall. Nannie and I would sometimes pick her up at the convent and take her with us to Woolworths. She always ordered a fried egg sandwich and a glass of chocolate milk, and Nannie paid. She'd spend a long time in the aisles at Woolworths, rosary beads clicking at her waist, lifting her head up from her permanently bent-over body so she could read the words on the boxes of stationery she would take back to the convent. That was her favorite thing to buy.

As long as family gatherings weren't on the first Saturday of the month, the busiest day for Condon's shoe department, Aunt Theresa and Uncle Martin could come out to Gibson Island, too. Uncle Martin would usually bring Aunt Alicia a pair of special shoes for yard work when he came, and she would take them out of the box and say "Well, thank you, Martin!"

"These are supposed to be the best," he said today, showing her the soles and tapping on the heels with his knuckles, but I knew she would just keep wearing her same old brown scuffed-up boots that came up above her ankles and had broken laces popping out the sides.

Uncle Donald was there, too. Daddy called him a whiner behind his back and told Mama not to encourage him, but Mama still listened to him anyway. She was always very polite that way. "Ever since Fannie died," he complained as soon as he arrived, "all I got left is Alicia here, who just wants to live with her dogs and drive a tractor around all day. Sis is too busy saving the world, and Theresa stays in her dream world with Martin, who thinks that running a shoe department is like running a small country. No offense meant, you understand, but I ask you—what am I to do now?"

"I'm getting tired of Uncle Donald's woe-is-me stories," Mama whispered to Daddy as she brought more iced tea out to the porch. "Why doesn't he just move back out here to the country instead of going on and on about it?"

"Your uncle Donald is like the rest of your family. He likes to hear himself talk," Daddy teased, and Mama nodded in agreement.

The other regular guests for Big Sunday Dinner Day, and probably the most interesting to me, were Dr. Meg Spencer and Judith Moore. Dr. Meg was a woman's doctor. She'd delivered my mother as well as the four of us at St. Francis Hospital downtown. Aunt Alicia had been her good friend and private accountant for many years. Meg Spencer's short red hair was cut close like a man's, and she dressed like a man, too, wearing pants and suits. I think she even wore a tie once in a while. She lived with Judith Moore, who was a very well-known painter in the Lowcountry. One day when Nannie took me on a trip into Charleston, we went to Gibbes Art Gallery, where she showed me some paintings by the local artists. Judith and Meg Spencer just happened to be in one of the side rooms hanging Judith's new paintings in preparation for a special show coming up at the gallery.

They insisted on us going back with them to their apartment, which was like a huge studio on top of an antique store on King Street. There were canvases and brushes and cloths and different paints everywhere. Dr. Meg laughed and said they didn't have much room to sit, so when they weren't working, they spent most of their time on the little screened-in balcony that overlooked the side alley. From there, they could see Dock Street Theatre and the comings and goings of the actors and stagehands and singers and dancers. Judith liked to work with watercolors the most and painted scenes of Charleston life. I could tell Dr. Meg was really proud of her because she kept pulling out paintings from stacks against the walls to show us. As we left the apartment, Judith gave me a set of charcoals and pastels in a wooden box so I could practice with them at home. From down in the street, I watched Meg Spencer take Judith's hand as they went back in from the balcony, and I said to Nannie, "They sure are the best of friends, aren't they?"

That Big Sunday Dinner Day while everyone was finishing up eating, Dr. Meg and Judith came over and asked me if I was still enjoying the art set they'd given me last year because they were worried my supplies might be getting low. Judith then sat by me and brought out a sack of new brushes and paints, and as we looked through them, I heard Dr. Meg talking with Mama.

"Louisa, Thomas looks great. You doing okay?" she asked. Mama always said Dr. Meg was the best doctor in the world and how lucky she was to have her when all her children were born.

"Yes, just kind of tired. Makes me appreciate how much Mama did for me and how much she helped me every day," Mama answered softly.

"I know you miss her," Dr. Meg said. "Even after these few months, I still can't believe she's gone. It just seems like a mystery to me. A perfectly healthy woman with no heart issues . . . it just doesn't make sense knowing her like I did."

"I guess we'll never know for sure," Mama said.

"Well, you be sure and take good care of yourself. Do like I tell you now and try not to rush back into everything so quickly. Give yourself some time. Call my office, and let's do a follow-up in a few months, okay?" Dr. Meg gave Mama a hug, and she and Judith left, soon to be followed by the rest.

Although those Big Sunday Dinners had always been nice at Gibson Island, at the end of this one, Aunt Alicia confessed to Mama she didn't really want to do them anymore and was glad when everyone finally left. She and Daddy and Mama had a talk about it as we started gathering trash and cleaning up the porch. Those social times were more of Nannie's doing, Aunt Alicia said, and while Aunt Alicia had tried to keep it up these past months, Mama agreed that they stop entertaining at Gibson Island for a while. It just wasn't the same anymore.

"Y'all will still keep comin' after Mass on Sundays, right?" she asked.

"Of course we will," Daddy said, "as long as you come over to Bailey's Place more often!" Recently, Daddy had noticed she was needing more help around the island. She'd been forgetful and misplacing a lot of tools, and much of the property was overgrown with weeds and tall grass. He'd recommended James and Ryan start taking on some odd jobs for her, and she agreed and paid them money for it, too. I think they also helped keep her company. The boys got to ride on the tractor with her and work in the yard and fix things like the loose boards on the little wooden bridge and the shed doors that were hanging off their hinges. They worked up quite a sweat and never complained like they did at home. After they were done working, she'd teach them about stamp and coin collecting, and then they'd go on their bottle-hunting adventures in the mud, things I had absolutely no interest in.

James and Ryan couldn't get enough of Aunt Alicia telling what happened when she lost two of her fingers in a car accident many years ago, so they asked her again while we were in the kitchen doing the dishes. "I was headin' home one afternoon after work, and a car swerved into mine on Savannah Highway. I had my elbow propped in the open window, and this left hand here was clutchin' the top of the car's window frame like this . . ." And she showed them how it was. "My car must've flipped two or three times, and when I landed, I looked at my hand and saw I'd lost my two middle fingers!" I never understood how Aunt Alicia could make a joke out of something like that, but somehow she did. Now, with her Polaroid, she took silly pictures of James and Ryan pretending their middle fingers were gone, too, resting their chins in the space where the fingers were hidden, and of course, she then posed with the boys, holding a glass of bourbon with her three-fingered hand.

My brothers didn't mind Aunt Alicia's oddness—how she fed the possums and raccoons dog kibble at night; that she wore the same clothes almost every day; how all her dogs slept on the bed with her and that her bedroom floor was covered with dirty dog papers next to the magazine heaps. Aunt Alicia asked James and Ryan to take Lady and the little dogs outside for a run, and while I was drying the remaining dishes, she brought out a folder with papers and handed them to Daddy and Mama.

"This is kind of interesting, Jim. Your employer's son came to see me last week, and I meant to show you these," she said.

"What do you mean? Jeffrey Landry?" he asked as he looked at her and then took a pile of jumbled-up papers out of the folder and spread them out on the kitchen counter.

"Well, yes—he seemed like an okay guy, after all. Since he bought the oyster factory last October, he says he and his partners convinced the Mercers and O'Connells down the road to sell their property, so he wants to talk to me now about some other Gibson Island options and—"

Daddy cut in. "What? What options?"

"He's giving them a huge payoff, and he says something could be in it for me, too, and with very little risk," Aunt Alicia said.

"Aunt Alicia! What are you talking about? You know just last month, Graham Pierce wrote another follow-up article about the oyster factory that said there was going to be an environmental study, and it's scheduled for early June. There was nothing about anyone selling any property out here," Mama said with a tone of voice like she just couldn't believe what was happening.

"Alicia, what did Jeffrey Landry say to you? Tell me exactly." Daddy looked very worried as he looked through the messy papers.

"He said the Mercers and the O'Connells are really excited about the deal they're getting and that they'll have more money than they ever dreamed of. He says he knows with Fannie gone now, I might be worried about my future and taking care of this big property. He says he can help, and I don't have to lose my home at all. If I sign these papers, it just means he can tell his partners he shared the information with me about some of my options. He's coming back tomorrow," Aunt Alicia said. "What? Why are you both looking at me that way? I didn't sign anything yet!" she added when she saw their faces. Mama and Daddy looked at each other and shook their heads.

"Alicia," Daddy said, holding up the package of papers. "If you had signed this paper, you would have agreed to sell all forty acres of Gibson Island to build a cannery and a road that would cut directly through the island to Hollywood. Look at the document here in the back. It clearly spells out that there is only *one* option and that is to release all forty acres to the Landry-Folson Partners Development Project for the construction of the oyster cannery and new road network at an agreed price to be discussed April 11, 1966. That's tomorrow!"

"No—that's not what he said!" Aunt Alicia shouted. "I didn't know! I thought if the Mercers and the O'Connells are doing it, I should at least hear about the other kinds of options. He tricked me!"

Mama looked at Daddy worriedly and took Aunt Alicia's arm gently. "It's okay, Aunt Alicia. That's right, you didn't know. But now you do, so Jim and I will help you sort this out. I'm so sorry he took advantage of you like that," Mama said.

"He's the one who's gonna be sorry tomorrow," Daddy said, and he put his arm around Aunt Alicia, who had covered her face with her hands.

Chapter Seven

April 10, 1966

WHILE MAMA AND DADDY TALKED MORE with Aunt Alicia about the trick Jeffrey Landry had tried to pull, I went upstairs. Things sure were a mess. I could tell how worried Mama and Daddy were, and I didn't know what it all meant. All I knew was that Nannie had worked so hard to try and protect Gibson Island, and I couldn't imagine losing it.

I stopped at the landing upstairs and looked around. Ever since the funeral, whenever I came over to Gibson Island, this is where I felt closest to Nannie—around her books and in her room. I sat on the floor next to the rows of bookshelves that lined the landing walls outside Nannie's room. The landing circled around the top of the stairs and had four bedrooms off of it, each with its own screen and solid doors. The books were all mixed up; some were lying sideways; some were stacked on top of each other; some were old books with yellowed, crumbly pages; some had book jackets; and some forgotten ones were buried way in the back.

The April showers started back up again, tapping on the tin roof over my head, and I found myself going back to times with Nannie here. Sitting in the middle of all her favorite books used to be the best way to spend rainy days, when we had no choice but to stay inside and disappear into another world. Nannie used to say, "Books take you somewhere better than any real place on earth, but not just any book will do." She said you can tell a good book just by the smell of it, so we would open our books and put our noses to them, taking it all in. Mama said Nannie meant it was the quality of the paper you could smell, but that wasn't what she meant at all; it was the smell of a good story. Nannie and I talked about the way different books smelled, and we took turns outdoing each other's descriptions. She liked one of mine best — if it smelled more like the new black asphalt roads in Hollywood on the hottest day in August, this was not our kind of book. I liked one of hers best. She said, "There is a split second when you can smell it. After you unfold a crisp white tablecloth and pop it into the air . . . right before it lands on the dark wood of the dining room table — it is the smell in that tiny breeze that you catch. *That* is the smell of a good book." And then she handed me *Rebecca* from the bookshelf, and I smelled it, and she was right.

I looked through them all now and found *Rebecca* again, and I took it off the shelf, leaving in its place a slice of dark wood surrounded by a thick coating of dust. I knew that Daduh wasn't able to make it up the stairs anymore, so no telling when this place had had a real good cleaning.

Probably the last time Daduh had been upstairs was the day before the funeral. That day she came up with her arms full of linens, and she found me on the floor of the landing going through all the books. We'd come over to Gibson Island that morning to help Aunt Alicia get ready for the gathering after the funeral, but I didn't feel like helping, so I slipped away from everyone. I kept feeling like Nannie was still around and was going to show up any minute, and I wanted to be ready for her.

"Child . . ." Daduh spoke with a soft voice, setting the linens on a chair in the corner. "Now, let's go ahead and get everything cleaned up for comp'ny comin'." Daduh extended her hand to pull me up.

"No. I don't want to, Daduh," I said, pulling my hand back from hers and staying put. I had stacked up a pile of books I wanted to look through.

"Oh, child," she said, and her words cracked in half with sadness. I stayed right there while Daduh dusted around me. Nannie's sweater was draped over the corner chair, and out of the corner of my eye, I watched her pick it up, hold it close, then tuck it under her arm. "It's gonna be all right, Genevieve," she said. I stood up quickly and hugged her. I knew she missed Nannie very much. "It'll do ya good to cry some," she added, putting her arm around me.

I shook my head. "Mama won't let me go to the funeral," I said to her.

"Well, that's her decision to make. She knows what's best for you," Daduh said.

"No, I don't think so. She's forgot all about me," I said.

"Now, that's not true. Your mama's real busy gettin' ready for tomorrow. It's a sad time, and there's a lot to do with all the people comin'. Help me put these books away. Come on now. Hurry up 'cause your Daddy's downstairs waitin' to take you back to your own house." I saw Daduh's eyes were watery, and I didn't want her to cry, so I helped her, and then I left.

The next day was the day of the funeral. It was beautiful and sunny, and I thought this was a day Nannie sure would like.

Daddy sat in the car waiting for Mama and asked me to go check on her. I went into the back of the house, where it was quiet and still, and I found her sitting on their unmade bed with her hands folded in her lap. She didn't look at me, and I didn't look at her.

Finally, I said, "Mama, please let me go with you."

"No, Genny. No. This is not how you're going to say good-bye." She didn't understand how I felt—like I was being left out of something very important.

"But how am I going to say good-bye? I heard Daddy tell James that's what funerals are for."

"Funerals are not for children," she said quietly and firmly. "I want you to remember Nannie the way you last saw her—laughing and talking together the way you did—instead of going to a funeral service and cemetery with sad words and sad music."

"Okay then," was all I said. She kissed me on the cheek, and I followed her to the back door and watched her go down the kitchen steps to the car. I thought at that moment she looked brave. I had never seen my mother wear black before.

I watched them drive away to this grown-up event where children were not allowed, where Nannie was waiting—at St. Anne's with Father Cuddihy and her friends and her family. And then, I had the strangest thought. I wanted to run after the car, stop Mama, and tell her Nannie wasn't going to be there at the church at all and to come back. It was a mistake for her to go. Nannie was here with me. Mama should come back and be with us.

The day after the funeral, people continued to gather at Gibson Island, but finally, when things quieted down in the evening, I tiptoed up to her bedroom. The ceiling on both sides of her bedroom slanted down so far that I sometimes bumped my head when I peeked through the circular window that overlooked the river. Underneath the window, a white porcelain basin and pitcher sat on a small table, and I wondered how many times she had washed her face in that basin over the years. Daduh had cleaned everything nice, especially Nannie's room. The pale-yellow nubby bedspread was freshly washed, and on the nightstand there was an empty dish that used to hold Nannie's reading glasses and a lamp with pink roses and a brass key sticking out to turn it on and off. I put my hand inside the dish and then turned the key on the lamp.

I sat on her bed, then lay down and felt my head sink into the worn middle of her pillow. I wanted her to call my name again like she'd done earlier that day at the bottom of the stairs. I wanted it to be true. It was peaceful and nice to be in Nannie's room, and I had the feeling once more like a soft, warm blanket around me. I felt tingly all over. I heard the whirring sound in my ears. It was happening again. From her bed, I could see myself in the dressing table mirror.

It was then that I noticed the piece of paper taped to the corner of the mirror. I'd sat at this very dresser many times with Nannie brushing my hair, and I'd never seen this. I tried to scrape it off, but it was old, and I was afraid it would tear. I read the typed words out loud. "They that go down to the sea in ships, that do business in great waters. These see the works of the Lord and his wonders in the deep. For he commandeth and raiseth up the stormy wind, which lifteth up the waves thereof . . . Then they cry unto the Lord in their trouble, and He bringeth them out of their distresses. He maketh the storm a calm, so that the waves thereof are still."

I immediately ran downstairs and pulled Mama from her sisters and brought her up to Nannie's room, so she could see what I'd discovered. She frowned slightly as if she was trying to remember something. "It looks like it's from the Bible, but I don't know why she put that on her mirror. She never mentioned it, and I don't know what it means. I never saw it before." She stood very still. She looked exhausted, and her eyes were swollen from crying.

"Mama, remember last Sunday when Nannie said she dreamed she died? Do you think she really knew?"

My mother closed her eyes tightly. "Genny—I don't want you to do this."

"You don't want me to do what?" I asked her, but I was really begging her.

"Nannie liked to tell all kinds of stories, and she had a special way of connecting with you through those stories. Sometimes she got carried away, and I don't want you to mistake them for real life. It's not real life."

I couldn't believe my mother, Nannie's own daughter, was saying this. Was she blind or in some kind of shock? I felt as if Mama was trying to ignore Nannie and who she was. These words Nannie put on her mirror—about going down to the sea, about great waters—and waves—this was something important, wasn't it? Did Mama forget she'd dreamed Nannie got lost in the waves and couldn't find her and how she woke up crying in the middle of the night? How could she think the stories Nannie told over the years didn't matter? I didn't know what to say to her, so I said nothing. I thought it had to be because she was so exhausted and just couldn't deal with anything else about Nannie.

A couple of days after the funeral, Rachel came over, and I wasn't sure how to talk about what I was feeling. She tried to cheer me up and tell me about the new records her sisters had and how we needed to start practicing more songs.

"You have a good voice, Genny. I think you should start singing more. We haven't practiced since last . . ." She stopped her sentence because she was going to say last week—the Sunday Nannie went missing. We lay on my bedroom floor with our feet up against the wall under the window.

"Thanks. You have a good voice, too."

"I know you miss your Nannie a lot," Rachel said softly. "I

have two grandmothers, but I don't ever see them much, and I don't think we could ever be as close as you two were. I think that's unusual." She was right about that. No one could be as close as we were. "My mama says it takes a long time to get over what y'all went through. But soon you'll get used to her being gone. Soon you'll be feeling better, and you can always remember her and how much she loved you. Right?"

I sat up and looked at Rachel, and I saw how hard she was trying to help. It was at that moment I knew what a good person she was and that she really could be my best friend. I also knew I could never tell her the truthful story—that my Nannie was not gone.

I needed to talk to someone about this, though, so I decided I would talk to Father Cuddihy after Mass the following Sunday, which also happened to be my birthday. All the parishioners loved Father Cuddihy, even if he was from the North. His Boston accent always got stronger when he told stories about growing up in a big family and how he decided to become a priest. I liked Father Cuddihy because he always tried his best to help others, including me. He had said the funeral Mass for Nannie, and Daddy said he did a perfect job at it because he knew her and our family so well.

While everyone hovered over cookies and juice at the rectory, I asked Father Cuddihy if we could talk. "This sounds serious. Of course, Genevieve. Let's go outside," he said. He led me away from the loud laughter and chattering, and we sat on the front steps of the rectory. The leaves swirled around us like little tornadoes in the crisp autumn air. He asked me how I was doing, and I realized it was the first time anyone had asked me that question since the funeral. That made it easier for me to tell him.

"I have this feeling that Nannie is still around me, Father." I just came out and said it and waited for him to be surprised—or not surprised, being who he was and all.

"Genevieve, your feelings are perfectly natural. I've never seen a girl love her grandmother as much as you loved your Nannie. I used to watch the two of you whispering to each other and trying not to laugh during Mass." I smiled remembering that, too, but I wasn't sure he understood what I was saying about Nannie still being around. "I know losing her was so hard, but she's still here in your heart, and that will help you as time goes on."

"But Father, I didn't lose her. That's the thing. I thought I did, but I still hear her and can feel her around me. Isn't that something different? Is that normal?" I twisted the small diamond ring on my finger and thought if Father couldn't answer this question, no one could. I had certainly tried telling Mama about these feelings lots of times, but she definitely did not want to talk about Nannie with me.

"Yes, that's normal, Genevieve. Each person has different feelings after they lose someone they love. You have yours. Your mama has hers." He pointed with his chin toward the parking lot where she was leaning against the car laughing with Daddy and a group of people. "See how she mingles with others and laughs? It's not that she's not sad on the inside—of course she is, but she's just trying to take each day the best she knows how, so sadness won't take over."

"Mama doesn't want to talk about Nannie at all, really," I said, looking up at him and searching for something more than what he was giving me.

"Losing her own mama like that was very hard. Give her time. I know you want to talk about your Nannie and your feelings, but try not to do that too much till she's ready." I really needed Mama to hurry up and be ready. Father smiled at me and patted my hand.

I sat on the steps for a few more minutes and watched Mama mingle as the people in the church parking lot started to leave. She was talking to the Griffin sisters, but I didn't see Marylou anywhere, which was unusual because she was always with them. I got up from the steps of the rectory and walked through the rows of cars, winding back along a narrow path behind the church. I had never been back there before and was surprised to find a small garden area, without flowers or green grass, ready to rest for the winter under its thick blanket of dried leaves. Next to it was a small white stone bench and a statue of St. Francis of Assisi holding a bird in his hand, and there was Marylou, sitting in her wheelchair under the crooked arms of an old oak tree that had two connecting trunks. The main trunk of the tree spread out wide like a pleated robe, and way at the top was a wrinkly, tired face buried in a beard of gray and white moss that reached all the way to the ground. The other trunk was narrow and curved like a walking cane. A bony arm branch with long fingers clung to the cane trunk.

Marylou's arms were quiet in her lap now but twisted much like the wise old man tree bending over her. She looked like she was enjoying the view of something far off through the dense trees, so trying not to disturb, I walked quietly toward her to see for myself. Suddenly, with the heels of her hands, she managed to push her chair around to face me, and I smiled when I realized she had pretty good control over that wheelchair and could make it move on her own.

"Hi, Marylou," I said. She moved her head around in a circle, and I got the funny feeling she was expecting me. I sat on the stone bench. "Did you come here by yourself?" She moved her head around for the answer, which I could tell was yes. We sat there together for a minute. "Today's my birthday," I said.

She moved her head around again and with the heel of her hand pushed the brown sweater that lay across her legs onto the ground. I saw she'd done it on purpose, but I jumped to pick it up for her.

"Here you go, Marylou," I said, and as I handed it to her, I saw a small book on her lap. She nudged it toward me, and I took it from her. It was called *The Little Prince*. This didn't seem like a book Marylou would be reading—it looked like a children's book. It had a picture of a small boy up in the sky, standing on top of a planet with stars around him. She moved her head around, so I opened it and read the message inside: "To Marylou Griffin on her 10th birthday. From your friend, Frances Gibson Cooper, 1956." This was Nannie's name. This was her handwriting. I looked at Marylou, searching her eyes for what this meant. I ran my fingers across Nannie's name and imagined her writing this message in the book and giving it to Marylou a long time ago when she had turned ten years old. I stared at it for a minute thinking about Nannie going over to Marylou's house all those years and taking books that she hoped Marylou would love. I wondered why Marylou had this book with her now.

I set the book gently back on her lap. "My Nannie used to tell me about visiting you and how you loved to read. She said you had more books than the whole Charleston County Library." And then, in a sudden, jerking motion, Marylou swept the book off her lap onto the ground. It landed at my feet, and I looked at her and asked, "Why are you doing that?" I picked it up and put it on her lap. She was smiling. "Oh, Marylou, you want me to read this book?" She started to push it off again, but I caught it just in time. I was starting to understand. "You want me to keep the book? Marylou, I don't think you should give it to me. My Nannie gave it to you." But I wanted it. I wanted it badly.

At that moment, her mama came to the top of the path, called out to Marylou that it was time to go, and started heading in our direction. Marylou just ignored her and stared at me smiling and turning her head in circles faster and faster. "Thank you," was all I could think of to say.

I thought that I would help her now and pushed her back up the path. I went around to the back of her wheelchair, and as I did, I could see the view she'd had through the trees. It would have been easy to miss, but from this angle, I could see tall, thick marsh cradling a sliver of the Toogoodoo Creek that had broken off somewhere and crept back into this secret place behind St. Anne's. Then, I noticed the small clearing of land covered in autumn leaves that sloped up from the left side of the marsh. Chalky stones stuck up out of the ground, and I thought it must have been an old cemetery. The wheelchair rolled back a little, and Marylou turned her head to me to make sure I had the handles. As I started to push Marylou up the path to her mama, I kept Nannie's book tucked tightly under my arm, feeling like this really was my birthday after all, and barely noticing out of the corner of my eye the clean white headstone in the distance.

The landing had grown dark around me, and the light tapping of April showers on the tin roof suddenly turned into the drumbeat of a downpour, getting louder and louder. Wiping the dust off the shelf with my hands, I put *Rebecca* back in its place and went into Nannie's room. I sat down at her dresser, and I looked again at the Bible quote still taped to the mirror. "So, Nannie," I said aloud to her. "No more Big Sunday Dinners—they're all over." I waited until Mama called my name from the bottom of the staircase to tell me we were going back to Bailey's Place. With my hand on the banister, I stood at the top of the stairs and felt an overwhelming heaviness—a feeling that Gibson Island was never going to be the same again, and there was nothing I could do about it.

Chapter Eight

July 2, 1966

THE NIGHT WE SAW FLYING SAUCERS hovering over the river behind our house was also the night Daddy brought home a new washing machine, icebox, TV, and stereo. All that traveling he'd been doing had sure paid off.

"Are we rich?" Ryan asked him as deliverymen wheeled in the surprises one by one. We all gasped, but it was Mama who was the most surprised.

"Jim, what is all this?" Mama stood in the living room turning around in circles. My father grinned, pointing to an empty space next to the gray velvet sofa for the deliverymen to put the stereo.

"It's an early Christmas, darlin'!" he announced and added that he'd gotten a raise, so we were finally getting the things we needed and deserved, especially after all that had happened in California. "You are now looking at the senior site manager, which means I have three sites now instead of just one. We have

Mr. Landry to thank for this. You should've seen his son's reaction when my promotion was announced at the meeting. He is definitely not one of my fans, especially after what he tried to pull on Alicia. I think he might've been counting on getting the promotion himself, since his oyster factory project seems to be fallin' apart. Things should get interesting when he has to report to me from now on."

"I kind of feel sorry for him in a weird way," Mama said.

"Well, you need to get over that fast!" Daddy said, pulling her toward him.

Mama laughed. "Yes, I'm over it already!" she said, as we jumped up and down around my parents, cheering our good fortune. Not only had Daddy been moved into a very important position in his company, but it looked like he'd also saved Gibson Island. Last week's newspaper article reported the oyster factory project was stalled for now and maybe even permanently. After what had happened, Aunt Alicia put Mama and Daddy in charge of all decisions about the Gibson Island property, and Daddy told Jeffrey Landry to stay away from Aunt Alicia and to deal with him directly from now on.

"Mama, are we rich?" Ryan asked again. The front porch filled up as Rachel and her brothers and sisters and Tracy and Pat Butler all came over to see what the excitement was about.

"We're not rich. We're just lucky is all," my mother said nervously, bringing us back down to earth for a minute and running her hands across the top of the TV. But it sure felt like we were rich, especially compared to the Robertsons. I suddenly felt guilty celebrating like we were doing in front of my best friend. I saw Rachel quietly lead everyone back outside. With seven kids and not much money, their family struggled to make ends meet. It seemed Mrs. Robertson worked all day and into the night. I'd seen her washing the family's clothes in an old machine that had a roller on top to squeeze out the water, and there was always laundry hanging outside and something cooking on the stove with lots of vegetables from their own garden out back. Although Rachel had to wear hand-me-downs from her older sisters, she never complained.

After almost a year, Rachel and I had learned a lot about each other. We were the same in some ways but opposites in other ways. For one thing, we looked opposite — she had a thin face that stayed tanned all year long, and mine was round and pale. Her hair was light blond and straight as an arrow, and mine was dark and curly. Unlike me, Rachel was very athletic and limber and could do cartwheels and handstands in the Carpet Grass, our name for the plush green lawn that stretched between our house and the Baileys'. I recognized early that her being moody was the main thing that made her most different from Ellie, but it didn't get in the way of us being friends. I was really hoping Rachel and Ellie could meet this summer and was disappointed when I learned Ellie couldn't come down. Mama said they had to spend their vacation time this year with Uncle Peter's family in Rhode Island, so she and Aunt Marjorie were still trying to figure out how we could get together.

I followed Rachel outside. We'd had a big day together and were pretty tired. We started off the morning singing for hours with songs from Petula Clark — like "Downtown" and "Don't Sleep in the Subway" — the Lettermen, and the King Sisters. Between our clothesline in the backyard and the Nuthouse, there was a slab of concrete in the ground that looked like a shed once sat on it, but for us, it was the Stage, where we brought our pretend microphones to entertain the world. After we were finished with that, Rachel, Curt, James, and I did one of our favorite things, which was boggin' in the mud at low tide. This turned out to be a bigger adventure than we expected because James got stuck in a deep spot, and the mud quickly turned into quicksand.

Rolling our shorts up as high as they could go, Curt and Rachel and I were boggin' close by each other when we noticed James was having trouble.

"James, come back!" I yelled at him as he bogged out too far from the Edge. The Edge was where the real land met the riverbed and where we would build mud forts until the tide came in.

"Genny! I'm stuck!" James yelled back, and we could see that he had sunk into a mudhole up to his thighs.

"Oh no!" Rachel said. "What are we going to do?" James was trying not to topple over into the dark mud, and the more he moved, the deeper he sunk.

"Stop moving, James! Stay still—I'm coming," I shouted, but I could see James was panicking.

"Help me. The tide comes in soon!" he cried out.

Curt and I looked at each other and knew we had to do this together, so we started out across the mud, bogging carefully and lifting our feet up high and quick as we walked. "Hold onto my hand, Genny," Curt said. "We have to help each other to get there."

"Hurry!" James yelled, and then we saw, with horror, that he had sunk to his hips. Now James was crying, and we could hear Rachel yelling behind us. Somehow, Curt and I got to James before the mud swallowed him alive. Standing next to him, we were able to each take an arm and pull him up partway, and then we lifted from his hips and pulled the rest of the way. Lucky for Curt and me, we were not near a mudhole, so we were able to get James without sinking deeper than our knees. When we got back to the Edge, we collapsed into the mud fort we had started working on earlier. We agreed not to tell anyone about the boggin' incident because then we wouldn't be allowed to come down here by ourselves anymore.

After that, James and Curt and Rachel and I had to work fast to finish our fort before the tide came in, creating a room, a tunnel, and a roof made of dried marsh. It was such a hot day, and I rested my face against the cool, hard-packed mud floor, listening to the faraway river sounds deep in a world I couldn't reach. When we left, we looked back at our work, and we were okay knowing it would be gone in the morning, and we'd have to start all over again.

As the deliverymen pulled away from our house that evening in July, the air was heavy and still, and I joined Rachel at our favorite spot, the oak tree we named Dora after the hurricane that Nannie tracked dutifully for days a couple of years ago. She reported on it each morning, along with the low and high tides, and made Aunt Alicia stock up with batteries and canned food. When it finally hit, it was no longer Hurricane Dora but still a frightening storm with high winds that brought down trees and branches. Gibson Island was spared, but when we moved to Bailey's Place the following year, we could see the damage the storm had done to the wharf and many of the trees—except for Dora, who seemed untouched.

Whenever any hurricane was building out in the ocean, Nannie started tracking it, and she would be anxious but thrilled at the same time—like she got at Christmas. It was easy for everyone to get caught up in it—the planning, the charting, the watching, then as the time grew closer, the last-minute instructions: Put on shoes with rubber soles, fill up the bathtub with water, get the kerosene lamps ready and set out extra candles, turn off everything except the icebox, don't open the freezer door if we lose power, and most of all, close windows and doors on opposite sides of the house.

"Lightning can ride in on drafts between open windows and doors," Nannie explained in an official-sounding voice. "I remember one time when I was a little girl at Gibson Island when lightning shot in like a ball of fire through an opened front door and then went right through the house out an opened back window!" Daddy kind of chuckled when Nannie told us that, and most people thought she exaggerated when it came to hurricane and storm stories, but I believed her. I always believed her.

Dora, though, was more than a tree—she was like an older friend who gives good advice about almost anything, and more importantly, she was the keeper of our dreams and secrets. Dora held herself high and tall, and she reached her long arms out to the river, one of them so far and low it almost touched the Edge. She was in charge here in this world and got respect from the river itself as well as from all the other trees. When Rachel and I sat underneath her, we felt we were part of her world and no one could see us.

This evening, I could hear my brothers shrieking from inside the house, and I knew that pretty soon, the new TV and stereo would be interrupting the familiar stillness this time of day at Bailey's Place. As we sat there, I was so tired I thought I would fall asleep, but it seemed Rachel was in one of her moods.

"Remember when you first moved here last year, and you came outside and lied to us and told us you had a sister?" she asked me from out of nowhere. I did, in fact, remember but didn't say so.

Rachel said, "You played a song on your record player from your bedroom so we could hear it from the window. You came outside and said it was your sister singing."

I felt trapped suddenly. She'd never confronted me with this before. I'd always wanted a sister, and when we moved to Bailey's Place, I saw the Robertsons' big family and Rachel with her four sisters. I wanted to say I had a sister, too. I think I convinced myself I did have one, because for some reason, that's what I told the Robertsons when I met them that day underneath Dora. To make it worse, I told them to wait outside, and I'd go and get my sister. I put my favorite record on and opened my bedroom window all the way. It was Annette Funicello, but I told them it was my sister singing and she was too busy to come outside. They all shook their heads, and Curt said, "That's just a record." Then they all walked off, except for Karen, the oldest one, who gave me a little pat on the shoulder and said, "It's nice to meet you, Genevieve."

I'd tried to put that embarrassing moment out of my mind. It was such a stupid thing to do, and Rachel had never mentioned it—until now. I could feel my face getting hot. She leaned against Dora and stared at me, waiting for my response. The way I'd seen it back then was Rachel had four sisters, and I wanted just one sister, so at the time, I didn't see any harm in creating one. I just didn't think it all the way through.

"Genny—come on in for supper!" my mother called from the screen door on the side porch. I wished Mama would ring Nannie's bell when she wanted us to come inside, but she never would do it. The bell was old and tarnished with a black, leathery handle and made a loud, annoying clanging sound. It had been in the family for a long time, and Nannie liked to ring it for us to come in for supper just like her own grandmother, Genevieve, used to do. When James and Ryan and I wouldn't come right away, Nannie would say, "We used to pretend we didn't hear our grandma ringing this god-awful-sounding bell, too. Just like the three of you, we were never ready to come in from playing."

Mama called out again. I decided to ignore Rachel's comment and figured she might just be jealous because we had a new stereo and TV. "Yeah. Well, I gotta go in now." I walked away from Dora and from Rachel. As I passed through the living room, the bell, now sitting quietly on the mantle over the fireplace, caught my eye.

As soon as I turned the corner from the living room, I heard the loud clanging of the bell behind me. I stopped without turning around. I could feel my eyes widen, and I took a breath and held it.

"Genny! James! Ryan! Stop fooling around in there and come sit down for supper!" Mama was saying from the kitchen.

I turned around. The bell was on the mantel. It was still and quiet. I went over to it. "Nannie?" I whispered. These things kept happening, and for some reason, they didn't surprise me much at all. I felt excited—like a big day with Nannie was coming soon.

"Hey, Angel Baby! Let's get some supper." Daddy's voice made me jump as he walked in the room.

As we finished up our Friday night TV dinners, I heard Mama and Daddy talking in the kitchen.

"Are you sure we can afford this, Jim? I mean—I'm so happy about this promotion, but it makes me nervous to—"

"Stop worrying. Please. I have everything under control. Mr. Landry sees what I can do for him and the plant, and I really think this is the job for me. No more changes. We're settled here. No more worries, either, okay?" I heard Daddy go out the kitchen door, dragging some of the boxes the deliverymen left behind. Suddenly, what started out to be a big night with all Daddy's surprises got even bigger when he came rushing back into the house.

"Come on outside. Everybody! Right away!" He stood, holding the door open as we scrambled out. Mama picked up Thomas, and we followed Daddy to the Edge. Our family lined up on one side of Dora, and the Robertsons lined up on the other. Before long, the Butlers and the Cooks came down, followed by Miss Sylvia and Mr. Bailey.

Up in the clear, black sky dotted with stars, there were three pale-green, circular orbs floating above the river. For a second, I thought we were seeing some kind of early Fourth of July show, but that wasn't it. We all stared up silently as the glowing disks glided by slowly, then darted quickly, then glided again, coming in and out of view for at least a half hour. Daddy announced he was going inside to call the Air Force, the weather station, and the police. Tracy and Pat Butler started crying. Cynthia and Ray Cook held onto each other tightly and never said a word. Mr. Bailey paced with his hands in his pockets, shaking his head back and forth. "Never seen anything like this. Never," he kept saying. Mrs. Robertson rested her hands on top of the twins' heads. James and Ryan sat at Mama's feet, while Thomas squirmed in her arms. It was an eerie night, and we all felt very uneasy, like we might be in serious danger. Rachel came to me and linked her arm through mine like best friends do when they have no differences between them.

Once the flying saucers went back where they came from, we all went back to our houses. Daddy was pretty mad no one called him back to answer his questions, and nothing was in the newspaper the next day either. On Monday, there was talk of some type of Air Force exercises or weather-related tests that might possibly have explained it, but it was all just guessing. Daddy was always a man to do the right thing by people, and if he thought there was some confusion or wrongdoing, he would get involved and demand a straight answer. The best way to do that, he said, was to write to the newspaper, so he wrote to the *News and Courier* about what we saw that night, pointing out that "people get nervous when the government and people in authority don't communicate, so if there is something to say, they owe it to folks to say it." The paper never printed his letter, although they had printed plenty of his before.

One that got a lot of attention in the newspaper was his letter about the Magnolia Drive-In Theater and how it was shameful to show adult movie previews on family movie nights. Our family had loved going to the drive-in together, and after a lot of preparation, we were all set to watch *That Darn Cat!* one Saturday night We had picked up our barbecue sandwiches and milk shakes from Piggie Park; the speaker was hanging on Daddy's window going full blast, the mosquito coil was lit, the pillows were propped around us in the backseat, and the next thing I remember is Mama saying, "Oh my God! Kids! Put your heads down right now! This is unbelievable."

We celebrated on the Fourth of July, plugging our ears from a few noisy firecrackers on the sidewalk and running across the Carpet Grass swirling sparklers in the air, but compared to our experience with the flying saucers Friday night, it was boring. That Tuesday morning after the holiday, we sat in the kitchen at breakfast, still in disbelief. Even Ruby and her husband, Jackson, had seen the flying saucers that night from their house and commented on it when they came up to the kitchen door.

"Mr. Jim, we know what we saw, and that sure looked like somethin' from outer space, no doubt about it," Jackson said. He had an old red car he'd pretty much built himself, and he'd drop Ruby off every morning in it before he went out to the fertilizer plant. Jackson had to work a couple of different jobs, but he worked at the plant with Daddy most days of the week.

After we had talked all we could about the flying saucers, Jackson told Ruby good-bye at the kitchen door and asked Daddy if he could come in late to the plant that morning because Daduh needed him to tend to a broken water pipe at her house.

"Family first!" Daddy said as he and Jackson walked out together.

Because her legs were too short for her body, Ruby wobbled a little from side to side when she moved fast. She took Thomas out of Mama's arms.

"Mornin', Little Sweetman," she said in the high-pitched, singsong voice she saved just for him. Ruby made me feel happy every single time she was around.

"Ruby, Thomas feels a little warm to me, so I might leave the bank early today if he doesn't feel better. I'll call you in a little while." Mama kissed us good-bye and hurried out to catch her ride. Cynthia Cook waited patiently and waved to me as I watched Mama climb in, her navy-blue high heels the last to swing into Cynthia's little white sports car.

Ruby said from behind, "You sure can tell if folks have children by the car they drive."

Jackson and Ruby were a quiet couple who kept to themselves, and they were hard workers. I was glad Daduh had recommended Ruby to come work for us after Nannie left. Ruby was real short and chubby and laughed easily; she had kind eyes that were brown with black freckles in them; and I could tell she loved the boys and me. She treated Thomas like her own baby. She and Jackson didn't have any children, but Daduh said if they did, her grandson and his wife would make the best parents in the world, and she prayed for it every day. Jackson was the type of person who could do just about anything—he could fix cars, build sheds, and do heavy lifting. In addition to working for Daddy part-time at the fertilizer plant, he worked for Western Auto, Davidson's filling station, and Champ's Country Store and Motel. He was popular out in the country because people could count on him, and as Mama described him, "Jackson is very trustworthy and has the nicest disposition—plus he loves his Ruby!"

Jackson and Ruby lived up a few miles on the side road, which was past Bailey's Place on the way to Hollywood. There were two rows of twenty little yellow houses that lined the railroad tracks across from the loading station and the sheds where tomatoes and other produce were kept. All the houses looked exactly alike and had three rooms—a living room and kitchen together, a bedroom, and a bathroom. One time when we took Ruby home, she invited us in, which was a real treat.

"Ruby," Mama said with her hands on her hips, "You've done quite a job of decorating, and this place is clean as a whistle. I don't know how you do it plus take care of all us Donovans!" They lived next door to Jackson's sister, Gloria, who sometimes came to watch us on days when Ruby couldn't come. We liked Gloria okay, but she wasn't as good a worker as Ruby and liked watching her soap operas on TV more than she liked watching us. Not to say that Ruby didn't enjoy a soap opera. She and I watched *Another World*, but that was only during ironing time and only if Thomas was napping. I preferred *Dark Shadows*, but Ruby would never watch that because "it was evil doings." Gloria had one child of her own she called Rooster because she said he woke the whole town of Hollywood up before dawn every day, but his real name was Benjamin Frederick. Ruby said that was a mouthful for a baby name, but it was sure better than Rooster.

When we went to Ruby's house, we got to meet little Rooster when Gloria dropped him off for Ruby to babysit so she could go out. Gloria had on long, dangly earrings and a short skirt, and her fingernails were painted bright pink. Rooster was cute but kind of funny looking with hair that stood straight up on his head and eyes too big for his face. I felt sorry for him because he didn't have a daddy that lived with him, and Daduh had told us that her granddaughter was always hurting for money and trying to find regular work. When Gloria did get some work, which was cleaning houses, she'd leave Rooster with Daduh, and sometimes on Saturdays, instead of going to Gibson Island to clean, Daduh would send Gloria in her place so she could make the extra money.

That evening at Ruby's, Rooster came over to me and wrapped his chubby little arms around my leg. He didn't even notice his mama leaving, swinging her shiny gold purse as she practically danced out the door and into a long green car that waited in the driveway. I looked down at those eyes staring up at me. I sat down on the floor with him, and we looked at each other for a long minute. He just wanted to look at me and touch my face with his fingertips. Then he climbed into my lap and put his head on my shoulder. He smelled like breakfast—bacon and pancakes—and I stayed there on the floor with him and patted his back until Mama said it was time for us to go. Ruby took him into her arms, and his big eyes watched me walk away. As we drove home, I thought it was too bad Ruby couldn't be the one to take care of Rooster all the time. It seemed she would be a great mama for a little boy like that. Mama said everyone was always trying to help Gloria, but she needed to help herself. Even though Daduh kept trying to send her granddaughter over to Aunt Alicia's for the extra work, Aunt Alicia finally had to put a stop to that and told Daduh to never mind, she could do without the substitutes on cleaning days. That included Gloria as well as Daduh's daughter, Lumpy, who was Gloria's mother. Daduh kept hoping that Lumpy would be able to get a good job and make some money of her own, but Aunt Alicia made it clear it would not be a job working for her.

"Gloria is not good at this work, and Lumpy is worse," Aunt Alicia told Mama. On those times when Daduh sent Lumpy over to Gibson Island to work, Lumpy walked from Daduh's house, but it took her a whole morning to get there. Lumpy didn't ever notice she was late for work, though. She'd finally arrive, walking slowly up the driveway. Then she'd sit on the front steps, emptying out all her pockets and her satchel, and hundreds of little rocks and oyster shells would spill out onto a patch of sun on the porch. According to Aunt Alicia, "That's why she's always been called Lumpy. Because she *is* lumpy. She's slow as all get-out, and she weights herself down with all that crap she picks up on the side of the road. She looks like she's got lumps stickin' out all over her body where she stores things she's collecting when she's out wandering around. Her seventy-five-year-old mother can walk all the way here in thirty minutes, clean the whole house, cook dinner, iron, and walk back home before Lumpy even gets started."

No doubt about it, Aunt Alicia had no patience for Lumpy. "She shuffles around here in her bedroom slippers that she brings with her in that old ugly bag she carries. For some god-awful reason, she wears two blouses at the same time and a skirt that looks like a horse blanket with some kind of colored stains all over it. Lord." On top of that, Lumpy didn't have a lick of sense, Aunt Alicia said. She couldn't cook one bit, and if she tried, she'd ruin it in no time. In fact, Aunt Alicia was afraid Lumpy would burn Gibson Island to the ground if she didn't stand right there and watch her every second. When she'd had enough of Gloria and Lumpy filling in for Daduh on Saturdays, she told us she finally had to sit Daduh down and have a serious talk. Aunt Alicia told me that there are two categories of maids: the ones that come and go and don't care a hoot about anything but themselves and can't be trusted, and then the women who take care of you like family—and that would be Daduh and Ruby.

The previous Saturday, over at Gibson Island, Daduh had been snapping string beans on the little screened porch off the breakfast room, and she'd given me a bowl and shown me what to do. "You're a big help to me, Genevieve," Daduh said, smiling at me as I tried to snap the beans as fast as she did.

"You do a lot of work around here, Daduh. Seems like you never stop," I said.

"I've been takin' care of Miss Alicia and all the Gibsons since the beginnin' of time, but I'm not getting' any younger, that's for sure, so I need some help now and then."

"I can help," I said, but I knew what she meant.

"Well, your Aunt Alicia and me—we've come to an understandin' about things. I'm going to slow down a little and come maybe just two Saturdays a month. That'll help some. The house doesn't need as much tendin' to these days, I guess. And she sure doesn't want to have my Lumpy or Gloria around here anymore. And I can't say as I blame her," Daduh said and sighed like she liked to do. "I can't have those two messin' things up."

I followed Daduh into the kitchen and took out a couple of her cinnamon sugar cookies from the big glass jar on the counter. "You know, these cookies are a secret recipe my mama taught me," she said, taking one for herself.

"They're the best I ever had. Maybe I can help you make 'em some time," I said.

As Daduh rinsed the beans, she shook her head like she was in the middle of another conversation, so I just waited for her. "Your Aunt Alicia says some things different than how your Nannie would say 'em, but when it comes to Gloria and Lumpy cleanin' here and takin' care of folks, I have to agree with her. Gloria's got her priorities mixed up, but her mama's another story and always been kinda different." Daduh smiled and looked up at the ceiling like she was remembering something a long time ago. "You know, I named her Matilda Arabella."

"Lumpy?" I asked. I never thought about her daughter having another name.

"Yes. Matilda Arabella. Isn't that pretty? That was a real name of a Negro woman doctor—the first one ever in the state. She was like your Dr. Meg and smart, and I wanted my baby to have a name of someone who did somethin' important like that," she said. "Lumpy lives in her own world, that one, but she's got some talents—just not the kind that amount to much in this world, I guess. She's my daughter, and I can see her for what she is, yes, I sure can. Only thing is, Gloria is just like her mama and don't understand hard work that makes you sweat is God's work. I try to put the fear of God in her and keep her on the straight and narrow, but Lord knows, it tires me out still. Thank the Lord for Ruby and Jackson helpin' to take care of my great grandson. At least those two got their heads on straight." I thought about Rooster and how much she loved that little boy, always bragging that he was the smartest one in the whole family for as far back as she could see.

Daduh plopped a big scoop of Crisco in the skillet. She wiped her hands and looked at me. "Genevieve, a lot of young people are out for themselves—don't you turn out like that, you hear?"

"You don't have to worry about me, Daduh," I assured her. I smiled to myself when I thought about how Daduh tried to keep everybody in line, which was most obvious on Sundays when she and her family would take their long walk to Hope Baptist with Daduh and little Rooster leading the way.

In spite of our strange Friday night with the flying saucers, that summer day started like it was supposed to. After Mama and Daddy left for work, Rachel called for me outside my bedroom window as I dressed hurriedly; I could smell the freshly cut grass as Robby drove off on the Bailey's riding mower, its popping noises fading in and out of the morning as it tossed chewed-up sticks and rocks to either side. Our dog, Fella, stretched out beneath Dora, keeping his one good eye on Queenie, the Robertsons' German shepherd, as she fed their new puppies in the shade of the Robertsons' back steps. Fella was a great dog, and although he had lost an eye to a raccoon earlier in the year, it didn't slow him down one bit.

Halfway through the morning, Rachel and I were walking through the Orchard when Cynthia Cook's white car drove back up the road fast and stopped at our house to let my mother out. I saw Mama running into our house, so I knew something was wrong. I'd been outside with Rachel since they left. Could Thomas have gotten sick after all? Ruby must have called her at the bank to come home. I took off running, too, and before I burst into the kitchen, I noticed Cynthia Cook was still sitting in her car in front of our house.

Ruby sat at the table staring up at my mother, who was now holding Thomas. I looked him over for signs he was sick, but he looked perfectly fine. Ruby didn't look fine, though. Her face was gray—she was frowning and leaning toward Mama, listening hard and trying to make out what she was saying.

"Miss Cynthia is in her car outside. She's going to take you home," Mama said slowly to Ruby. She handed Thomas to me, and I watched her take Ruby's elbow and walk her out to the car, and then Cynthia Cook drove away with Ruby, who was just staring straight ahead.

Despite my pleading, Mama waited till Daddy got home to tell us what happened. I'd decided Ruby must have caught some kind of sickness or fever from Thomas. But Thomas wasn't sick, so that didn't make sense. And why did we need to wait for Daddy to come home to tell us what was wrong? Before our minds could wander too far, Daddy called us in to sit at the kitchen table, his face pale and his shoulders slumped as he tried to talk. This was bad news coming, I was certain of it. James and Ryan and I waited for what seemed like a long time. Thomas slept against me.

"It's very bad news," Mama said to help Daddy get started. She cupped both hands over her mouth and searched our faces for a first reaction.

"It's little Benjamin," Daddy said. For a second I was confused. I didn't know a little Benjamin.

"Rooster," my mother added.

"Yes. Rooster," he said. "Gloria's little boy. He died in a car accident this morning."

We didn't speak. I'd never heard of a child dying before. I couldn't picture it. I couldn't understand it. I held onto Thomas. I could smell the baby sweat from his little blond head full of damp curls. I could feel the warmth of his body and the steady in and out of his breathing against my chest.

Mama and Daddy said some words, and James and Ryan said some words, but I don't know what they were. When my brothers left the room, Daddy told me Ruby and Jackson wouldn't be around for a few days because there was something else I should know. I was going to hear about it anyway, so it was best to just tell me the real story.

"Jackson went back home this morning to get his tools so he could fix the leaky pipe at Daduh's. When he backed the car out of his driveway, he ran over something, and he thought it was a toy from Gloria's house." Daddy paused.

Now that Rooster was walking, there were all kinds of toys and balls left in the yard — too many toys, Jackson had said once. "Miss Louisa, that little boy is spoiled rotten," Jackson told our mama, when she told him how cute that little Rooster was. "My grandmother talks like she's so strict, but when it comes to that baby, she melts like butter."

"Angel Baby," my father said. "Jackson didn't run over a toy this morning." He lifted my chin gently so he could look me in the eye.

Rooster had wandered out of his house next door and crawled under the car to get his toy. My father said there was no way Jackson could have seen him, and it was just a terrible, terrible accident. Daddy's eyes filled with tears, and he shook his head hard as if that would make the awful truth go away. He said there were no people anywhere on the planet right now sadder than Jackson and his family.

Clouds were gathering unusually fast. Before it got too dark, I carried Thomas with me out on the back porch and looked up at the sky. I wished hard that Rooster was still alive, that Jackson hadn't gone back home, that Daduh hadn't asked him to fix her leaky pipe, that Gloria had watched her baby better. Most of all, I wished Nannie was here with me, and I wished she had been with us when the flying saucers sailed across the sky over the river. That would sure be a story she could tell.

At that very minute, I knew Nannie understood this sadness everyone was feeling, and I was sure she also knew more than we did about those flying saucers and the aliens that flew them. I remembered then how she gave *The Little Prince* to Marylou Griffin because she knew that Marylou loved the planets and stars. After Marylou gave me that same book on my tenth birthday, I read it over and over, first because it had been from Nannie, but then because I loved the story of the little boy who fell to Earth from an asteroid and who thought this world was so odd. And I had to agree, this world was kind of odd. Like the others that night looking up at the flying saucers, I was afraid at first, but for some reason now, I didn't feel that way at all.

Marylou—or Nannie—had underlined a part in the book that said, "Here is my secret. It is very simple: It is only with the heart one can see rightly; what is essential is invisible to the eye." I asked Daddy about those words once, and he said it was like how he loved me. "You can't see love," he said, "but you can feel it, and you can't live without it." I thought it was like that with Nannie now. I couldn't see her, but I knew she was there, and I knew that I would never have to live without her.

A strong breeze that smelled like a storm coming swept across the porch, and the aluminum folding chair in the corner tipped over, landing with a loud clanking sound and shaking for a few seconds until finally stopping. I held Thomas close, and turning to go back into the house, I saw it. As the sun dipped down behind the river, the heavy, dark clouds shifted with the wind and showed me the twinkly lights of the flying saucer. And then just as quickly they swallowed its soft green glow.

Chapter Nine

September 24, 1966

I'D NOTICED MORE THAN ONCE WHEN Mama walked into a room that everyone stopped what they were doing. She loved the attention, and to thank them she returned it, but in a way that made them each feel like the most important person there. She was the perfect hostess at every party, even when it wasn't her party. No matter who they were, Mama had a way of making everyone feel at ease and appreciated—but she also expected politeness. I wouldn't be exaggerating to say that in her eyes rudeness was a sin and one not easily forgiven.

Her feelings about rudeness became very clear not long after little Rooster died. Jackson and Ruby and Gloria and Daduh were going through a bad time and had a lot of healing to do. Aunt Alicia said that no one cried as hard as Daduh did at the funeral, and Gloria fainted right in the middle of it. Ruby couldn't be around all of it too much longer and came back to work after about a week.

"How's Jackson doing, Ruby?" Mama asked her on her first morning back. I had never seen Mama fix Ruby coffee before, but here she was pouring the coffee and setting out the milk and sugar like she did when Miss Sylvia came over.

"Not so good, Miss Louisa. Even though his sister knows it was an accident, they can't even be in the same room together five minutes without one of 'em havin' to get up and leave. Jackson says he won't ever forgive himself and that the good Lord must want him to do somethin' soon on this earth to make up for this terrible thing. He can't sleep or eat. He just needs to get back to work and get his mind on somethin' else."

I put some oatmeal cookies on a paper plate and set it on the table. Mama smiled at me and said to Ruby, "What can we do to help? I know Miss Alicia is helping Daduh out, and Jim says Jackson can start back with the part-time work when he's ready. He knows Jackson wants a full-time job at the plant, so maybe one will turn up soon."

"Thank you, Miss Louisa. Daduh's having a hard time, for sure. Most people are kind to us, but I have to say, we're noticing some strange behaviors from people in town who are blamin' Jackson and callin' him names I won't repeat. It's mighty surprisin' to me. The police officer that talked to us that day asked if Jackson had been drinkin' whiskey, and anybody who knows that man knows he never touches a drop. But now some say he drinks all the time, and he's like his sister and the company she keeps. It's just not true. I don't know where all the ugliness comes from. Hope Baptist has been good to us, though. Reverend Baker says we just have to be strong."

"Yes, Ruby." I watched my mother as she touched the top of Ruby's hand and added more sugar to Ruby's coffee. "He's right.

You have to be strong, and you have to be around people who will lift you up, not knock you down."

But instead of getting better, Jackson's troubles just seemed to get worse. A couple of months later, most of his extra part-time work seemed to be drying up, and some of the attitudes in town toward him weren't much better. One morning when we were out shopping at the Western Auto in Hollywood, Jackson walked on in with his lunch bag in his hand and a smile on his face. That made my Mama and Daddy happy when they saw him come in looking so determined and hopeful. Even though things had been slow lately, Jackson had been doing a lot of weekend work there through the summer and even helped to start a new service — delivering car and appliance parts right to people's doors so they didn't have to drive into Hollywood. That Western Auto was a great store. It even had a box of records, just 45s, but I always found something I liked, and after rummaging through the stack, I picked "Yesterday" by the Beatles and took it up front.

I noticed Jackson was still standing by the register and looked confused. "Hi, Jackson," I said, setting the record down next to the items my parents were loading up on the counter. James and Ryan were stuffing pennies into the gumball machine, and Thomas was in Mama's arms, staring at Mr. Mike, the manager, but really at his hat that had an orange tiger on the front of it. Jackson was watching Thomas, and I wondered if Thomas reminded him of little Rooster and if it was hard to be around babies now.

"Hi, Miss Genny." He smiled warmly and looked back at Mr. Mike with no smile.

"I'm sorry, Jackson, it's just the way it is. I'm just not going to have any more work for you," Mr. Mike said. He started ringing up our things on the cash register and wouldn't even look at Jackson when he was talking. It took about half a second for Mama's antennae to go up and detect rudeness.

"Okay, Mr. Mike," Jackson said quietly. "What about deliverin' these orders here, though? Aren't these the boxes that need to go out today?" Jackson looked over at the pile by the front door. Mike didn't answer him and kept ringing up our items.

"Is that all y'all need?" he asked my parents. My mother looked at Mike, then looked at Jackson, then looked at my father, who was reaching in his pocket to give Ryan more pennies.

"Jackson asked you a question, Mike. Maybe you didn't hear him." Mama frowned slightly and squinted her eyes the way she did when she was figuring something out. She waited for him to respond. Daddy cleared his throat.

"I heard him," Mr. Mike said. "I told you, Jackson, I don't have anything for you today—or next week, either."

"Mike," Mama said a little too sweetly, "I thought Jackson worked here just about every Saturday. And I thought he started that great delivery service the Western Auto has now. Didn't you think that, Jim?" She turned to my father, who nodded. "You know everyone in Hollywood just lines up with jobs for Jackson to do. And it looks like there are a lot of people waiting on those deliveries there."

"Miss Louisa, that's fine. I better be goin' now." Jackson headed out the door to his old red car.

As soon as the door closed behind him, Mama said to Mike, "Can you tell us what just happened here with Jackson?"

"Listen, we don't know the whole story about that baby being killed this summer. They live out there by the railroad tracks and drink and carry on, and God knows what else goes on there. No tellin' the state Jackson was in when he killed that little boy. I can't have him going to people's houses deliverin' stuff to their doors. I can't have a baby killer working here." That was the wrong thing to say and all my mother needed. Her frown disappeared suddenly.

"Whoa there, Mike," Daddy said, trying to catch up with what was going on.

Mama spoke calmly and firmly. "Mike, that's just it. You don't know about the situation or Jackson and his family. First of all, you're wrong. Second of all, you have no right to treat people that way, especially someone like Jackson who has been nothing but good and honest and hardworkin' for you and the rest in this town."

"I don't want to get into this with y'all now," Mike said, taking out a large bag to load up what we were buying. Another customer walked in and noticed the tension. Mama exhaled a burst of air from her nose and handed me the record.

"Genny, put this back where you got it. Boys, come on. We're leaving this store." She walked out, and we followed right behind. James and Ryan didn't even hesitate; they knew she meant business. We could see Daddy through the store window, using his hands to talk to Mr. Mike and shaking his head, and then he walked out, too, leaving all our items on the counter inside the store.

Across the street, I saw Jackson at Davidson's filling station, putting gas in his car. He'd seen us come out with nothing and watched as my father slammed the car door shut. Another car in the lot, a big run-down-looking station wagon, had steam rising from the hood. Daddy looked at Mama and said, "I know what I'm gonna do," and he drove across the road and parked next to Jackson's car.

"Genny, you and your brothers go on in and get a Coke," Daddy said, handing me some change through the car window. We each decided on something different to drink, and while we stood in line at the counter, I watched Jackson introducing a man to Daddy. They shook hands, and Daddy wrote something down on a piece of paper and handed it to the man. The man gestured to the station wagon that was filled to the brim with clothes and boxes. A woman waved shyly from the window, and there were kids in the backseat. As we came out of the station, one of the little boys jumped out of the car and ran toward Ryan.

"My name is Adam!" he said proudly. "Are you seven?"

"Yes, I'm seven," Ryan said, surprised that he knew.

"I can tell 'cause you're as big as me," Adam said.

"Adam, come back in the car!" his mother called. Ryan pulled a gumball from the Western Auto store out of his pocket and handed it to him. Adam smiled, popped it in his mouth, and ran back to the car. Jackson was with the little boy's father, and they were looking under the hood of the car. There was a bunch of steam coming out of it, but I figured as good as Jackson was with cars, he could help these folks.

When Daddy came back to our car, he told Mama that Jackson might have just found him the night watchman he'd been looking for, and he was going to interview him next week. "Seems this guy's been goin' from place to place for a while, but he's got experience working night shift at factories and wants to settle down now here with his family."

"Well, how about that? And . . . did you tell Jackson *his* big news?" Mama asked.

Daddy nodded, grinning broadly. "Yep! I sure did. I made it official. Jackson will start as my full-time warehouse supervisor for the main plant site. I need to clear the start date with Mr. Landry, but I don't think there's gonna be any problem. Jackson said he couldn't wait to get back home to Ruby and tell her. I just wish I'd said it in front of that jerk when we were in the Western Auto. That would have been very satisfying," Daddy said.

"Well, you didn't know you were going to make a quick decision on the spot—and it was a good one, one you would've made eventually anyway. Mr. Landry won't mind. He likes Jackson and trusts your judgment, so deciding a little early on the warehouse supervisor is no big deal. Jim, it's all comin' together. It's true . . . everything happens for a reason," she said, looking at him with a big smile on her face.

Ryan turned around in his seat and stuck his arm out the car window, waving good-bye to Adam. As we pulled out of the filling station, Mama shook her head at Mike across the street, who was struggling to lift a load of delivery boxes into his car. "There's just no excuse for rudeness," Mama said, and she made sure we never went to the Western Auto in Hollywood again.

Chapter Ten

November 16, 1966

RACHEL AND I HAD BEEN PRETTY worried about where we'd go to buy our 45s in Hollywood, now that Western Auto was out of the picture, but then we heard the great news about a brand-new store called Hollywood General opening the day after Thanksgiving. The grand opening and the Thanksgiving parade were just a week away, and we talked about it all the way to school. When we got there, I began to get this funny, kind of jittery feeling in my stomach I'd been getting lately every time I stepped off the bus. The closer I got to my classroom, the worse it got. Mrs. Gardner greeted us at the door, and then I took my seat and looked over at him.

I couldn't be sure, but I think Joe Saylor liked me from the beginning, too. I wondered if he got the same feeling in his stomach that I did. Joe was really good in arithmetic, and I was really bad at it, so today he was my partner for this week's practice test, and we sat side-by-side, working on word problems.

"So," Joe said. "Here is the first problem. It takes Bill twenty-five minutes to walk to the car and forty-five minutes to drive to work. At what time should he get out of the house in order to get to work at nine a.m.?" Joe worked the problem quickly and asked me if I needed help with it.

"It's no use. I'm just not good at this," I said, putting my pencil down. I wondered if he thought I wasn't smart. I knew that I was, but I sure couldn't prove it to him this way.

"Genny, you're good at other things, like writing. I'm not good at that. I'll show you how to do it," Joe said, smiling, and he ended up explaining how to do all the word problems.

Joe was very quiet and very polite, and he loved baseball. I would watch him at recess hit balls way out over the playground, and I could tell this was a big deal because sometimes the principal of the school would come outside just to watch Joe hit, and then he'd go over and pat him on the back. He was the tallest boy in the fifth grade with very black hair that was much longer than the other boys'. He'd just started coming to our school, and every girl had a crush on him. Even Rachel said he was the cutest boy she'd ever seen at R. B. Stover Elementary since she'd been there.

It was most obvious that Joe liked me on the day we had to read our homework assignment in front of the whole fifth-grade class. The assignment was to write a report about something we love to do and that we believe could turn into a future career. Joe talked about baseball and how one day he would play professional ball, and I definitely believed that would happen. As I walked nervously to the front of the class, a whirring sound in my ears got so loud I couldn't hear our teacher talking. Everyone was staring at me, waiting. Then, I felt it — this tingling sensation in my neck and a comforting blanket of warmth settling around me. I took a deep breath, and I read my report aloud to Nannie, and I knew she was listening. I spoke about words, how I loved them, especially in books and poetry, and how they're the only real way to make dreams and truthful stories last forever.

"Truthful stories are gifts—like special powers," I explained. "The storytellers give the gifts to anyone who accepts them. My grandmother taught me when someone tells you a truthful story, it's not like any other story. You'll recognize it because it has a special message inside of it, and if you listen close, you'll find out what it really means. If you use its special powers, the words will jump out from the story and land inside of you and live there forever. They change you. When that happened to me, I knew I wanted to be a writer."

As I walked back to my seat, Joe smiled his lopsided smile at me with a look of understanding, and I could feel my heart beat a little faster. Later Rachel said that Marvin, Joe's best friend, told her Joe really liked me.

With Christmas coming in a few weeks, Mrs. Gardner told us to start thinking about the big class party and the gift exchange planned for the last day before vacation. She instructed we were not allowed to spend more than three dollars, and when the day of the party came, we were to bring in a wrapped gift that could be for a girl or a boy and put it under the tree. At the party, each person would pick a gift, but we wouldn't know who it was from, so it would be a big surprise.

For days, I prayed there would be a way I could give Joe Saylor my gift and that I could get his. From that moment on, all I could think about was Joe Saylor and what special present I could buy for him. I needed help, but I didn't want anyone to know. I decided to lie and ask Rachel's brother Curt what kind of baseball-type present I could buy for James, who didn't care at all about baseball. Curt told us that the new Hollywood General would carry baseballs and bats and gloves and also baseball cards, which a lot of boys liked to collect and trade.

The Truthful Story

The grand opening of the Hollywood General finally arrived. My father called the timing of the opening during the annual Christmas parade "brilliant advertising" and took us down to see the festivities. Balloons were tied to the front of the store, raffle tickets were being sold for prizes, the air was filled with the smell of Krispy Kreme doughnuts and coffee, and the marching band from St. Paul's High School was warming up in the parking lot. This was the perfect way to get in the holiday spirit. Pretty soon, Santa would be climbing on the back of the fire truck that Hollywood shared with all the neighboring towns, and for about ten wonderful minutes, I would believe it was really Santa who was waving at us and throwing candy up and down River Street instead of Mr. Tucker, who delivered the mail every day.

When Daddy dropped Rachel and me off at the Hollywood General to do our Christmas shopping, we took our time enjoying the new store. We found the baseball cards behind the counter, under glass. The teenager who worked there told us to get the Bobby Richardson card because he was like a local hero, and Richardson also happened to be his favorite. The problem was it cost four dollars, which really cut into the money I had earned, and was more than we were supposed to spend. Rachel convinced me that this was not a regular gift for just anybody, that Joe would love it, and that Mrs. Gardner wouldn't know how much a baseball card cost anyway. The card was shiny and colorful and came in a plastic sleeve.

Pleased with my purchase, I tucked the little bag under my arm, and Rachel and I split up in the store to look around. As I looked through the collection of paperbacks at the back of the store, I heard a man's voice.

"Hey—aren't you . . ." The man walked up behind me, and I suddenly became uncomfortable and very aware that no one could see us. I looked for Rachel, but my view was blocked. It was Jeffrey Landry, and he leaned down to me, so close I could feel the heat of his breath. Before turning away, I noticed all the little holes and scars across his face and that he smelled kind of sour and like the bourbon that the grown-ups served at parties.

"Hi, Mr. Landry," I said and smiled slightly.

He smiled back. "So, did you like the parade?" he asked, and without waiting for an answer, he said, "Where's your daddy?"

"Oh, he's outside waiting," I lied, knowing we'd be meeting Daddy at Corinne's Café down the street shortly.

"Okay, well, tell him happy Thanksgiving for me," he said and then walked off. I watched him go out to his truck and get in, but he just sat there watching what was happening in the parking lot and all the families and children laughing and shopping. I had a feeling he'd spent Thanksgiving alone.

A little later, Rachel and I left the store and headed down to Corinne's Café as planned. Daddy was waiting for us in a booth right next to the jukebox, which was perfect for Rachel and me. We ordered our hamburgers in a hurry, and then Daddy grinned and handed us some change and told us to pick out our favorite music. The first song we chose was "This Diamond Ring" by Gary Lewis and the Playboys. While we decided on the second one, I saw Jeffrey Landry walk up to our booth. "Jim, mind if I sit for a minute?" he asked, sitting down opposite Daddy. He nodded to me when I looked over at him, and I just smiled and went back to picking out the music. I could hear bits and pieces of their conversation through the music playing. "I know it's the holiday weekend and all, but I sure would like your help on somethin'," he said in a nervous way.

"What's goin' on, Jeffrey? You haven't been coming into work much lately, and I was starting to get worried. You comin' in on Monday?"

"Yeah, well, I've been busy workin' on putting the final touches on a real good deal that's goin' on right now—and I gotta move on it pretty fast. I'm tellin' you about this in confidence because it's so big, and I think you are going to want in on it," he said. He was smiling a lot at Daddy, but then he stopped—probably because Daddy wasn't smiling back. "I know my father promoted you 'cause you're smart, but I think you can do better than site manager at a fertilizer plant," he continued.

"Oh? How so?" Daddy asked.

"Now don't get all sore—just hear me out." Jeffrey Landry grabbed some napkins out of the holder and wiped the sweat off his forehead, and his hands were shaking. "My partners who wanted to invest earlier this year are back in on this deal to get the oyster factory opened. This is gonna be huge—we're gonna make a lot of money, Jim. But I need someone like you—with your smarts—to be part of this plan. I want you to say good-bye to that dead-end job with my father. Come on as an equal partner in this deal and become your own man—a rich man."

Rachel went over to the counter to get a Coke, and I waited by the jukebox, my ears perking up when I heard Jeffrey Landry say Daddy could be a rich man.

"Jeffrey, I don't have any money to invest in your deal," Daddy said.

"You don't need money," Jeffrey paused.

"Oh," Daddy said slowly. "Okay. I get it." He stood up over Jeffrey. "I see where this is going. You want me to turn over Gibson Island."

"Yes, but don't look at it that way. You and the aunt get money for the land *plus* it would belong to *your* company, and you would be an equal partner," he said.

"No, Jeffrey. That doesn't make sense. And it's not real. I just read in the paper yesterday that your partners pulled out. It sounds an awful lot like the project has been cancelled for good. I'm sorry you're stuck with that factory, but—"

"It's real, Jim! I just have to go back with the final plan, and they'll go for it. I guarantee it." He stood across from Daddy now. The waitress came up behind us with our hamburgers, and we all waited for Daddy and Jeffrey Landry to step aside so we could sit down, but they didn't seem to notice.

"Even if it was true, I would never do it. When are you going to understand that we're never selling Gibson Island?" Daddy said quietly but his face was getting red. Jeffrey Landry stuffed his hands in his pockets and shook his head back and forth.

"You have to do it," Jeffrey said, and he had a look on his face like he couldn't believe what Daddy was saying.

"I don't want to talk about this anymore. I got the kids here, so . . . ," Daddy said, sitting down and taking the hamburgers from the waitress. "Sit down, girls, and eat your lunch." It was kind of uncomfortable because Jeffrey Landry stood by our table for a minute while we started eating, and no one said anything. We kept our heads down, eating our hamburgers to Wilson Pickett's "In the Midnight Hour." By the time I got to my third bite, I looked up and he was gone.

On the way home, we sat in the backseat, we talked about the Christmas party, and Rachel told me she had a plan for how to get Joe my gift without Mrs. Gardner finding out. She was just as excited about the baseball card as I was and said, "Here's what you'll do: You'll take the wrapped-up gift to class and put it way in the back of the Christmas tree under the tree skirt. It's so thin and small, no one will notice. Marvin will have Joe hide his gift to you in the same place!" And so the plan was set. We'd know where each other's gifts were hidden and could exchange them without anyone catching on.

At dinner that night, Daddy told Mama about Jeffrey Landry's visit at Corrine's Café.

"It bothers me that he won't give up about Gibson Island," Mama said. "What's going on with him?" Mama asked. The boys came running into the room, and I put Thomas in his high chair. None of us could believe Thomas had started walking a month ago, especially since James and Ryan and I hadn't started walking till well after we'd turned one.

"He's been keepin' a low profile at work for a couple of months. In fact, he hasn't been coming to work much at all lately, and I told Mr. Landry I can't really count on him anymore. He just isn't reliable. What I did learn from his father is that Jeffrey's been running up some gambling debts in Charleston. I really think the guy needs some help, what with his drinking and gambling . . . but his father wants to stay out of it. His answer is to give him a job and pay him for not working and look the other way. He just doesn't want to deal with his son, even when the truth is right in front of him," Daddy said, setting a plate of cornbread on the table.

Mama's mind was on the oyster factory. "But if the partners he had before aren't going to invest now, all he has is a broken-down factory. What else can he do?" Mama asked, concerned.

"I think nothing. Coming to me today was probably a last-ditch effort." Daddy turned to James. "Say the blessing for us, James." James always liked saying the blessing. He'd sit up nice and tall and mix in his words with the church version, which made it more interesting.

"Bless us, Oh Lord, for these are our gifts, and we are about to receive them with this nice plate of cornbread and chicken and butter beans through Christ our Lord, Amen," James said in his serious voice. Ryan laughed until he saw Mama frowning at him.

Chapter Eleven

November 26, 1966

THE DAY AFTER THE HOLLYWOOD GENERAL grand opening, Daddy took James and Ryan and me to Champ's Country Store, which was out past Ravenel, down Highway 17. Champ was the nickname for Daddy's childhood friend who owned a little grocery store with one gas pump out front and a motel next door. He was called Champ because he won a lot of boxing matches in the old days. Whenever Daddy took us to Champ's, we knew we would be there for a while. We got to eat whatever we wanted, which was usually a Coke or a Yoo-hoo and a MoonPie and sometimes a Nutty Buddy. Daddy and Champ would sit at the front of the store at a table covered with newspapers and talk about politics and drink beer. There wasn't much for us to do around there, but sometimes Champ would pay us if we swept the store or arranged things on the shelves or in the stockroom. That day, Ryan and James and I made enough money to buy Christmas presents for all the people on our list. It was a good thing, too, since I had spent my savings already on Joe's baseball card.

When we were done, we took Cokes out on the back steps of the store, which faced out to a big woods. A yellow cat curled its tail around my legs, then ran off down what looked to be a dirt road leading into the trees. My brothers and I'd never noticed this road before, so we decided to go exploring. It was definitely a road, and it wound through the woods, taking us to an open spot where we saw clothes hanging on a line tied between two trees. There were some toy plastic buckets and shovels in a dirt pile in front of an old, broken-down school bus. The yellow cat had warned all the other cats, so about ten of them scurried off as soon as we got to the clearing.

When we heard voices, James and Ryan and I hid behind the trees. Ryan tried to say something, so I put my hand over his mouth. To our surprise, two little girls jumped out of the back of the school bus. It looked like tomato crates had been stacked up as steps to the back door, and then we noticed there were also curtains in the bus windows. James pointed to a pit in the ground that looked as if a fire had been built in it. Had some kids decided to make this their own hiding place? But who was watching them? Obviously, with laundry hanging and a fire pit, some adults had to be around somewhere.

We suddenly felt like this was supposed to be a secret. We did not want these people to know we'd discovered them or what was going on, so we got out of there fast. We ran through the woods back to the store and up to my father, who was standing out in front by our car.

"Where've you kids been? I need y'all to come when I call you," he scolded. "Your mama's going to be mad if we're out much longer. Aunt Alicia's comin' for supper, and you know if she doesn't eat by five thirty, the world comes to an end." Daddy tossed his keys up in the air and caught them with his other hand. "See ya next time, Champ." Champ waved and went back inside his store.

"Daddy, wait," I said. "There's people livin' in the woods. I think this is something real bad. We need to tell Champ right away."

James added, "We need to show you what's goin' on back there."

Ryan pulled on Daddy's hand. "You won't believe it!"

"Hop on in the car, now. Don't worry Champ with that. He knows what's going on. He doesn't need you kids to bother him with that stuff."

The three of us exchanged nervous looks as we drove home. At supper that night, Aunt Alicia told us about a band of gypsies that lived out in the country when she was a young girl. She leaned forward holding her glass with her three fingers and spoke in a low voice. My brothers and I all leaned forward, too.

"These gypsies are people who move around from place to place and trick you to get your money, and some say they steal little children."

"Alicia . . . ," Mama said in her warning voice.

"Well, they do. When we were little, the Griffins had a neighbor, Warren Mason, and he and his wife had a little boy named Warren Jr. He was about three years old, and one day he was out in the front yard playin' with his little sand bucket and toys, and next thing you know, he was gone. His wife turned her back for just a minute, and when she came back, he was nowhere to be found, and no one ever saw him again. All that was left was his little toy bucket."

I thought about the toy buckets and the old school bus. I suddenly felt very worried and gave my father an "I told you so" look, but he just kept eating his spaghetti. Mama and Daddy looked at each other. Aunt Alicia was becoming more confused lately and not getting all her facts straight.

"Why do they want to take children?" Ryan asked in a scared voice.

"Well," Aunt Alicia said as she took a sip of her drink, "some say it's so they can teach them how to steal from people because no one would suspect children stealing. Who knows why they do what they do?" After Aunt Alicia left, James and Ryan and I couldn't shake off what she'd said. We slept in the same bed that night wondering what and who it was we'd seen way back in the woods behind Champ's store that day and how many more were out there.

By the time my mother was ready for the office Christmas party, she looked like a princess, not the kind in fairy tales, but the real ones. The princesses who married famous men with yachts and islands—the kind who donated paintings to museums and served on committees that raise money for orphans; the kind invited to movie premieres but who never have time to go; the kind who played croquet on Sunday afternoons with their children while wearing white linen shorts. Princesses who owned a thousand dresses and had a room just for shoes.

It looked like she was covered in diamonds. The top of her dress shimmered in silver sequins, and the bottom was white and silky and swirled around her nylon-covered legs when she moved—just enough to reveal fuzzy blue bedroom slippers. The high-heeled shoes with thin straps lay on the floor outside the bathroom. With her face close to the mirror, she applied creamy pink lipstick, and I leaned to one side so I could see her better. My father appeared next to her reflection, and their eyes met in the mirror. She lifted her dark brown hair up carefully so my father could zip up the back of her dress. He had on his best suit, and they were ready for a special evening at his company's party. When I hugged my father good night, I could smell his aftershave and knew he was going to be thrilled with his Christmas gift.

Already wrapped and under the tree was the Brut cologne and the bonus gift — Brut soap on a rope, so he could hang it in the shower, which I thought was very practical.

As Mama and Daddy headed out the door to the office Christmas party, I thought they looked so romantic, and Karen Robertson took a picture of them with the Polaroid camera Aunt Alicia had given us when she got herself a new one. I'd never been this excited about Christmas before. I waved good-bye to Mama and Daddy as they drove off into the night and raced back to my room, anxious to check on the big secret I'd been keeping.

I pulled out the gift in my closet I was saving for Joe Saylor. This was the one time when I was not annoyed with Mama for insisting on Karen Robertson staying with us while they went out. I was old enough to babysit now, even late at night, but I didn't fight that battle this time. Tonight, while Karen kept the boys busy, I could sneak away into my room without being bothered.

In my room, I wondered how could I wait two whole days till the class party? I placed Joe's gift back in my closet for safekeeping and put on my new favorite record of Debbie Reynolds singing "Tammy." As I danced around in circles and sang the song, I thought only of Joe.

That night, Karen and I were curled up under a blanket on the sofa in front of the twinkling Christmas tree when Mama and Daddy finally came home from the company party. We wanted to hear all about it, and they said it had been wonderful but they were too tired to talk. They hurriedly paid Karen and sent her on home. Mama kissed the top of my head and told me to go to bed. "Sweet dreams, Genny." She said this as she walked away from me. I noticed that instead of taking off her high heels, which was usually the first thing she did when she walked in the door, Mama tossed her purse onto the sofa and headed straight to the kitchen, following Daddy with a worried look on her face.

The Truthful Story

The next morning, when I got up, Daddy was bringing in cardboard boxes and lining them up on the floor in the living room. Mama was busy stacking all kinds of canned food, paper plates, and red-and-white boxes of Carnation powdered milk on the kitchen table. They'd changed out of their party clothes, but they looked like they hadn't slept all night. Along with groceries, there were piles of my brothers' and my clothes stacked in some of the boxes. Ryan and James and I just stood there staring at them as they moved about with unusual energy.

"Well," Mama started, "at Christmastime, it's important to give to others in need and to make sacrifices, so today's our chance!"

"Who's all this for?" James asked as he peeked into the boxes and bags.

Daddy jumped right into the answer. "Last night, my new night watchman at the plant was accused of something he didn't do, and the police arrested him while the Christmas party was going on," Daddy said as he handed James and Ryan each a bag to carry outside.

"That's terrible, Daddy!" we said almost in unison.

"Mr. Landry's good-for-nothin' son is behind all this. Jeffrey says he caught my watchman stealing money and that he was attacked by him—but it's not true, and I can prove it. Now Jeffrey's pressin' charges against him. There's more to this than meets the eye, and I'm going to get to the bottom of it, you can be sure of that," he added sternly. Carrying another load of boxes in his arms, he stormed out of the house to put them in the trunk of the car.

"Daddy's upset," Mama said to me, tucking a box of candy canes in the corner of a box. "He's never trusted that Jeffrey Landry—and now he's ruining people's lives. Since your Daddy got promoted, it seems that things have gotten worse at the plant, and it always points to Jeffrey Landry."

"Why doesn't he just tell his daddy?" I asked, thinking that should fix everything. "Your Daddy has been trying to get Mr. Landry to understand, but it's his son, so I think maybe it's kind of hard for him to accept the truth," Mama said. "Your daddy calls Jeffrey Landry a loose cannon." I helped her put some cans in the cardboard box. I felt bad for Daddy, especially when things were going so well for him at work.

"What's a loose cannon?" Ryan asked, coming in from outside and picking up another bag.

"That means the guy just goes off sometimes for no reason," Mama said. "He's got problems, and he starts blamin' other people for stuff they didn't do and yellin' and sayin' things without thinking. That's what happened last night."

Daddy sat down and lit a cigarette. "Now, my watchman is going to be held in the jail over in Ravenel until bail is posted, and he might not have a Christmas. He has a wife and four children, and I know for a fact they're very poor."

Mama told us, "Jackson and Ruby went over late last night to check on the family and said they're really strugglin'. Ruby says they don't even have a Christmas tree."

We stood around Daddy, who was shaking his head. James put his hand on Daddy's shoulder, and I thought of the time I heard Mama describing her children to Nannie. "There's one word for each of them. James is comforting; Ryan is inquisitive; and Genevieve is stubborn." I wanted badly to be comforting or inquisitive.

Daddy looked at us and said, "Now, I need to ask you kids a big favor. I want you to think about giving up a toy or two so these children can have something to open on Christmas. No matter what happened at the plant, these children need to have Christmas."

James and Ryan and I went right to work searching for the right toys to give, while Mama finished putting together the boxes of food. I picked a jump rope, a Chinese checkers game, and a disappointing *Weekly Reader* bonus book I had gotten called *Jason and the Golden Fleece*. When I looked at my gifts to the poor children laid out on the bed, I realized these were things I didn't like and they probably wouldn't like them, either. I remembered what Daddy said about making a sacrifice, and I knew these things weren't much of a sacrifice on my part. I gathered up my Barbie and Skipper dolls. I was getting too old for them, anyway. I dressed them up nicely and brushed their hair before placing them in their cases.

"Genny, you don't have to give away your favorite dolls—just something small they would enjoy," Mama told me as we placed our donations in the last box. But I didn't mind at all. It felt good. Daddy was in better spirits and said we could all ride along to deliver our gifts in person. He felt it was important for our family to knock on the door together and wish them a merry Christmas and to do it in a way that didn't embarrass them.

Jackson and Ruby pulled up outside and helped load the cartons into both cars. I could tell Jackson was real happy to be helping these people out. Ruby said that he was not so depressed as he was right after Rooster died, and a lot of that had to do with Daddy getting him a full-time job at the plant. She said they'd also learned the more they did for others, the better they felt. We packed in the last of the boxes along with a little Christmas tree and a box of silver and blue ornaments. Jackson led the way as we drove behind him, and I thought to myself that this was what Christmas was all about.

Mama turned the radio on so we could listen to the holiday music. After driving a while, we turned in front of Champ's store and took the little dirt road in the back. I thought we must be lost, but we kept following Jackson. James and Ryan and I looked at each other, wondering what was going on. We pulled up next to Jackson's car, parking outside the beat-up school bus with the curtains. It was the gypsy place. What on earth were we doing here? There had to be a mistake.

"Daddy, this is the place we told you about. The gypsies!" I said, pulling hard on the back of the driver's seat as he tried to get out of the car.

"Genevieve, stop," Daddy whispered impatiently as he turned to look at us from the front seat. "This is where they live. They don't have a house yet, so Champ lets them live here temporarily and use the motel for the bathroom. Enough with all the gypsy nonsense."

"Now let's go wish them a merry Christmas," Mama said, "and wipe that strange look off your faces right this minute." Thomas was standing on Mama's lap looking back at us, too. He had on his little blue overalls and red-striped shirt. Mama zipped up his coat and kissed him. "Let's go, Sweetman!" At that moment, I could feel the big difference between what we had and what these people didn't.

I felt ashamed of myself. These weren't gypsies—they were poor people who had children like us, and their daddy was in jail at Christmastime because of something he didn't do. On the way over, Daddy said that the new night watchman was well liked at the plant and a good man, and all this was such a horrible mistake. We walked up to the school bus, and a lady with shoulder-length dark hair and pale skin came to the back door. Jackson set the boxes down by the crate steps.

"Merry Christmas, Mrs. Saylor," my father said.

I frowned at my father. *Mrs. Saylor?* I had only heard that name once before. Mama was saying to her how this had to be a hard time for her family. "So we brought a few things to help you and the children get through it all."

"Here you go, Mrs. Saylor," Ruby was saying. James and Ryan were proudly carrying the boxes with their toys. I was paralyzed. Mama looked at me, raising her eyebrows as a cue to bring my box and hand it over. I saw the children gathering behind their mother at the bus's back door to see what was happening. I recognized the two youngest as the ones we'd seen when we spied on them from behind the trees. They were smiling and clapping their hands.

A boy about Ryan's age came to the door. "Hi, Ryan!" the little boy said, and I remembered him from the filling station awhile back.

"Hi, Adam," Ryan said and handed him a box of toys.

Then, from behind the tired-looking mother, a tall boy with black hair approached the door to join his family. I dropped the box of dolls and ran away as fast as I could, tripping over a baseball bat on my way through the woods.

Chapter Twelve

December 25, 1966

"Now that's a fire, Angel Baby," Daddy said after trying for half an hour with newspapers and twigs to get one started in the living room fireplace. We'd used it before, but Daddy was determined to have it working on Christmas Day. A pinecone that had found its way into the bundle crackled loudly and threw out a burst of sparks. He sat back on the floor and grinned with satisfaction. As I warmed my hands in front of the fire, Mama brought a tray of coffee and hot chocolate.

"Daddy," I whispered so the boys couldn't hear. "How are they doing? The Saylors?" The sound of metal pieces clattering noisily to the floor pierced the air as James and Ryan's Erector Set building collapsed around them. The fire and the glow from the Christmas tree provided the only light in the room, and we felt cozy and safe.

All through the Christmas week, I couldn't stop thinking about Joe and his family. "Well," he answered, "I guess the Saylors are doing as well as can be expected." Mama joined us on the floor in front of the fire, wearing the Christmas red robe Daddy had gotten her. Anyone could smell both of them a mile away with their Brut and Evening in Paris colognes.

"Is Mr. Saylor still in jail?" I asked, piquing the attention of James and Ryan.

"He's out on bail, which means he can't leave town and has to report to court right after New Year's. Champ and Jackson have collected some donations for the family, so that should help in the meantime," Daddy explained.

"What will happen to the kids?" I asked Mama.

"Don't worry. They'll be fine. Nothing will happen. Daddy will fix it all up, right, Daddy?" Mama touched his arm, and he nodded.

"Yes—I certainly will," he said in a determined voice and went over to Thomas and lifted him high into the air.

It had only been a few days ago, and I still flinched at the thought of it—the fact that Joe Saylor was so poor and they had to live in a bus behind Champ's store. And on top of that, his daddy had just been arrested and taken to jail. It felt like the worst day of my life.

I was horrified when I realized who was living there, and I just couldn't let Joe see me or know that it was my family bringing them food and clothes and toys. I couldn't let him see the shock on my face. It was supposed to be about another family—one that we could help out and feel sorry for but then drive away from and back to our lucky lives, back to my house and my school, back to the Christmas party where Joe and I would carry out our plan and exchange gifts secretly. Soon, Joe and I would hold hands for the first time, and the other girls would watch us and be jealous. But instead, there I was standing in the dirt outside a broken-down school bus with curtains, next to my parents and my brothers and Jackson and Ruby, holding a box of Barbies, while my Daddy proudly held up a pitiful Christmas tree that had lost half its needles in the trunk of our car.

When I saw the tall boy with black hair and dark eyes was Joe, all I could do was run away. I didn't stop running until I was way down Route 17 past Champ's Motel. There was no one and nothing but bare woods and empty highway ahead. When I bent over trying to catch my breath, I saw the drizzle beginning to land like paint drops on the black road, and I heard her speak.

"Genevieve." There was nothing else. Just my name.

I knew this was Nannie trying to get my attention. I had to turn back. I also knew Mama was going to be furious with me for being so rude. Daddy, Champ, and Jackson were huddled out front of the store talking, and Mama and the boys were in the car. Ruby saw me coming and got out of their red car to meet me halfway, and she had a look on her face I hadn't seen before and never wanted to see again.

"Genny, you better explain yourself to your mama and quick. Where did you run off to?" I was taller than Ruby now and wondered when that had happened.

"Ruby, I know that boy. His name is Joe Saylor. He's the new boy I told you about at school."

"The one you went and bought that baseball card for and didn't tell your mama?"

"Yes." I hung my head that I'd been found out by Ruby. "I had to run. I didn't want him to see me. And I couldn't stand to see him like that. I feel real sick, Ruby."

Ruby stopped walking and took my wrists in her hands. "You aren't the one livin' in a school bus. You aren't the one whose daddy is in jail. You aren't the one who should be feelin' sick right now. You better fix your head right, Genevieve. Go and apologize to your mama. All she ever wanted was to make those people feel special for five minutes." Ruby watched as I got in our car. Then Jackson waved to Champ and Daddy, and he and Ruby drove off. Mama said this was not the way our family behaved.

"Genny, I don't care if you know the boy or not. You don't act that way to anyone. No one deserves to be treated like that," she said on the car ride back.

Daddy offered a voice of reason. "Your mama's right, Genny. Now, Mama, I don't think Genny meant to be rude. I don't think they even noticed, to tell you the truth. They were so happy to get the food and clothes and the toys, they probably didn't even see Genny run off like she did."

It was what I needed to hear because it gave me a glimmer of hope. Mama still looked at me all day as if I was a puzzle she couldn't quite figure out. I couldn't figure me out, either. The fact that Joe might not have seen me was one thing, but I'd seen him. It was enough to make me sick, all right. I was so sick I couldn't go to school the next day. So, I missed the Christmas party, and the baseball card stayed in its plastic sleeve up in my closet. I kept it tucked inside a box with a pair of Mary Jane black tap shoes I wore only one time to a dance class, back when Mama had the mistaken idea I was a natural.

When Rachel came over after school, she said it had been the best Christmas party ever. She said Joe hadn't come to school, either, and wasn't it strange we were both sick and couldn't come to the party after all that careful planning? I decided right then not to tell Rachel about the bus or anything about Joe's father or his family. I just couldn't bring myself to talk about it and tried to wipe it from my mind and get on with Christmas vacation like none of it had happened.

I figured out quickly, though, that it's not that easy to pretend something didn't happen. I tried every day, and I wished I could talk to Nannie about it all. I was getting used to the feeling I got when Nannie was around me—the whirring sound in my ears, the dizzy feeling in my head, the sound of her whispers. But it wasn't enough. I wanted to see her and talk to her. Last year, Mama had given James and Ryan and me a prayer card with Nannie's name on it and a prayer you can say for her soul. I didn't understand exactly why I should pray for her because I knew she was fine, but I thought it might help me, so on Christmas Eve morning, I pulled it out of my ballerina box and knelt down by my bed and prayed as hard as I could for Nannie to come to me in person.

Nannie used to say that Christmas Eve was the most magical day of all; everything feels brighter and happier—the multi-colored lights, the music of Andy Williams and Johnny Mathis on the stereo while the house fills up with smells of baked ham and pecan pie, presents wrapped in shiny foil paper and fancy ribbons tucked under the tree, new clothes laid out on my bed to wear to church, empty Christmas stockings lined up and ready to be filled with comic books and new pencils and Matchbox cars. To make it even more special, that afternoon Ruby and Jackson stopped by, bringing Daduh with them and a plateful of cinnamon sugar cookies shaped like snowmen and Santa Claus faces.

"We just came by real quick to wish y'all a merry Christmas and leave the kids these cookies," Jackson said.

"Why thank you, Jackson. You bring your grandma in here right now to say hello. Miss Alicia is here, too." Mama opened the door wide for them to step in. While Ruby went to get Daduh and help her in, Mama turned to Jackson and said, "Jim has gone on over to the plant to meet with Mr. Landry. Since the plant is closed today, no one else will be around."

"Did he take all the files with him?"

"Yes, he was able to pull 'em all together last night. Thanks for your help, Jackson," Mama said. "I think this is all the evidence he needs, so we'll see what happens." Mama handed me the plate of cookies. Thomas squealed next to me when he saw Ruby coming. "James and Ryan, you go on out and help Ruby and Daduh up those steps!" Daduh was wearing her favorite color, a brand-new sweater with purple flowers on the shoulders and down the sleeve—like the wisteria outside my bedroom window in the springtime.

Ruby said low so Daduh couldn't hear her, "Daduh is feelin' kind of blue today, so Jackson thought it might cheer her up to see Thomas." I remembered Rooster was born on Christmas Day, and he would have been two years old. Mama and Aunt Alicia and Ruby and Daduh went on back to the kitchen. I went over to Daduh and hugged her, and she hugged back the way she always did. While she and Aunt Alicia talked at the table, Mama and Ruby stood by the sink, which was still stacked with dirty dishes. Ruby acted like it wasn't her day off and started to wash the dishes, but Mama put her hand on her arm to stop her.

"Just habit, I guess," Ruby said, folding a dish towel. Then she nodded to where Daduh and Aunt Alicia were sitting. "Miss Louisa, she's gettin' pretty tired here lately—she's gettin' much worse since we lost little Benjamin."

"I know." Mama rubbed Ruby's arm lightly. "Aunt Alicia said she can't do much cleaning anymore. Gibson Island is just too much for her these days. Is there anything we can do to help, Ruby?" Mama asked.

"I think if Genny could take her out and let her stroll Thomas around for a few minutes outside, it might be nice for her," Ruby said, so I got the stroller out, and I walked with Daduh while she pushed Thomas for a ride down the dirt road toward the Cooks' house. The river moved alongside us in a hurry, and the tree branches quivered in the cold, so Daduh tucked the blanket around Thomas's legs as they dangled down from the seat.

"He's growin' like a weed!" Daduh exclaimed. "Seems like just yesterday he was born. You know your Nannie knew he was cookin' before your mama did," she said to me, chuckling.

"I know. She told me." I looked at Daduh to see if she was okay because Ruby had said she'd changed so much. She seemed like regular Daduh to me.

"Your Nannie knew a lot of things before they happened. I didn't wanta get too far into that, mind you, but I noticed it all the same. Her grandmother was the same way, you know." Daduh said this as if she was talking about the weather. She peeked around at Thomas's face and went back to pushing the stroller.

"Daduh, did you know my great-great-grandmother Genevieve?"

"Oh yes, I knew Miss Genevieve. My mama worked for her, and she would tell me about her aches and pains." I loved hearing this from Daduh—she always made me feel even closer to Nannie.

"That's right," I said, pausing and waiting to see where this was going next. Was she going to tell me about my great-great-grandmother's dreams or more about Nannie?

"I used to think she and your Nannie were a little strange, to tell you the truth, but I learned pretty quick that sometimes things aren't always as they seem." Daduh was a little out of breath. *Sometimes things aren't always as they seem.* The Orchard. Nannie's whispers to me. I watched her as she leaned down to talk to Thomas. "How you doin', Sweetman?" she asked, using Ruby's nickname for him. "I sure do miss my little Benjamin somethin' awful." Thomas looked up at her as if he understood. Daduh started singing in her gravelly voice, "Gonna put on my golden shoes, down by the riverside, down by the riverside, down by the riverside . . ."

And, suddenly, all I could think of at that moment was little Benjamin—Rooster—and I saw his face as clear as day right in front of me, just like when Mama and I were at Ruby's house. I saw him now laughing and laughing. I wanted her to know, but I didn't want to scare her. "Daduh, I think your little Benjamin is okay now. He's happy and laughing and wants you to be happy, too. It's his birthday, and it's Christmas. The best day of the year."

Daduh smiled a sad smile, but it was still a smile. "How you know all that, child? You're the same as your Nannie, aren't you?"

"I just know it somehow. I'm so happy you came today, Daduh," I said and took her hand. Nannie was right here with us, and so was Rooster.

Before Jackson and Ruby and Daduh left, Ruby said to Mama and me, "I don't know what Thomas did, but Daduh is a hundred percent better. Just look at the spring in her step. Merry Christmas! Enjoy those cookies Daduh made for you!"

"Genevieve, I almost forgot," Daduh called me over to the car.

"What is it, Daduh?"

Then she whispered close to my ear. "The secret ingredient . . . is molasses. Don't you tell a soul now, you hear? That's your gift from me to you."

"I won't. I promise," I whispered back.

"Merry Christmas!" Mama said.

"Happy birthday, Jesus! Thank you, Lord!" Daduh called out, just like she always did this time of year.

I watched as Ruby got Daduh situated in the front seat of their red car. Before she shut the door, Ruby reached down and scooped up part of Daduh's dress that hung to the ground. Then she kissed her on the cheek and got in the backseat.

Ruby was good to Daduh and more of a granddaughter than Gloria. Jackson's sister had up and left soon after Rooster died, and Jackson and Daduh had done their best to move on. It still wasn't easy, but everyone knew if it wasn't for Ruby, it would've been almost impossible. Ruby had a good understanding about family—just like Daduh did—and she had given me her clear message about that when we delivered our Christmas gifts to the Saylor family.

Daddy got home from his meeting at the plant just in time to put on his blue suit and head over to church. Instead of going to midnight Mass at St. Anne's like we usually did on Christmas Eve, we were going to the earlier evening service, and Mama wanted to make a stop on the way. Daddy pulled into Marylou Griffin's driveway. Their small white house had dark-gray shutters that matched the floor of the wide concrete porch and a wheelchair ramp next to the front steps. A porch swing sat still but inviting at the far side, and on the front door was a Christmas wreath made of magnolia leaves that must have come from the enormous magnolia tree that leaned elegantly against their house. I'd seen its creamy white flowers blooming in the summer, and I'd roll down my windows as fast as I could when we drove by after church, so I could breathe in their lemony perfume.

Mama said now, "I'm just running in to drop something off to Mrs. Griffin. Y'all stay right here." As she swung the car door open, I jumped out, too, realizing this was a chance I couldn't miss.

"Mama, can I go in with you?" I asked, smoothing out my dark-green skirt and tugging slightly on the neck of my turtleneck Christmas sweater, which was feeling snug and itchy and would definitely be coming right off after Mass. She nodded, and as I started to walk up the ramp, she waved her hand for me to stop, so I went up the front steps with her. I guessed that probably it wasn't proper to use a wheelchair ramp unless you were in a wheelchair.

"Merry Christmas!" Mama said a little too cheerfully. I knew she wasn't all that fond of the Griffin sisters, so she surprised me with the voice she was using; although, I had started to notice that Mama could pretend pretty easily when she needed to. I watched her hug Mrs. Griffin, who invited us in. "We're going to early Mass, so we won't see you later tonight. I just wanted to drop a little something off for Marylou," Mama said.

"Louisa, what a nice surprise. And Genevieve, too! Come in and say hello to Marylou. She's reading in her room. That girl is quite the reader, you know," Mrs. Griffin said, fluffing up a pillow on her living room chair and stacking a group of magazines into a pile on the coffee table.

"Jim and the boys are in the car, and Mass starts soon, so we just wanted to dash in for a minute," Mama said.

"Of course — please come on back." Mrs. Griffin led us down the wide hallway into a large room filled with all kinds of interesting furniture and decorations. It had a regular-size bed and a tall white headboard with built-in bookshelves that were overflowing with books; a sitting area with a daybed; and an overstuffed chair and ottoman. The long curtains landed in puddles on the pale wood floors and framed a double window that looked out on a shady, peaceful backyard with a garden area and a bird fountain that spouted water up into the air.

There were different sized tables around the room. One had a rock collection; one had seashells; another held a large fish tank with colorful fish; but most had books — lots and lots of books. I tried to be polite, but all I could do was think about going to those books. Marylou was in her chair seated at the largest table in front of her reading stand with a light that hung down above it. She had instruments that looked like long forks on the table, and she held one in her mouth now as she reached down to turn the page of the book on the stand.

"Hi Marylou," Mama said. "We won't see you at midnight Mass, so we just wanted to drop by and say hello."

I have to say this came as a surprise to me that Mama would want to come here like this, but I sure was glad. Marylou rolled her head in a circle toward me, as if to say, "Look around. I know you want to." So, I smiled at her and roamed quickly from shelf to shelf and table to table. The books were organized like a library. Medical-type books; travel books—about China, Brazil, Peru, England, and Germany; novels and short stories and poetry; books about space and the moon and planets. Marylou even had a telescope next to the window. I'd never seen one in person before and wondered how many folks could say they had their own telescope. I went over to it and saw that it was aimed at the darkening winter sky, and soon the stars would be popping out for her to enjoy. I thought about *The Little Prince*, and I thought about the night we saw the flying saucers at Bailey's Place. I looked over at her. She rolled her head, and I knew Marylou had seen them, too. She probably knew all about aliens and life on other planets and just couldn't tell us the secrets we longed to hear. She had read everything about them and even had a telescope to keep her eye on things out there. I sighed so deeply that everyone turned their heads to me suddenly.

"Marylou, you have the best room I have ever seen!" I said, walking over to her. She nodded proudly.

"So, Marylou," Mama said, "I know my mother used to bring you a book every year on your birthday, and even though today is not your birthday, I thought Christmas would be a good time to restart the tradition." Mama reached into her pocketbook and brought out a package. Now I was really surprised, and I watched my mother give the package to Marylou and help her open it. "It's called *Flight of the Falcon*," Mama said. "I don't know if you like Daphne du Maurier, but if you do, this is a good one and just out last year." It was hard to tell if this was the kind of book Marylou would like, but I was mostly happy to see Mama's face light up as she talked about it and thought that Nannie probably had that same look on her face when she brought Marylou a book each year. For that one minute, it was like I was watching Mama and Nannie together, talking, gesturing, leaning down to Marylou. It was as if I wasn't even in the room, yet I felt closer to Mama than I'd felt in a long time.

Then, I heard the whirring sound and felt Nannie near us. Marylou looked at me, her hands and eyes steady. I believe she sensed something, too, but I couldn't be sure. On the way out of her room, I heard her make sounds for the first time, and sure enough, she was saying, "Thank you," or at least that's the way I heard it. I turned back and noticed that Marylou was dressed for Christmas—a full red skirt and a white, long-sleeved blouse. She leaned back in her wheelchair, her head tilted so that her neck looked longer and thinner than usual, and so that I could see that the wide collar of her blouse was trimmed in lace and embroidered with a tiny red cardinal on each side. At Mass, Mama made sure we all sat in the pew where my great-great grandmother Genevieve used to sit, and I made sure I sat right next to Mama.

Christmas Day ended with everyone falling asleep in different places. Ryan and James were under the Christmas tree, so Daddy carried them one by one back to their room. Thomas, his cheeks still rosy from the fire that was now dying down, squirmed in Mama's arms, but as soon as she started humming "Silent Night," he was out. Aunt Alicia was spending the night with us, and she was nodding off on the sofa holding a drink in her hand, so at Mama's silent direction, I took the drink so it wouldn't spill, and Aunt Alicia got up and went on to bed, too. While picking up the Christmas toys scattered around the room, I twisted Nannie's ring on my finger and began to feel nervous, like something was about to happen, and then it did. I heard the phone ring and Mama called out from the kitchen.

"Jim—come here!"

"What is it? Who was on the phone?" Daddy asked.

"I don't know. A man. He said, 'Tell your husband merry Christmas and that sure is a pretty tree you got there tonight.' Then he hung up," she said.

"It's gotta be him—Jeffrey Landry," Daddy said flatly. "He's probably by himself somewhere and drinking too much. I know his father said they don't spend Christmas together." He went to the living room window behind the Christmas tree and looked out.

"Jim, do you think Jeffrey knows you went to see his father yesterday? I mean—this call is awfully strange," Mama said.

"No, he doesn't know," Daddy answered.

"Well, do you think he really came out here to our house and saw our tree? You should tell Mr. Landry about this, too. This is going too far," Mama said, bringing me close to her on the sofa.

"Is anyone out there, Daddy?" I asked.

He turned the porch light on. "I don't see anyone. I doubt he came around here tonight." Even though Daddy seemed calm about it, I could tell he was worried because he opened the front door and walked out on the porch and then came in and closed the living room curtains. "Don't worry, Louisa. It's going to stop—and soon." Mama let me lie on the sofa between her and Daddy. She stroked my hair, and they talked very softly, the Christmas tree lights fading behind my eyes as I started drifting off to sleep.

"Jim, you did the right thing by going to Mr. Landry and laying out the truth. I know there's a risk, but at least now there'll be a real investigation about what happened and not just Jeffrey's made-up story. It makes me sick someone like him can ruin people's lives."

"Yeah, and now he's starting on us," Daddy said.

"I just hope that—"

Daddy stopped her. "I know. The job. Let's don't worry about it tonight." The Christmas music was still playing low in the background. "It was a nice Christmas, though."

"Yes, it was. And I really like my new red robe," was the last thing I heard Mama say, and then Christmas was over.

The next day, Mama and Thomas took Aunt Alicia back to Gibson Island and brought Ruby and Daduh along to do some cleaning. Since Daduh wasn't able to do as much cleaning as she used to, Mama and Daddy gave Aunt Alicia a Christmas present—two days a month of Ruby's maid services, so of course, this made everyone happy. Ruby was glad to make the extra money, but she said it was on one condition—that Daduh come along for the first time to "explain how Miss Alicia likes things done at Gibson Island." Ruby sure understood how people's minds worked.

Right after Mama left, Daddy got a phone call, and he told James and Ryan and me to come with him quick to Champ's store. I was pretty anxious about going back there, but he reassured me. "Genny, the Saylors don't live in the bus anymore. Champ thought it was best to get them out of there for now, so he found them another place, a better place, at least for the time being." I was glad to hear that and glad the Saylors had a friend l ike Champ.

Before we left the house, I sat on the floor of my bedroom closet, taking Joe's baseball card out of the shoebox and turning it around in my hand. When we got to the store, Daddy and Champ sat down at the table with their beers as usual; only this time, Jackson pulled up right after we got there and joined them in what looked to me like a serious conversation. Champ had set up a checkers game for us in the back of the store next to the ice cream box, and as soon as James and Ryan started playing, we heard the little bell on the front door ring.

"Now, what do *you* want?" Champ demanded, and the shuffle of chairs scraping the floor meant everyone was standing up.

"I came to buy cigarettes. You sellin' or not?" the man said. Then he laughed. "What's going on here anyway? Am I missing a meeting about somethin'?"

"Nope," Daddy responded, with three snaps of his lighter—open, light, close.

"We're fresh out. You're not wanted here," Champ said. James looked up at me from the checkerboard, and we crept along the aisle toward the front of the store.

"I have to say, Jim. You do keep interestin' company. An ex-con, a baby killer, and a pathetic, old alcoholic boxer. Haven't you learned anything yet?"

"Jeffrey, get on out of here. You think we weren't going to find out that you went over and threatened Roy and his family last night? You leave him alone. We know what you're up to."

"You and your boys here can't prove a damn thing. I'm just trying to protect my father and his company like any good son would do." He made a chuckling sound. "You think you're so smart, comin' in and takin' over things at the plant, don't you? You're in a mess of trouble for hirin' that no-good criminal Saylor. You knew what he was, Jim, and you kept it a secret from my daddy. That looks real suspicious, doesn't it? This guy comes in from nowhere with your recommendation and then tries to steal us blind. Makes us wonder if you were in on it all along," Jeffrey said calmly.

Before they could react, the door slammed shut hard, the little bell ringing away like crazy.

"That son of a bitch!" Daddy said.

"Mr. Jim, don't pay any attention to him. You got more important things to think about right now." Jackson's soothing voice broke through the tension.

"We need to keep cool heads here, Jim. You did the right thing. You turned in the files. You came clean with your boss about hiring Roy. Now we just gotta hope Mr. Landry will do the right thing. We gotta be patient," Champ added, and the chairs pulled back out for them to sit.

"When Jeffrey finds out, everything's gonna hit the fan. In the meantime, you two let me know if Roy and the family need anything, okay? Until his hearing comes up, I don't want Jeffrey near them. They don't need this," Daddy said.

"We got it, Jim. You just focus on Mr. Landry and stick to your plan," Champ said.

"I just hope it's not too late," Daddy said, and as James and I leaned forward across the aisle, a stack of Texaco motor oil cans came crashing down. "Okay, kids, y'all go on outside, you hear? We're leaving shortly."

"What do you think Daddy's plan is?" James asked me as we went out back. "I don't know for sure, but somethin' bad is going on here," I said and started after James and Ryan as they headed for the path toward the bus. Just then, I heard the loud idling of a car engine next to Champ's, its dirty white exhaust billowing out from around the corner. When I walked around the side, I saw Jeffrey Landry sitting in the front seat of his black truck, lifting a beer to his mouth. I wondered how he'd threatened Mr. Saylor. He probably told him he was going to jail for the rest of his life and would never see his family again. I imagined Joe overhearing this and being scared for his daddy. I felt a chill come over me, and I looked up above the hood of the black truck and saw a red cardinal sitting on a low-hanging tree branch.

155

Nannie used to tell us, "When you see a lone red cardinal in a tree, it means someone you love who has gone to heaven is here with you now and knows how much you need them and miss them." I turned to see if James and Ryan saw it, but they were far down the path. A gust of wind blew through the trees, the branches scraping noisily back and forth against Champ's motel sign next door. Jeffrey Landry threw his beer can out the window, and his truck took off, knocking over a trash can on its way out.

I ran up ahead to the boys, who were standing outside the bus. Curtains still hung in the bus windows, but no one was around, except for the same cats. The little Christmas tree we'd left was tossed into the woods. While James and Ryan poked at the dead pile of ashes in the fire pit, I walked up slowly to the back door of the bus. I thought about the little children's smiles when they saw us, and I pictured them excited when they opened the gifts we'd brought.

I tugged at the door handle, but it wouldn't budge. I cupped my hands to peek through the cloudy back window. All the bus seats had been removed to make room for them to live. I could see a table and folding chairs, an old sofa with no legs, a rug, and some clothes hangers on the floor. It was obvious they'd just left in a hurry. On the table were jelly jars used for drinking glasses and a few paper plates. In the corner, leaning against a stack of folded blankets, there were a couple of boxes and a baseball bat. They still had things here that belonged to them, and they'd need to come back. That meant Joe would be coming back, too.

I wished I had another chance. I wished I had stood there and looked at Joe and said, "Merry Christmas" because I had a strange feeling I was never going to see him again. I took the baseball card out of my pocket and slipped it under the door of the bus. I pushed it with such force that it scooted to the middle of the floor, and I could see it through the window, sitting there on the dirty floor right next to an empty red-and-white Carnation milk box.

As we drove home, I repeated Nannie's words to myself over and over: "Remember that things aren't always as they seem," but I forgot what those words meant as soon as I saw the police car waiting for Daddy in our driveway.

Chapter Thirteen

December 26, 1966

With Thomas in her arms, Mama smiled stiffly and started introducing us all like she was hosting some kind of party. "Jim, this is Officer Flynn. Officer Flynn, this is my husband, Jim Donovan. And these are our other three children — Genevieve, James, and Ryan." We all nodded and stood there staring at him, and Daddy and Officer Flynn shook hands. She said, "So, can I get you some tea? Would you like to come in?"

"Holy cow!" Ryan said walking over the police car and looking it over.

"This isn't good," James whispered to me, obviously considering all the other things that had happened that morning.

"No thanks, ma'am. Mr. Donovan, can I have a word with you?" he asked. We all just stood there with Daddy, until we realized that he wanted to have a word with him alone.

"Oh. Okay. Well, kids, let's go on inside. Jim, you'll let me know if y'all need something?" My mother placed her hand on each of our backs, one by one, to guide us firmly toward the house. We watched Daddy as he nodded and listened, walking down toward the river and along the Edge with Officer Flynn.

Inside, Mama paced around, looking out the window constantly.

"Why's the policeman here, Mama?" James asked again, looking out the back door.

"Is Daddy in trouble?" Ryan asked.

"No, honey. Officer Flynn just needs Daddy's help on something," she answered, leaning forward over the sink to get a better view of them talking. "Oh no!" she said as a car pulled up in the driveway. "What are the Mitchells doing here? Oh for God's sake, it's poker night!"

"Connie, Lloyd — come on in!" she called from the back porch. Mama acted as if she hadn't forgotten their monthly poker night at all. They were staring at the police car, and Porter, their son, was pointing to Daddy and Officer Flynn. "It's just some disturbance at Jim's work," Mama said quickly. "Nothing to worry about. Hello, Porter." We had automatic instructions from Mama to keep an eye on Thomas any time Porter was around, and Mama gave me the reminder look.

Porter Mitchell was the only person I ever hated. He was two years older and mean as all get out. The problem was he was smart-mean. That is, most adults couldn't see right away he was evil, but kids knew as soon as they met him. The other problem was he was the only child of Mama and Daddy's best friends, Lloyd and Connie Mitchell, which made it hard to get rid of him. Since James and Ryan and I dreaded being around Porter, James ran next door and got Rachel and Curt to come on over, too. Rachel and Curt liked to play board games and cards so while the grownups played poker, we decided we'd play Spoons, a card game where the loser of the game is forced to eat a spoonful of whatever awful concoction the rest of the players come up with. That would help make the evening go by faster.

When Daddy came back in, the police car had left, and he and Mama talked for a minute in the kitchen before coming into the living room. "Hi, folks. Merry Christmas!" He kissed Connie and shook Lloyd's hand. "Just some excitement over at the plant," he said casually. "All kinds of challenges come with supervisory responsibility, isn't that right, Lloyd? So let's get started—who's ready to win tonight?"

Daddy unfolded the card table and laid the green felt and the carousel of poker chips on top. Lloyd worked in insurance and had some kind of problem with his neck, so when he looked at something, he had to turn his whole body in that direction. Daddy said when he did that, Lloyd reminded him of Ed Sullivan. Connie was very tall and skinny and the only woman I ever knew who had a moustache. It wasn't like Mr. Bear's moustache, which was bushy and curled up on the ends. When you went to Bear's Store, if you took too long to pick out your candy at the counter, Mr. Bear would get impatient and twist and twirl the ends into little moustache ropes. Connie had grown up with Mama and Aunt Marjorie and Aunt Viv, and Daduh said she was the kind of friend who dropped everything when they needed her. Around Nannie's funeral, Connie had taken charge of arranging for all the food we ate—for weeks—and she also helped Mama and my aunts with the service arrangements. Daduh said to me in private, "How such nice people like Miss Connie and Mr. Lloyd could have a boy as mean as that Porter is beyond me. He is bad news. You stay clear of him, you understand?"

I did understand. The main reason we didn't like Porter was because of what he did when he came with his parents to see Thomas right after he was born. As soon as he got there, instead of going in to see our new baby brother, he headed for our backyard, and James and Ryan and I found him poking a stick at our dog Fella's face as if he was trying to take out his good eye. Poor Fella was growling and barking and crouching low to the ground like he was going to pounce on Porter.

"Stop, Porter!" Ryan yelled out. "Leave our dog alone!"

Porter laughed. "Stupid blind cur dog and stupid cur family," he said and threw the stick at us. We took Fella and left Porter standing there by himself. As we played in the Carpet Grass with the Robertsons, Porter just watched us from our sidewalk for a while and then disappeared into the house where the grown-ups were, which was fine with us. Later, he came back outside and sat on the porch steps, grinning. Then, suddenly, Porter did the strangest thing. When Ryan went past him on the steps to go inside, Porter pushed him so hard that Ryan fell backward down the concrete steps. We all rushed over to Ryan, who luckily wasn't hurt, and brought him back with us over to the Carpet Grass while we waited for Porter to leave.

"Are you crazy?" I shouted at him. Porter just sat there until his parents came out, and we didn't dare walk near him. Soon after, we watched as Lloyd and Connie hugged my parents good-bye and got into their car.

"Maybe next time, Thomas will stay awake longer for you. He's such a good baby and never cries!" Mama was saying proudly. Along with the Robertsons, we watched with relief when the Mitchells finally drove away, Porter's chubby, red face still grinning at us from the back window of the car.

Later, I was glad to hear Mama tell Daddy, "Somethin's not right with Porter. He makes me uncomfortable." She picked

Thomas up from his bassinet, and we heard her gasp.

"Jim, come here. What is this?" She lifted up the light-blue blanket around Thomas. Daddy and James and I went over to the bassinette. There was a red welt on Thomas's outer thigh, and it was already turning into a bruise.

"What in the world is that? Is it a bug bite?" Daddy asked as he ran his finger across the mark.

Mama started checking him all over. "Jim," she said quietly, "this is a pinch mark. Someone pinched him so hard it left a mark. You can tell—look at it."

"That can't be. How?" My father turned and looked at us. Ryan was looking up from where he was sitting on the floor, and James and I walked over to him. Ryan burst into tears.

"Porter pushed Ryan down the steps today," I said.

"And he tried to poke Fella's eye out with a stick," James added.

"What?" Daddy said. "Ryan, are you okay?" Ryan came over to them, and they checked him over, too.

"I'm okay," Ryan said, his bottom lip quivering, "but he's real mean."

"Was Porter with you the whole time?" Mama asked.

"No, he never plays with us when he comes over. After we told him to leave Fella alone, he went in the house while we played with the Robertsons in the Carpet Grass."

"Jim, I never saw Porter come in the house. Thomas was asleep back here in the bassinet while we were up front." Mama had a frantic look on her face.

"Honey, let's don't jump to conclusions here. Thomas would have cried if Porter had done something," my father said, taking my perfect little baby brother from her and kissing his head. Mama's eyes searched Daddy's face, and she took Thomas back from him.

"He never cries," she said.

After that visit, we lucked out because we didn't see much of Porter, and I wondered if Mama had spoken to Connie about her son. But this particular poker night after Christmas, he was back. Ryan steered clear of Porter and refused to play Spoons with us, deciding instead to play with Thomas on the floor while James and Curt set up the game. When I went to the kitchen to bring back some Cokes, Mama and Daddy's poker game had already started. Just as the door swung behind me in the kitchen, I heard Lloyd saying he wanted to know the real reason why the police officer was here.

I heard Daddy take a deep breath. "Well, it's all going to come out anyway, so I'm going to let you in on what I know right now. So, you remember when I got promoted this past summer? Well, right after that, I learned Mr. Landry's son, Jeffrey, had been stealin' from the company, and I've been gathering the proof I need over time to take to his father. When I brought Jackson on board, he also ran across more problems with the warehouse financial records." Ice cubes clinked in all of their glasses of bourbon. "Meanwhile," he continued, "the night watchman I hired, Roy Saylor, had been pretty down on his luck, but I took a chance, and he turned out to be a real winner." I could almost hear Lloyd and Connie nodding as he spoke.

"So, last weekend, right before our Christmas party started, Mr. Landry called to say he'd be arrivin' late. While the party was underway, Roy, who was on duty, came and got me and said he'd just caught Jeffrey taking money out of his father's payroll safe and putting it in a bag."

"What?" Lloyd interrupted loudly.

Daddy continued, "Roy knows no one has access to the payroll except his father and me. He didn't want to jump to conclusions about the owner's son, naturally, but he was suspicious. When he asked Jeffrey what he was doing, Jeffrey started screaming and became violent with him. When I went out to handle things, Jeffrey had called the cops and reported to them that he caught *Roy* stealing the money and that Roy had tried to stab him." The sound of rattling poker chips was deafening. Mama said something, then Connie said something, but I couldn't catch it. Finally, the poker chips were quiet.

"They took Roy away, and Jeffrey said he'd tell his father that I'd hired Roy knowing he was an ex-con and that once the police saw Roy's full record, his fate would be sealed. And then he said once his father knew what *I* had done, *my* fate would be sealed."

"Jesus, Jim. What a son of a bitch," Lloyd said.

"Yeah, well. That's what I've been dealing with. The problem is I did know Roy was an ex-con, so technically I could get fired. I was wrong to keep that to myself." When I heard Daddy say that, I felt scared because I didn't want him to lose his job, and I didn't want to come home one day and find our icebox or stereo gone.

"So, on Christmas Eve," Daddy continued, "after Jackson helped me organize all the evidence, I met with Mr. Landry and I told him everything. I gave him the boxes of financial records that prove his son stole thousands of dollars from him. The thing is . . . Jeffrey's been getting himself deeper and deeper in debt and in trouble, and the biggest blow or the last straw—however you want to look at it—was when his oyster factory partnerships fell through. Officer Flynn took some more information from me just now, and I'm sure we'll be talking a few more times this week."

Connie said, "This is like *Perry Mason*. How did Mr. Landry react when you told him?"

"Not that good really—but not shocked, either. He's very cold about his son, and they've never had a good relationship, especially since Jeffrey's drinking and gambling problems have gotten worse. On the other hand, Jeffrey gets what he wants as long as he stays out of his father's life."

"That's pretty sad," Lloyd said. "Is the old man taking any of this out on you?" "Well, he's still processing it all. He obviously believes it because he went to the police today. I didn't want to be the one to do it, but I was prepared to. Officer Flynn says they'll finish the investigation this week, and they want us to keep it quiet until then. I think once it's completed, the plan is for Mr. Landry and me to talk to Jeffrey at the office next week and convince him to turn himself in," Daddy said.

Suddenly, James interrupted, running through the room and bursting through the swinging door, practically knocking me down. "Genny! Hurry up!" He grabbed the Cokes off the counter. "We're waiting on you!"

As I walked past the poker game, I heard Lloyd awkwardly change the subject and say to Mama, "Louisa, that must be a wicked hand you're holding. Give us a break this time, you hear?" Mama smiled back weakly.

"Hi, Angel Baby," Daddy said. They'd forgotten I was in the kitchen.

"Hi, Daddy." I went over to him.

"Don't give my hand away now," he said, holding his cards up so I could see them. I put my hand on his shoulder, and he patted it without taking his eyes off his cards. "Genny, turn on the stereo and liven things up for us. Put on some Herb Alpert and the Tijuana Brass!" Daddy said cheerfully. Once I got the music going, I headed to the party in the back of the house.

"What's wrong with you?" Rachel asked when I sat down and started our game of Spoons.

"Nothing." Something else I couldn't tell my best friend about. "Let's just play," I said. Curt started dealing the cards. Rachel had told me a while back she thought her brother had a crush on me, but I didn't pay much attention to that because I still thought about Joe all the time. Then I noticed Thomas was not in the room, and Ryan was now playing alone with his collection of army soldiers on the floor.

"Ryan—you're supposed to be watching Thomas!" I said angrily and ran toward the back bedroom. Thomas had moved fast to a basket of magazines and was tearing up a Sears catalog. Just as I got to him, I felt hands grab my waist from behind. I swung around, and it was Porter. He had followed right behind me.

"What—" Before I could finish my question, he took my head in his hands and pushed his mouth on mine, his tongue jamming against my front teeth. I shoved him so hard, he fell backward to the floor. "Keep away from me, Porter!" I yelled at him. But he just got up calmly and walked away. I stood there, feeling stunned and nauseous, and wiped his spit off me with the back of my sleeve. He brushed past Curt, who was standing in the doorway.

"You okay?" Curt asked, coming over to me. Thomas started crying.

"Yeah. He's so gross." I picked up Thomas and the Sears catalog and walked with Curt back to the Spoons game. I was shaking and felt disgusted and angry, but Porter sat there and acted like nothing had happened. I stared at him, frowning. Did he think he had kissed me? I'd never been kissed before, and I certainly wasn't going to count that. I could see Curt was bothered and kept looking back and forth from Porter to me. I felt embarrassed he'd seen what Porter did. Mostly, though, I was sick and tired of Porter trying to hurt us every time he came around.

As I thought about what I should do next, we continued to play cards, and when Porter lost, Curt said, "Well, you win some, you lose some, Porter. We'll be right back with your spoonful. Come on, Genny." We went to the kitchen, and Curt said eagerly, "We have to make this really awful." I agreed, so we mixed up the worst one ever and had a great time doing it. We put in ketchup with a lot of hot sauce, peanut butter, and a raw egg. "Wait—the best thing of all . . . ," Curt said and took a spoon of Fella's wet dog food out of his dish. I gasped, but then I started laughing until I had tears streaming down my face, and the laughing tears turned to crying tears for just a minute.

I covered my face, remembering what Porter had done and how he put his hands on me. I was thinking about Joe and his family and Daddy and how he might lose his job. Curt had no idea what I was feeling inside, but he tried to help.

"Genny, Porter's weird," he said. "Everyone knows it. You're okay now. Come on. Let's give him what he deserves." I nodded, surprised by this new friendship. Curt finished mixing it up, disguising Fella's food, and we presented Porter with his punishment.

"I'm not going to eat this," Porter said, shaking his head.

"You have to—you lost. If you don't, you're a cheater," Curt argued.

"Yeah, Porter. You can't be a sore loser. That's how the game works," James said. Ryan jumped up from the floor and came over to the table to watch.

"Yeah!" Ryan chimed in.

Finally, Porter gave in. He held his nose and put the spoon in his mouth. Curt and I watched with great satisfaction as he gagged once and swallowed it down. Porter washed it down quickly with his Coke, and while we were all laughing at him, he started turning beet red and grabbing his throat. His nose started running, and he was having trouble breathing. James ran for help.

"What happened? Oh my God. Porter . . . Porter!" Connie yelled out. Porter was having trouble talking. "Are you choking?"

"Genny—what happened?" Mama asked.

"I don't know. He just started grabbing his throat and turning red. We made a spoonful for him 'cause he lost. He had a Coke, then he started doing this . . ." We were all scared, and Daddy called for an ambulance. Porter's daddy laid him on the floor.

"What was in the spoonful, Genny?" Lloyd asked. I didn't want to tell him about the dog food. Dog food was not supposed to be for people. This was awful. We had poisoned him. I looked at Curt, my eyes pleading for his help.

"Well, it was ketchup and uh, an egg, and some, well, a little of Fella's food, and . . . ," Curt started. Mama looked at me like we were crazy. "And peanut butter," he finished.

"Oh my God, Louisa!" Connie looked up at Mama. "Porter is allergic to peanuts—tell the ambulance to hurry, Jim!" Connie yelled out.

The ambulance came and gave Porter a shot and took him to the emergency room. Later, Mama and Daddy finally came back home and told us he was fine now, and that we weren't to feel too bad about it because none of us knew about the allergy. They never even mentioned anything about us putting Fella's food in the spoonful.

"Well, it's real bad that it happened. But at least he didn't die," Curt said outside as they were leaving. I did hate Porter, but I didn't want to kill him—just get back at him for all the mean stuff he always did.

"And it wasn't the dog food that did it," I said. We both started to laugh and stopped ourselves. As he and Rachel walked across the yard, Curt turned around and gave me another smile and waved, and I knew three things: Curt would not tell anyone about the terrible thing that Porter did to me; we would not be playing Spoons for a long time; and Porter would never have friends as good as mine. As I shut the back door, I wondered what everyone at Bailey's Place was thinking about the Donovan family having a police car and an ambulance coming out in one night.

And then the phone rang—piercing the silence that had finally settled around us after a long night. Somehow we weren't surprised when the caller hung up.

I couldn't sleep at all that night. I heard Mama wake up, and I knew she was having a bad dream. I could hear Daddy's voice calming her from the bedroom. After a while, I got up and walked by their room. The door was half opened. It was quiet now, and I saw I wasn't the only one up after all. I could see Mama's dark silhouette as she knelt on the floor with her back to me, at the end of the bed. Her head was down, and she was praying. I knew she was praying for Daddy and for us and for the Saylor family. As I backed away quietly, my eyes drifted up to the bed. Daddy was sleeping.

And then I realized it wasn't Mama who was praying at the end of the bed. She was lying next to Daddy, sleeping too, her arm draped over his side in what had started out as a hug.

Chapter Fourteen

January 3, 1967

THE FIRST TIME NANNIE VISITED ME in person, she said, *"It's a special occasion,"* as she sat at the foot of my bed. I felt the mattress sink down slightly, and I lifted the blanket over my head so that I couldn't see.

"Is it my birthday?" I asked sleepily in the dream, then said quickly, "No, it's not my birthday." I heard myself talking out loud, not in a dream at all.

"Silly. It's my birthday!" she said. *"Genevieve, look at me. Don't put your head under the covers! That's what your mama always does."* So I looked at her. She looked younger than the last time I'd seen her and very happy. Wasn't it just like Nannie to come for a visit on her own birthday? But where had she been at Christmas and before that in November for my birthday? I had been praying with her prayer card every day since Christmas, so I wasn't that surprised to finally see her in person, but I *was* surprised it had

taken so long. I'd heard her, felt her, dreamed of her, but this was something quite different, and it really was perfectly natural.

"Nannie, where have you been?" I asked her, blinking to make sure she didn't disappear. I had so much to tell her, so much to ask. I wanted to know if she'd seen the aliens and if Rooster was there with her. I wanted to ask her about Joe and his family and if they would be okay.

"I've been so busy, but I didn't forget you. I tried to talk to your mama, but she'd have none of it. I can't get through at all to your Aunt Marjorie or Aunt Viv, but I can with your mama. She's just too stubborn to pay attention. I need to tell her something, and I'm going to need your help."

"I wasn't sure if I was sleepwalking, but I saw you kneeling next to Mama's bed," I said.

"Yes," she answered and smiled.

"I miss you, Nannie." I meant those words more than anything I'd ever said or felt in my life. The room was oddly peaceful and still, but I felt electric and alive, a part of me newly discovered after being in hiding for so long. I thought that if someone saw me now, I would stand out like a bright lightbulb in a dark place.

"I know you do, Genevieve, but I've been with you the whole time."

I nodded and breathed a sigh of relief. She was here, and it seemed like just yesterday when we sat on the porch having our warm saltine milk. I held up the back of my hand to show her I was wearing the ring. "Look."

Nannie smiled again. *"Perfect. I knew it would be. I needed to hurry and get that to you. Now you understand why."* She tilted her head, studying me. *"Genevieve, this is the beginning now for you. Things will start happening that might seem confusing, and you'll have to pay close attention from here on out. And if something scares you, I want you to push through it. Remember the time you cut your foot on an oyster shell when you were boggin'?"*

"Yes. There was a lot of blood everywhere. You told me I didn't need stitches, and you bandaged it real tight to make the skin grow back together. You kept tellin' me to push through it," I answered.

"That's right. If you try, you can push through anything and get to the other side of where you are," she said.

"Okay, Nannie," I said quickly, smoothing down the hairs on my arms. I wasn't quite sure what she meant, but I was okay with whatever she told me.

"Now, Genevieve — I'll try and tell you things as best I can. You've always been able to know things, to hear and see things even without my help. I knew that from the minute you were born. Your mama's the same way, but she doesn't want to admit it. I wish your mama could help you now with some things, but you're going to have to be the one to help her for a while. She doesn't understand that she can't fight or hide the gift we have. It's part of who we are." She paused for a second. *"No matter what, I will never leave you, okay?"* I couldn't believe how lucky I was to have this time with her now and that she was going to stay with me and help me. The love I felt coming from Nannie was filling me up. I sat up straight and squinted hard in the dark room. She was gone again.

"Nannie? Nannie?" I got out of the bed and walked around my room. "Come back," I pleaded softly. "Please stay." For a minute, I felt panicky but then remembered she was always here.

The early winter morning hours—and minutes—crept by until it was finally time to get up. Hugging the covers around my shoulders, I leaned over from my bed and lifted the curtain. Frost like white lace draped across the top of the lawn. The day's colors hadn't started yet—everything was still black and white, except for the golden glow in the Robertsons' house as they all took turns in their one bathroom. Normally, I leaped out of bed on school mornings. But this morning I crawled back under the blankets, holding onto my dream. Only it wasn't a dream.

It was the first day back to school since Christmas vacation, and usually on school mornings, Daddy poked his head in and said, "Morning, Glory!" his special greeting meant just for me. I waited, but he didn't come. I could hear the other rituals starting back up, though—floors creaking, toilet flushing, Thomas's demanding baby voice from his crib, Fella's tail thumping happily against my door—all reminders of a new day. But this wasn't just any day.

"You know what today is, Mama?" I asked as I sat down at the kitchen table. James and Ryan were eating their usual cereal, and Thomas was in the high chair playing with a plastic cup. He threw it on the floor.

"First day back to school!" Ryan offered, drinking the milk from his bowl. Mama handed me a glass of juice, set Ryan's bowl down on the table, and gave Thomas his cup back.

"No, not that," I said to Ryan, waiting for Mama to answer my question as she rushed around the kitchen.

"Where's Daddy?" James asked. The boys had fresh crew cuts and wore new clothes they'd gotten for Christmas.

"Daddy left for work early—something came up at the plant, and he has a meeting with Mr. Landry. Now finish up, James," she answered. I stared at her, still waiting.

"Mama, do you know what day it is?" I asked impatiently.

She turned around and looked at me, finally answering. "Yes, I do, honey. How did you remember?"

"She told me," I said bluntly.

Mama smiled. "Yes, well, she sure never let us forget her birthday, did she?"

"No. I mean she really told me." As I spoke, Ruby came in the back door, carrying an armful of ironing she'd taken home with her. I wanted to talk to Mama more, but now wasn't the time with the boys talking over each other and Ruby noisily carrying laundry in and Thomas throwing his cup again on the floor.

"Mornin', Miss Louisa. Still can't get that stain outta Mr. Jim's new shirt. Daduh says to try a vinegar soakin', so we'll give that a try today. How is the Sweetman this mornin'?" Ruby went over to Thomas, who squealed with delight to see her. Mama and Ruby continued talking, and the boys jumped up from the table and ran out the door, so they could play outside for a little while before the bus came.

"Mama, can you help me tie my hair back?" I interrupted. Maybe if I could get her alone for a minute, I could tell her.

"Sure. Ruby, can you get Thomas another cup?" Mama and I went back to my room, and she tied a strand of green yarn in my hair. "There. How's that?"

I decided to say what I needed to say quickly before I changed my mind. I'd tried so many times before. "Do you ever feel like Nannie is around, Mama? I have lots of dreams that I don't think are really dreams." Father Cuddihy had advised me once to stay away from this subject, but I thought now that Nannie was around more, I really needed to tell her.

She looked uncomfortable. "Yes, I can feel her. I guess when you love someone so much, they stay in your heart forever. That's what you're feeling, too."

"Well, no, not really," I corrected. That's what Father had said, too. "I mean she *is* in my heart, but I feel like it's more than that. It's like she's really here. There are lots of things I see and hear that I can't explain. I'm not imaginin' it, Mama." Everyone always said I had a good imagination, and I didn't want to hear that again. That, and they said I was sensitive. If I heard that one more time, I would scream.

"I didn't say you were, but when you're young, it's normal to have a vivid imagination. You're a very creative person, Genevieve, and you have a way of looking at the world that's very different from other people. Maybe you should write a story or a poem

174

about Nannie; that'll help you feel better. It's okay to be sad just for today, but you need to move on and think about other things most girls your age think about." She was talking faster than usual. "Your hair looks nice. You better hurry on out to the bus stop."

"Mama, I'm not sad at all." I wanted to help Mama at that moment, just like Nannie said I should. Then I told her in a loud whisper, "It's because Nannie *isn't gone.*"

Mama looked at my reflection in the mirror, and her face changed. "Genny, I need you to stop."

"But . . ." I could feel the tears welling up fast. Why was she acting this way?

"She's gone. That's it. I don't want to talk about this. Don't you understand how painful this is for me?"

"But this is something different. Something special."

"We are not special." She said each word slowly and sternly. She put her hands on my shoulders and turned me to face her so she could look me straight in the eye. "We are *not.* She's dead. She's gone. These dreams or these feelings won't change anything." I pulled away from her and pressed my hands to my ears. "Now go, so you don't miss your bus."

With that, Mama walked out and left me standing alone with my reflection, my hands still pressed tightly against my ears. I wanted to run from the room. I wanted to scream.

As I walked down to the Wishing Well alone, I pulled my coat around me and held my books close to my body. "Happy birthday, Nannie," I said, tucking my chin down underneath my collar. The January wind slashed across my face and made my eyes fill with water, which was good because I wanted to feel the pain, and I wanted to cry. I was disappointed in Mama, and I felt sorry for her at the same time. I felt confused and relieved. Relieved that Nannie was finally all the way back, but confused about what Nannie said—how things would start happening and to pay close attention and to help Mama—and how all this fit in my regular life. My regular life was one where I couldn't speak about this, not with Mama, for sure, and not even with Rachel.

At the bus stop, I could tell the Robertson twins were in an argument with the Butler girls again. It happened at least once a week. As we lined up to get on the bus, I noticed Mr. Oakley, the bus driver, had stepped off and was talking to Rachel's father. As I climbed up the steps, I heard Mr. Oakley say, "It's a mess at the Landry plant now, so we'll get more news as the day goes by." I paused to hear more, but Mr. Oakley was right behind me, ready to go.

"Genny, you okay?" Rachel asked, taking my arm, as I sat down next to her. I saw Mr. Oakley's worried eyes in the giant rearview mirror as he looked at me.

"I don't know yet," I said to her as I looked back at my house, while the bus groaned into gear and headed away from Bailey's Place. I remembered Daddy had to leave early this morning, which was unusual. Was that why Mama was so tense and rushing around? What was the mess at Landry's plant? I still hadn't said a word to Rachel about Joe living in a bus or about Joe's daddy being arrested. Today, Joe would be waiting for me at school, and I would finally get to see for myself how he was doing.

As the bus rattled along the dirt road and jumped up onto the smooth, paved one leading into town, I knew whatever mess was happening at the Landry plant had something to do with Joe's daddy. Just as we turned off of Bailey's Road, a black truck went speeding by us toward town—Jeffrey Landry's truck. I turned to watch it go by and then looked to Rachel, but she was reading her book. I looked up in the rearview mirror, but Mr. Oakley's eyes were staring straight ahead.

I waited outside our classroom with Rachel and some other friends and watched as kids poured into the hallway from their

Christmas vacation, looking only mildly enthused. I searched the faces in the crowd. I searched for Joe's face. When the bell rang, I was the last one to take my seat. I watched the door, waiting to see Joe and his crooked smile. As Mrs. Gardner closed the door and welcomed us back, I thought I saw, through the small glass pane at the top of the door, a glimpse of his coal-black hair. I stared at the door handle, but it didn't move.

Mrs. Gardner asked us to share the most interesting part of our Christmas vacation, and there was not one thing I cared about that I could say out loud. I went down the list in my head. I thought I had a boyfriend, but then I found out he lived in a bus. Then I acted badly and probably caused him to be hurt even more. There was trouble at Daddy's work, and he might lose his job again. His boss's son was making threatening phone calls to our family. My Nannie was visiting me regularly now but no one knew. Mama wasn't herself, and we weren't getting along at all.

I couldn't talk about any of this. Everyone around me at school went about their business, unaware of what I was thinking, and at recess, the boys still played baseball, even though their best player didn't show up.

Chapter Fifteen

January 3, 1967

"We're going to Gibson Island," Mama announced when we walked in the door after that first day back at school. "Just for a couple of days." Ruby was packing up some of Thomas's things.

"What about school, Mama?" Ryan asked.

"It's okay—I'll drive you each day. It'll be fun. Daddy has the rest of the week off, so he'll join us, too. It'll be just like the old days." But Daddy wasn't there. She moved around quickly, stuffing clothes in the overnight bags, and I knew something was very wrong.

"Mama, what happened at the plant today? We heard there was something going on there?" I asked.

She started to lie, I could tell, but she couldn't go through with it. She sat down on the velvet sofa, her voice shaking. Ruby came over to her with Thomas. "I'm sorry. I need to just tell you the truth." James touched her arm and sat on the other side of her, and he seemed like the strongest one in the room at that moment.

Ryan moved closer to me, bracing himself for what Mama was going to tell us. "Daddy is okay, so I don't want you to worry. But Mr. Landry was found shot in his office this morning. At this point, all we know is Mr. Landry has been taken to the hospital and is in critical condition. Your daddy is with the police. He wants us to go to Gibson Island and stay there and wait for him. He doesn't want us to have to deal with all this craziness."

"Mama, who shot Mr. Landry?" James asked.

"When will Daddy come?" Ryan asked.

"Why are we going to Gibson Island now?" I asked.

"That's a lot of questions for your mama right now. Let's get movin'. Most of your things are in a bag on your bed. Last chance to add a few more of your own, and grab a couple of games and toys while you're at it," Ruby said, standing up.

"Ruby's right—we do need to hurry. Aunt Alicia is on her way over to pick us up. We don't know who shot Mr. Landry. Your daddy found him this morning when he went in early to meet with him. I've only been able to talk to Daddy once today. I wish I could tell you more. In the meantime, Daddy feels like Gibson Island is the best place for us to be until everything's settled. So, go get your things now."

I heard the telephone ring, and I grabbed my overnight bag and came back into the living room just in time to hear Ruby tell Mama, "That was Jackson, Ms. Louisa. Seems Roy Saylor didn't show up for court this mornin'. Jackson went over to pick him up at the motel, but the station wagon and the family were gone."

"What? And Jim said the police are out looking for Jeffrey Landry. Now, they're both gone? What's goin' on here, Ruby?" Mama asked, not waiting for Ruby to answer. "There's Aunt Alicia pulling up. We'll talk later on as soon as things calm down."

On the way over to the island, I wondered what was really going on. There were so many questions here that needed answers. Where was Roy Saylor? Where was Joe and why wasn't he at school today? Where was Jeffrey Landry? What did Daddy see when he got to Mr. Landry's office? Would Mr. Landry die?

Even though our minds were on bigger things, Aunt Alicia seemed to be celebrating that we were coming over to stay. When we arrived, all the dogs came running as if they knew this was more than one of our Sunday morning visits. I was glad Ruby was going to be helping out around Gibson Island now because it really needed some attention. Aunt Alicia didn't seem to notice how dirty it had gotten. Once we settled in the red breakfast room with iced tea and cookies, all she could talk about was us staying with her again and how she wouldn't be alone anymore.

"Now, Aunt Alicia, you know we're here for just for a couple of days till all this gets settled at the plant," Mama said, looking at her with a slight frown. She reached over and patted her hand. "We really appreciate this."

"Okay, that's fine. I just thought for a minute . . ." Her voice trailed off.

When Dodie and Markie curled up next to Thomas, who was falling asleep on the floor, Mama said, "Looks like I need to put the little man down for a nap. I'll be right back."

Aunt Alicia told the boys she had a surprise for them and took them into her office. I could hear them exclaiming over an old coin collection she'd never shown them before, and she was laying it all out on the table. I watched from the dining room screen door as they stood over it with magnifying glasses and small polishing cloths, and as happy as I was for them—especially today—I couldn't imagine anything more boring. I heard the familiar, heavy tocking of the hallway clock.

Nannie always said, "That old, broken clock doesn't tick—it tocks. Doesn't chime anymore, doesn't keep the right time, either, never has, but it keeps on tocking away, pushing through to try and get it right." As I passed by it now, one of its hands was drooping downward, looking more like five than three.

I picked up the boys' and my bags and went upstairs. Naturally, I headed for Nannie's room to settle in, but when I got to the screen door, I saw Mama lying next to Thomas on Nannie's yellow bedspread. He was tucked into her safe arms, and they lay with their noses almost touching, fast asleep. I didn't expect to find her in Nannie's room. As far as I knew, she'd avoided coming in this room, especially after I showed her the Bible verse on the mirror. "Well, it's about time," I thought. "Maybe if she rests here, it will help her."

And so I headed down to the wharf—another place that Mama avoided. She had not stepped one foot on this wharf since that day. Everyone else had gone back to how it was supposed to be—sitting on the wharf, fishing off the wharf, leaning over its railings, walking in the pluff mud as the fiddler crabs danced around, normal things you do when you live on the river. But Mama would not step onto the wharf. The funny thing was—I don't think she even noticed that I would not go on the wharf, either.

Standing on the edge of the first wooden step, I stared down at my feet—willing them to move forward. The wide cracks between the wooden boards let me see the signs of the tide coming in beneath me—river water turning the mud from parched gray to slick black as it crept in, filling up the little, bubbling crab holes and pushing the loose oyster shells forward to the dry banks, away from the baby oysters who needed them for shelter. "Right on time," Nannie would say, checking her tide chart and her watch. With one hand on the railing, I thought about going out onto the wharf. I wanted to. I would start slowly, one board at a time, then move with confidence down its long aisle, leaning here and there, taking the shaky steps at the end down to the small floating section of the wharf. Then, I would dangle my legs over the side, splashing, and not think about anything except how the river is beautiful and fun. Not think about anything else.

But I couldn't—not just yet. I turned away and headed down the path, picking up the stray oyster shells along the way and tossing them back into the river. "Back where you belong," I said to them. I wondered when Daddy would come home and how things were going to end up. The temperature was dropping. The clouds were turning the dimpled water gray, and except for one small white wave rising briefly along the marsh line, the river was eerily still.

I thought, then, about what Ruby said about Jackson going to pick up Joe's daddy and about him being an ex-convict. I hated to have any of these thoughts, but what if Joe's daddy had been the one who shot Mr. Landry and he was running away? I didn't know why he'd been in prison before, but it must have been pretty serious. By now, the police would know who did the shooting, so why didn't Daddy tell Mama who it was, and why wasn't he back yet?

I ducked as a branch cracked loudly above my head and watched it fall in slow motion into a pile of dead leaves. Twisting the ring on my finger, I felt an overwhelming sense that something was terribly wrong. The old, boarded-up oyster factory lay ahead, and the marsh rustled around it as the wind started to pick up. Then the sounds grew louder, but it wasn't the marsh. I heard the sounds of more branches cracking and dead leaves crunching, and they were coming up fast behind me. Someone was running up the path. I flattened myself against the side of the half-naked oak tree that had lost most of its bark, and she grabbed my arm.

"Genny!" She pulled me into her, and like I had wanted her to do for so long, she held me in her arms till I could barely breathe. "Are you all right?" she asked.

"Mama! Yes. Yes. What is it?" I pulled back so I could see her face. She looked different, scared, her eyes wildly searching mine, her hair falling across her face while she took in big gulps of air. She had run from the house, down the path, looking for me. I'd just seen her asleep next to Thomas, so what had happened?

And then she stared past me, and I followed her gaze to the oyster factory. A shiny black truck appeared behind the factory building, coming to such a violent stop that the dirt around it blew up like a bomb, hiding the truck from view for just a second.

"Not again," Mama said, placing her hand over her mouth.

"It's his truck," I said, referring to Jeffrey Landry.

"Yes, it's the same truck," she said.

"The same truck?" I repeated.

She looked at me, and her brown eyes filled up. "I dreamed it, Genny. I dreamed all of this." She spread out her arms.

"Oh, Mama!" Her fear was new to me. "What did you dream?"

Mama whispered to me. "Just now, I had the same dream I've been having for the last couple of weeks. Let's get out of here." She grasped my hand urgently, pulling me away from the oak tree, and I pulled back.

"Please tell me! What did you dream?" I pleaded with her.

She spoke low and held my face in her hands. "I dreamed I was running down a long path looking for you and calling your name. I thought I heard you up ahead, but it was a branch falling from the sky, landing in a pile of leaves. You were gone. And then I saw the factory surrounded by oyster beds. The black truck—just like that one—came rushing up and parked on top of the oyster bed, crushing them, sinking into them. And you were in the truck—sinking with it, and your hands were pressed against the window. I couldn't get to you."

"That's Jeffrey Landry's truck, Mama," I said. At that moment, just as Mama described, the black truck at the oyster factory suddenly lurched and sped forward to the edge of the large oyster bed in front of us. "Hey!" his voice echoed angrily across the marsh. The man in the black truck climbed out and started running right at us, then stumbled and fell.

"Oh my God. Why is he coming at us like that? Run, Genny!" As we turned away, we saw him reach back into his truck and pull out a gun. The tide was low enough for him to cross the small strip of marshland that led to Gibson Island. The rain started with fat drops, slapping the path, and we ran fast, slipping on wet leaves and drawing our arms and shoulders in from the spear-like branches that swiped at us. I fell hard, twisting my ankle as I landed, and Mama lifted me up, but I could barely put weight on my leg. "Push through it, Genevieve! You can do it!" *Push through it, Genevieve!* We were almost to the wharf, almost to the house.

"You're gonna pay. You trash are gonna pay!" he screamed out.

We knew we couldn't make it up the steps of the house and across the porch without being seen, but we could make it to the smokehouse. We crashed into the door, slamming it against the wall and knocking a loose board out of its center. We landed on top of each other, and Mama scrambled up to throw the latch. We crawled along the dirt floor and hid up against the bait freezer, huddling under a hole in the tin roof where one single raindrop at a time landed on my head. We could feel each other's hearts thumping as we clung together.

"You have no place to hide! You're going to get what's coming to you, just like the old lady did! Lucky for me that bitch couldn't swim!" He screamed and howled outside the smokehouse, louder than the rain that pounded against the fragile metal and wood of our only shelter.

"Oh my God," Mama whispered.

"What are we going to do? I'm scared, Mama."

"Shh . . . *You're okay. You're okay.*" I could feel the warm breath of her words mixing with Nannie's words in my ear.

We both saw it at the same time. The grimy lightbulb next to the door flickered twice just as the muzzle of a gun pushed its way through the hole in the door and pointed straight at Mama. It went off.

I held on, and Mama held on. The soft, warm blanket feeling wrapped around both of us. And when we opened our eyes, we were both still there in each other's arms. Outside the door, we heard voices. Headlights bounced through the cracks in the wall. Mama got up shakily and called out, "Jim?" And when she heard his voice, she unlatched the door, carefully, calling his name over and over. "Jim? We're here!"

Mama opened the door, and Jeffrey Landry lay at her feet in a pool of bloody rainwater. Confused, we looked up and saw Aunt Alicia standing there in her flannel shirt and baggy green pants, holding a shotgun with her three-fingered hand resting on its trigger.

As Daddy moved toward her to take the gun away, she yelled, "Louisa! Drag his ass over the threshold!"

Chapter Sixteen

January 3, 1967

THE POLICE ARRIVED RIGHT AFTER DADDY took the shotgun from Aunt Alicia. While the police and medics were swarming around, Ruby came over and took the boys and me upstairs. She wrapped my swollen ankle and told me to stay put with my foot propped up, but there was no way I was going to stay there after what had just happened. As soon as Ruby's attention shifted to the boys, I limped down the stairs, and the second my hand gripped the dark wood banister for support, I heard Nannie's voice.

"Be strong, Genevieve. It's not over yet. Go to her." I felt dizzy and paused, the tocking of the broken clock on the wall in front of me growing louder and louder.

Mama stood on the top step of the front porch, framed by the spidery silhouettes of the Spanish moss hanging unusually low from the weight of the rain. I came up behind her, and she jumped when I touched her. She cupped her hand across the back of my head, my hair still damp and curly from the storm's assault. "I thought you'd gone upstairs," Mama said. We watched the smokehouse disappear into darkness as the last remaining police car turned off its headlights. Officer Flynn walked with Daddy up the steps, exhaling loudly and taking his notepad out from the inside of his jacket.

Daddy swept me into his arms like I was a little girl. His voice shook with fear and relief. "Oh, my Angel Baby."

Officer Flynn, Aunt Alicia, Daddy, Mama, and I sat together in the parlor, going over the details of everything that had happened that day. Aunt Alicia didn't kill Jeffrey Landry, but she wished she had. Daddy told her to keep that to herself because we really wanted to get all this over with as soon as possible. She'd shot him in the shoulder before he'd had a chance to pull the trigger, and Officer Flynn said he'd be in the hospital for a while and in prison soon after that.

As Aunt Alicia and Mama brought coffee in for everyone, Officer Flynn explained Mr. Landry was in serious condition but had finally gained consciousness this afternoon and was able to describe how his son had shot him.

"Jeffrey was waiting at the plant for his father early this morning—before Mr. Donovan got there—and he'd been drinking heavily," Officer Flynn said. "He didn't realize we already knew the truth and that Mr. Donovan and Mr. Landry were getting ready to confront him. So, Jeffrey described to his father how he'd discovered this elaborate scheme of Mr. Donovan's to steal from the company that involved Jackson and an ex-con—Roy Saylor."

"But that's so ridiculous," Mama interrupted. "There's no basis for any of it."

"That's right, Louisa, but I'm not sure, until today, I understood just how desperate Jeffrey had gotten," Daddy said. Mama nodded and pulled a stool over for me to prop my foot. Daddy continued, "Mr. Landry said he'd heard enough, so before I could even get there, he told Jeffrey he was a loser and a thief and that he was going to put him in jail." Daddy paused and looked down. "He told him he was disowning him as a son, and that's when Jeffrey shot him."

"What took so long to find him, and why did he come here?" Aunt Alicia asked.

"At first we didn't know for sure who'd done it. Jackson had called saying Roy Saylor was nowhere to be found, and he never showed up at his court hearing. Then, we heard Jeffrey was spotted tearing around town in his truck," Officer Flynn answered.

"I figured I was next on his list," Daddy said. "That's why I sent you all to Gibson Island." Daddy pursed his lips and took both of Mama's hands in his. "I sent you here so you'd be safe."

"He killed my mother," Mama said flatly, looking right at me. We both knew it was true.

Her words drifted heavily around the room like the buoys I'd seen on the Ashley River. Mama described what Jeffrey had yelled while we were in the smokehouse, and Officer Flynn gently explained to Mama we had to be careful not to jump to conclusions. He said everyone in town, including Jeffrey Landry, had probably heard about her mother's accident. Just because Jeffrey was trying to scare us didn't necessarily mean he was responsible for Nannie's death.

"Officer Flynn, I know it sounds bizarre," Daddy said, "but there's something to this. Louisa's mother was very much against Jeffrey's oyster factory plan and was very vocal about it. If it wasn't for her, the *News and Courier* wouldn't have started covering it. They ran stories about that place for almost a year. In fact, two nights before Fannie died off this very wharf, she led a town hall meeting and got a huge petition signed against the plan. Jeffrey confronted her in the parking lot afterward—I saw him."

"Did he threaten her?" Flynn asked.

Aunt Alicia stepped in. "Not in so many words, but he could be intimidating. He tried to trick me into signing papers to sell the property. Isn't that right, Jim?" Daddy nodded at her.

Mama leaned toward Officer Flynn. "I want you to write it down in your notepad." She waited for him to pick it up off the table. "I don't know how Jeffrey did it, but I heard what he said to us today—he said he was lucky she couldn't swim. My mother disappeared off this wharf, a stone's throw from that oyster factory, and he either caused it or he did nothing to help her. But either way, he killed her." Mama pulled me closer to her. I could feel her body starting to shake. Nannie was right. I needed to be strong for her.

"Mrs. Donovan, this has to be very hard on you, and I'm not discounting anything here, so I promise you we'll be looking into this. Mr. Donovan, I think it's best to call it a night, though. It's been a long, emotional day, and we all need to have clear heads tomorrow." Officer Flynn shook Daddy's hand and gave us his direct phone number in case we needed him. He knelt down in front of me and asked if I was okay, and I nodded, my head resting against Mama's shoulder.

After Officer Flynn left, Mama made Daddy check all the doors and windows twice, and he said, trying to make a joke, "Who's going to bother us now? I bet the word about Aunt Alicia has spread like wildfire—I think we're more than safe." Aunt Alicia chuckled and went to her bedroom.

"Genny, it's so late. Go on up to bed, and I'll be there in a minute to tuck you in," Mama said. I climbed up slowly, nursing my ankle, and stopped on the circular landing at the top. My parents spoke in hushed tones.

"Louisa, come here." I imagined my father standing at the foot of the stairs and taking her into his arms. I heard her crying softly.

189

"Jim, do you believe me about Mama? I know he killed her."

"Of course, I believe you," he answered. "I was there before it happened."

"What do you mean?" she asked. I heard the rustling of their clothes as she pulled out of his arms.

"I was there with you the night you dreamed it. It was him standing behind you on the bank of the river, refusing to help her, and watching her drown." Daddy said this with kindness and absolute certainty. I would probably never find anyone who could express love better than my father did for my mother that night.

"Yes," she said. "Yes. You were there, too. Thank God you were there, too."

I held my breath, remembering my mother's last dream before Nannie went missing. As I turned to go into Nannie's room, I heard the clock downstairs chime and my father say, "Well, look at that. It's finally telling the right time after all these years. When did Alicia get this old thing fixed?"

Right before the sun came up, Mama laid down next to me in Nannie's room. She was the first to fall asleep, and as she did, she murmured something I couldn't understand. I opened my eyes to see Nannie standing over her daughter, lightly stroking her hair the way mothers do.

We stayed out at Gibson Island for a couple more days, and when we got back to Bailey's Place, I got up early Saturday morning before anyone else. It was cold out, so I wrapped a blanket around me and went to Dora. I sat underneath her and immediately felt her calmness. She'd missed me, and I leaned my head back against her and settled into the warm pocket in the ground at the base of her trunk. The whirring sound in my ears started, and I could tell Nannie was here now.

"Nannie, I've been waiting for you. I want to know what happened to you. How did Mama know to come find me?"

"She's starting to pay attention, and you're helping her — just like I knew you would," Nannie said proudly.

"Did Jeffrey Landry hurt you, Nannie?" I hated to hear the words come out of my mouth.

"I'm fine, Genevieve. That's what's important for you to know now. You don't need to worry about anything. I'll help your mama understand about this, and I'll bet you'll be able to help, too, but be patient. I'll let you know when it's time."

"But when will it be time? I don't understand how we can be so different — Mama and me." I could tell the stubbornness in me was bubbling up to the surface. "I know she talks to Daddy about her dreams, but she won't talk to me. She doesn't believe anything I say half the time. I try to tell her about you and me, Nannie, but she doesn't want to hear it." I brought the blanket up around my nose and sunk further into Dora's pocket.

"Your mama used to not talk about them at all. She's afraid of her dreams — it's not easy for her. I know it seems like she doesn't believe you, but things aren't always what they seem, remember?" Her voice faded like it always did right before she left, and I felt the hairs on my arms stand up. Nannie was not very predictable when it came to communicating. I would hear her in my sleep or early in the morning when I first woke up; sometimes I would see her, but not for very long; and sometimes, like today, her voice would fill my head like she was sitting right next to me. She always seemed to have a special message, but I didn't always understand what the message was. I tried not to be discouraged about Mama. I knew she loved me, but I couldn't help feeling like she wanted to keep me at a distance.

"Genny!" Daddy called from the porch. "What are you doing out there with a blanket?" he asked. "Come on in and get dressed.

Want to go to Champ's with me later?" I did want to go. Daddy was anxious to catch Champ up on everything that had happened over the last few days.

"Hey!" Rachel called out from her window. "Can I come?"

As Rachel and I climbed into the backseat of Daddy's car, she said, "I saw you were back from Gibson Island. I was worried when you didn't come back to school this week. Then, I found out what happened. I couldn't believe it!" Rachel reached over and hugged me. We talked nonstop all the way to Champ's, and when we got there, we got Cokes and sat on the back steps while Daddy and Champ sat inside. It was cold and damp, and we pulled our coats tightly around us as we sat shoulder to shoulder, still talking about everything that had happened. She'd heard about Joe's daddy being wrongly accused, and I didn't mind talking about that part much, but I just couldn't bring myself to tell her about Joe living in the school bus. When the big yellow cat came up and wrapped his tail around Rachel's legs, she reached out to pat him, but he darted off, and she started following him down the little dirt road.

"Rachel—wait! Where are you going? Don't go down there! We'll be leaving in a minute!" I called after her. What was she doing? I had to stop her.

"Maybe he needs a home!" she called back to me. I followed her, trying to get her to come back.

"You already have too many cats at your house, Rachel. Come on back!" I yelled. "Look at this, Genny!" Rachel said, her eyes widely taking it all in—the firepit, the clothesline, the dried-up Christmas tree off to the side, and the bus with the curtains still in the windows.

"Yeah. Look at it," I said quietly. "I don't think we should be back here, Rachel." She ignored me, shaking her head in disbelief.

"It looks like someone lives here. This is creepy," she said, picking up a small pink sand bucket and dropping it back on the ground.

"We should go, just in case," I said. "Let's get outta here."

"Genny, it looks like whoever lived here is gone. Come on! Let's go look inside," she said, climbing up onto the tomato crates and tugging on the bus door. I was horrified. This was a private place, and she had no right to be here. Just as I ran up behind her, the bus door opened, and she looked back at me. "Well, it's open. Let's check it out."

Part of me felt like grabbing Rachel and dragging her back to Champ's, but the other part of me leaned into the open bus door. Rachel went in first, stopping at the card table and chairs and picking up the jelly jar glasses.

"Wow. Someone really did live here," she said, walking over to one of the bus windows and touching the thin yellow curtains.

I stepped in guiltily, feeling like I was betraying Joe by letting Rachel come into what used to be his home. I wondered where they'd ended up, the Saylor family. No one seemed to know. They just disappeared. I walked around inside the bus, imagining what it was like to live there. Something was different now. After Christmas, when I came back here, the bus door had been locked. Now it had opened easily. I looked across the floor. The Carnation box was there as I remembered, but the baseball card was gone.

Before, when I peered through the back window, there'd been some blankets and a pile of boxes in the corner. Now there was just one box — like a shoebox — leaning against the wall. More importantly, I remembered seeing Joe's baseball bat through that bus window. Where was it now?

"What is it, Genny? What are you looking for?" Rachel asked, frowning.

"Nothing. Let's get out of here. It's freezing," I said, and Rachel climbed down from the bus. I looked around once more. The bat was gone. The baseball card was gone. Someone had taken it. I walked over to the box and saw that it was partially wrapped in

Christmas paper. I took the lid off, and I knew. I knew Joe had come back since I'd been there last. I reached inside the box and pulled out a small red notebook that said "My Journal" on the outside.

"Genny! Come on!" Rachel called from outside.

It had a string tied around it, and my fingers shook as I untied it and opened it. Inside the cover, in neatly printed handwriting as nice as a typewriter, it said, "For your truthful stories." The journal was filled with fresh, clean white pages, waiting for someone to write on them. Waiting for me to write on them.

Chapter Seventeen

June 3, 1967

THE DAY WE FOUND OUT THAT Jeffrey Landry got sentenced to prison, we went over to Gibson Island, and Mama planted a live oak tree not far from the path that led to the oyster factor. Daduh made us chicken salad sandwiches, and we ate outside on the porch with Aunt Alicia while Ruby took care of some Saturday cleaning upstairs.

"I think it's real nice how you're goin' to plant a tree for your mama," Daduh said as she poured our iced tea.

"I think she would like it, Daduh," Mama said. "That part of Gibson Island is so bare compared to the rest, and last week when I took a walk, I noticed the riverbank has started to erode. I think this tree, along with some other plants, will help."

"What will the tree do, Mama?" Ryan asked, taking cookies from the plate Daduh handed us.

"It'll help protect Gibson Island's river life and environment," she said, sounding just like the way Nannie talked at the town hall meeting. "This new tree will provide shade and help keep the river from getting too hot, which the fish will like. And it will grow deep roots in the ground, which help keep the soil from washing or blowing away, and the branches will give birds a nice place to live," she explained as Ryan listened closely.

"Like cardinals?" I asked, picking up the little cardinal salt and pepper shakers on the table.

"Yes, like cardinals." Mama smiled at me. "And lots of others, too. Here's a picture they gave me when I went out to the tree farm in Ravenel. This is what it will look like when it's all grown. There are some others like this on Gibson Island that have been here a long time, but there's a real old one that's dying down the path at the end of the island, so we'll put this baby one nearby."

"That's goin' to be one beautiful tree!" Daduh said, holding the picture up.

"Boys, you get the shovels out of the shed, and meet us outside," Daddy directed. They pushed the wheelbarrows behind us as we headed up the path that led to the oyster factory. We came up on the oak tree that was losing all its bark—the one where I was standing when Mama came running down the path looking for me on that terrible day.

"Now, this is the tree that's dying, so we're going to plant ours behind it—back over here," she said, and we started clearing out the area.

"And it'll grow to be real big and wide and reach out over the oyster beds, and it will fill up with Spanish moss and block out that eyesore over there," Daddy added, pointing to the factory across the marsh. We all nodded eagerly in agreement and got to work with our shovels.

As I watched Mama shoveling and arranging pine straw around the tree, she reminded me of Nannie when she would arrange her fishing and crabbing gear on the wharf. They both moved the same way and had the same kind of determined look on their faces when they worked on something they loved.

And then I heard this soft whooshing noise in my ears, and my head was filled with Nannie's voice. *"This is better,"* was all she said.

"Yes, this is better," Mama said, resting her shovel against the dead tree and looking at the new one, freshly planted in the ground. Had she heard Nannie, too? I started to ask her but then stopped myself. "Don't you think so, Genny?" she asked.

"Yes, and Nannie would really like it, Mama," I answered.

Jeffrey Landry had gotten five years in prison for assaulting his father and trying to assault us (even though we called it attempted murder) and for stealing money from the company. His father had started to regret pressing charges and fought to lessen Jeffrey's sentence, which made Daddy mad, but he said it was because Mr. Landry was feeling guilty about certain things. At least he was in prison. Mama couldn't bring charges against Jeffrey based on what he told us about Nannie, and he denied ever saying it, but we knew he was responsible, and we were just going to have to be patient until we could prove it one day.

Daddy didn't get in any trouble at his job for hiring Roy Saylor, but he had to get another watchman since Mr. Saylor never came back. Daddy said it was too bad because that just put Mr. Saylor in more trouble with the law by not showing up at court like that, but there wasn't much more Daddy could do to help. Jackson and Champ tried hard to find the Saylor family, but they were pretty sure they'd left the state. I didn't know what to think. All I knew was I missed Joe.

Rachel thought it was so strange that Joe never returned to school, but I never really wanted to talk about it with her anymore. Fifth grade was over, and I had a busy summer planned to keep my mind off of it. I got a job helping Mrs. Pratt in the bookmobile, so about once a week, I got to go with her on her route and help people check out books. The best part was when I got to go see Marylou at her house. I would set aside the newest books about astronomy and geography for her, and she would get pretty excited when we wheeled her into the bookmobile.

One stop we always made was at the St. Anne's church parking lot. Like clockwork, we'd pull in at ten a.m., set up a table outside with some sample books, and before long, folks in the area would walk or drive over and get a book or two. As we were getting ready to leave one day, I noticed Lumpy walking around in the parking lot, putting rocks and little flowers in her pockets. It was not surprising to see her out on one of her walks, but she lingered near the bookmobile like she wanted to come over.

"Hi, Lumpy!" I said and waved. She smiled and waved, picked some stuff up off the ground, and looked back up at me. "Do you want to see a book?" I held one up from the table, and she came on over. She wasn't much for talking or reading, but she seemed to really like the books with all the pictures.

"Make sure she doesn't put any in those big pockets of hers," Mrs. Pratt whispered to me.

I never thought Lumpy would do that, so I explained to Mrs. Pratt, "Oh — she doesn't put those kinda things in her pockets, Mrs. Pratt. She just likes stuff from along the roads and the river."

"Okay, well, let's pack everything up now," she said, and Lumpy wandered off again, leaving a book open on the table that was filled with photographs of beautiful flowers.

The best part of the summer was Ellie. Our dream came true because she got to spend almost a whole month with me. Aunt

Marjorie and Sam came, too, but Uncle Peter stayed up in New York, which everyone knew was for the best. Every day was filled with all the things we wanted to do. Ellie had gotten real good at dancing since I saw her last, so when Rachel and I would sing on the Stage, Ellie would dance, and we'd have real performances for the neighborhood. On Friday nights, we charged ten cents a person to come and watch us. Mostly, it was Mama and Daddy and Aunt Marjorie and the Robertson kids, but sometimes Cynthia Cook and her husband would bring their lawn chairs over for a few songs. Since the Nuthouse was right next to the Stage, Crazy Robby would come by and pretend he was working, but he'd end up sitting on the front step of the Nuthouse watching us, and I even saw him tapping his foot while we sang. We didn't mind him anymore.

Ellie and I finally finished another edition of our magazine, and this time we added real photographs we took from our Polaroid camera. We even put a true ghost story in it about Nicodemus and Goat Island. Ellie was the reporter and did an interview with James and Ryan and Sam, who swore they saw him during their latest porch camp-out.

"Look at this picture, Genny!" James told us excitedly, coming in from the porch late at night. We'd given him the camera to use during their camp-out, and sure enough, James had gotten a picture of blurry, white figure on the porch, and he was convinced it was Nicodemus. When he showed Daddy, he just scratched his head and said he didn't have a clue what it was, but it was most likely Nicodemus himself.

One of those summer nights, Ellie said we should have a séance. She said she did this with her friends in New York all the time, and she knew how to set it all up. Once it got dark and while the grown-ups were outside having their drinks on the back porch, James, Ellie, Rachel, and Curt and I met in my bedroom, sitting in a circle on the floor. Ellie had gotten some matches out of her mama's pocketbook, and she lit a candle and set it in the middle of our circle. We held hands just like Ellie told us to do. Curt was holding my hand, and I couldn't tell if it was my hand or his that was so sweaty, but I had a hard time concentrating because of it.

Ellie said in a low voice, "Now close your eyes and free your mind up of all other things. Take a deep breath. Just imagine now that you are going to talk with someone who has died recently. Who would you like to ask for?"

"How about Vivien Leigh? She just died a couple of weeks ago. I loved her in *Gone with the Wind!*" Rachel said.

"Or Buddy Holly. He died a long time ago, but I still love his music," Curt said.

I kind of laughed at them but stopped when Ellie gave me one of her serious looks. She said, "Okay, let's do Vivien Leigh." Then, Ellie asked for Vivien Leigh to come and give us a sign that she was here. We waited and waited for a long time, keeping very still and quiet. I thought about Nannie and almost laughed out loud, knowing she absolutely would not show up at a time like this, especially if everyone was wanting to hear from Vivien Leigh.

Ellie asked "Vivien Leigh, are you here? Are any spirits here with us?" I peeked at the candle flickering, dripping wax onto my floor, thinking that any minute Mama and Aunt Marjorie would bust in the room because they smelled smoke.

Then Rachel let out a gasp and said, "I felt someone touch my hair. I swear to you someone touched my hair." We all lifted our bowed heads slowly to look at her. She was frozen, still holding hands with Ellie and James, staring at me as if afraid to move or breathe. The flame of the candle danced wildly and reflected in her eyes. Rachel's blond hair was tucked as usual behind her ears, but the tousled, straight bangs that always hung down too long now moved slightly as if her own personal breeze lifted them up as it passed by. It was eerie to watch, but it didn't bother me.

"Did y'all see that? My hair was blowing!" Rachel said.

"Okay, that's enough for me," James said and pulled his hand away from her.

"Yeah, maybe you're right." Ellie pulled her hand away and blew out the candle. Rachel screamed out, but only because it was pitch black now in the room, so James jumped up to turn on the light. As soon as he did, I realized that Curt and I were still holding hands, and when I pulled away gently, he kept his hand on the floor, still slightly open, where mine had been.

Later that night, after the grown-ups went inside and Sam and Ryan and Thomas were asleep, we all sat on the porch and drank Cokes and talked about what had happened.

"Maybe there was a window open somewhere," Rachel was still trying to explain. She was always the practical one in the group, and even though it was her own hair that had been blowing, she was going to find a way to make sense of it.

"We closed all the windows, remember?" Ellie said. Her long legs hung over one arm of the lawn chair, while her back rested against the other. A lone lightning bug flashed over her head as if getting ready to make an announcement, then took off to join the rest of its kind, hundreds of them flickering and twinkling above the freshly mowed Carpet Grass.

"Please let's just change the subject," James said, leaning back sleepily on the front steps next to Rachel and looking up at the stars. Then, as if on cue and special ordered for just us, James yelled out, pointing, "Look! A falling star! Make a wish—quick!"

And there we were, James and Rachel, Ellie and Curt and me standing in our front yard, our mouths open and our heads tilted back to the summer sky as one star streaked across it, taking our wishes to a special place that we all believed in. I thought about this Wish Place, where different wishes, like falling-star wishes and birthday-cake wishes, would be stored for the people wishing them. They would be organized by importance and type, and they would be kept separate from prayers, which were much more personal. I wondered who was in charge of the wishes, what the rules were, how it was decided which wishes would come true for each person, and how long they would have to wait. And for some, it would be decided that the wish would not be granted at all.

"What did you wish for, Genny?" Curt asked me.

"The rules say you can't tell because then it won't come true," I said.

"I thought that was just the rule for when you blow out your birthday candles," Curt said, smiling.

"Nope. Same rule," I said and headed back for the porch. I wasn't about to tell him my wish no matter what the rule was.

I leaned against the stair rail watching James as he disappeared into the darkness, whistling for Fella to come home. Ellie and Rachel gathered up the Coke bottles behind me and took them inside. It was getting late, but I didn't want to go in yet. Curt followed me up the steps and stood next to me. He didn't say anything. He didn't look at me. He just took my hand. And I thought that whoever was in charge of wishes tonight had heard mine and decided I didn't have to wait another minute.

Toward the end of the summer, we all got involved in planning a giant picnic for Labor Day weekend at Gibson Island. This was going to make up for all the Big Sunday Dinner Days we had stopped having, and Daddy said this was going to be a celebration of the end of summer and the beginning of new memories. It was time Gibson Island returned to how it used to be — just like it was when Nannie was there.

Chapter Eighteen

September 2, 1967

"Poor ol' Gibson Island," Daduh said to no one in particular over a boiling pot of potatoes that morning. "Been in mournin' or in shock for too long now, so it sure is nice to see her comin' back to life!" Daduh was right. Besides the fact that Lloyd and Connie Mitchell were bringing their son Porter with them, it was a beautiful day for our Labor Day picnic. From Nannie's bedroom window, I watched Thomas jump out of his red wagon, his powerful little legs running as fast as they could away from James and Ryan, his blond hair flying and in bad need of his first trip to Fox's Barbershop.

Over the last year and a half, we'd watched Thomas turn from a baby into a very smart, very curious, and—as Ruby would nicely put it—"very active" child. He was the center of our lives. I often thought about the time Nannie told Mama she was pregnant—the week before she went missing. The connection between Nannie and Thomas always seemed natural to me and didn't go unnoticed by Mama. She told us that giving birth to him after losing Nannie had saved her during all that sadness.

Today, though, was a special, happy day. Even though summer was barely hanging on, with Ellie getting ready to go back to New York and school starting up in a couple of days, none of us thought about that as we scurried around setting up for the picnic. Since it was Labor Day weekend, most of my other cousins were able to come from out of town for the big event. Even some of Daddy's family came all the way from the beach. It seemed every corner of Gibson Island was filled with family and friends, and cars were parked all the way to the rickety wooden bridge. I wanted to finish what I was writing, but I knew there was a lot of work to be done for the picnic, so I wrapped the string around my red journal, which was reserved for special thoughts, and placed it back in Nannie's dresser drawer.

With the help of Mama and Ruby, Aunt Alicia had finally turned her office back into the family dining room, its centerpiece once again the long black walnut table, which was now piled high with covered dishes of comfort food rather than stacks of useless papers and magazines and files. As people arrived, they proudly dropped off their contributions to the picnic, which included everything from Marylou Griffin's macaroni salad (which I wondered how she could make herself but figured maybe she just liked it, so her mama named it for her) to platters of boiled shrimp from Dr. Meg and Judith, to Old Aunt Vivian's fruit cocktail cake squares. Rachel and her family came, too, and Curt and the twins each carried in Mrs. Robertson's famous coconut cream pies. When eating time came, we would transfer all the food outside and then bring out all the desserts and put them on a special table with Mama's strawberry sheet cake at the center.

Everyone had a job to do to make sure the picnic was a success, and since Mama and her sisters were the hostesses, that meant all of their children had to work extra hard. I watched Ellie as she loaded up a stack of paper plates to carry outside. The boys were putting out tables and chairs along the river's edge and under the trees, and Daddy was firing up the grill for hamburgers. Curt and Rachel lugged heavy coolers and started passing out soft drinks and tea to the guests. Curt went over to Marylou's mother and then came back to the cooler and poured tea into a cup and added a straw. I watched as he went over to Marylou and knelt down next to her, offering her a sip. It was the first time Marylou had been to Gibson Island, and she sat there now in her chair in a pink and white dress and white sandals, turning her head in circles to Curt.

"Marylou, this is my friend Curt. He is our next-door neighbor and my best friend's brother," I explained as I stood over them and opened up a couple more folding chairs.

"I was just telling her the same thing," Curt said. He smiled at me, and I noticed he was blushing a little. I had never seen him do that before. He gave her another sip of tea, and she raised her eyes to mine. I recognized that look on her face. It was the same one that she gave me when our family would sneak out of church early, or when she tried to communicate after the Robby situation, or when we sat behind St. Anne's and she gave me *The Little Prince*. It was the type of look that made me feel we had a secret, but I didn't know what the secret was this time.

Curt stood up, and it seemed that almost overnight, he had gotten a lot taller than me. I was thinking just then that he and Rachel were really not much like brother and sister. His hair was not blond or straight like hers, but a warm-brown color and wavy, and he had a tiny shock of white hair above his right ear. He said it was a birthmark because no matter how short he cut his hair, it always grew back the same way. "Genny, do you want me to get you some tea?" Curt asked. He seemed like he was paying me more attention than usual. I nodded, and when he went over to get the drink, Marylou started moving herself around like crazy.

"Marylou, what is it?" I asked, putting my hand on hers. She looked at Curt getting the drink. "Oh. He's just a friend." She moved around some more. "You think he likes me?" I knew now where this was going. I looked around to make sure no one else could hear me. "Well, I guess I am starting to think that he does really like me more than just a friend." Marylou smiled the biggest smile I'd ever seen on her face. Then it was my turn to blush. When Curt came back, I took the drink from him and raced off because I still had a lot of work to do.

I couldn't wait for the big surprise this afternoon — the variety show that Rachel and I had been planning for the picnic entertainment. We'd practiced all our favorite songs and we had to admit we were pretty good, so naturally we were the main act. Ellie was going to perform a dancing number, Ryan and Thomas were doing a comedy routine, and James and Curt were doing a magic act. Curt was not particularly interested in being a part of the talent show, but I had a feeling he was doing it for me. With costumes and props to get ready and some more practicing still to do, we hurried to finish up all the party chores.

As I headed down the hallway from the dining room, I heard Mama and Aunt Marjorie and Aunt Viv laughing and talking over each other, and for just a minute, I remembered back to that day when their muffled sobs and whispers drifted down to me from a private, sad place upstairs. In the kitchen now, someone turned up the radio, and the Lettermen were singing "Goin' Out of My Head." I stood at the door watching the three sisters sing along — Mama carrying the tune, Aunt Marjorie not carrying the tune, and Aunt Viv tapping the counter with salad tongs to the words "day and night, night and day . . . and night . . ." Then, in unison, they shouted more than sang the chorus, "I love you, baby, and if it's quite alright . . ."

I saw Daduh watching them and grinning away, and I knew she was thinking about when they were young girls. She used to tell Ellie and me, "Whoo-ee! Your mamas was a force to be reckoned with back in the olden days. Don't get me started." But she really did want you to get her started. Daduh liked to be the source of all information worth knowing. That's how I learned why Mama got kicked out of the private school in Asheville. Daduh said that she'd come to Smith Street for a little while to help Nannie out after the divorce, and dealing with three beautiful, strong-willed teenaged girls was no easy task.

Mama was the biggest challenge, she said. "She was stubborn as the day is long. Your Nannie thought it'd be good for Miss Louisa to go to the Asheville girls' school and learn some proper manners and study subjects to get her ready to be a secretary. She went all right, but no sooner had her bags landed on the floor they were calling your Nannie to come and get her. Seems she got caught smoking in the bathroom and sneaked out the same night with some other girls to the boys' private school on the other side of town. Now, I shouldn't be tellin' you all this, but I think it's plain funny how your mama's gonna do what she's gonna do no matter what! And she hasn't changed a bit."

Daduh and Ruby were working alongside each other, Daduh keeping her eye on Ruby, who was tossing Nannie's special bean salad in the huge yellow ceramic bowl meant just for that dish. This would be the first time Nannie wasn't the one making it.

"Okay, time to test," Ruby announced, sliding the bowl down to me as I propped myself up on the stool. The bean salad had been soaking in its dressing and spices all night in the icebox, and if it wasn't as good as Nannie's, we weren't going to serve it, Daduh said. I plucked a tangy wax bean out of the dish, then another. Everyone fell silent, and Aunt Viv turned down the radio.

"Well?" Aunt Marjorie asked.

"Do you think it tastes like hers?" Mama asked.

I chewed slowly and smiled. "Just like it! It's perfect!" I said.

Daduh wiped her forehead with the back of her hand and said, "Whoo-ee! That was close." Ruby covered it with tin foil and clapped her hands together. Aunt Alicia reached up in the cabinet and brought down a bottle of special bourbon. "No Jim Beam today! Time to break out the good stuff," she said on her way out to the porch. Everyone grabbed something to carry and headed outside. Mama moved her large strawberry sheet cake to the back counter for safekeeping and smoothed out the icing with a spatula. Then she stood still, staring down at it like she was frozen.

"I wish she could've seen Thomas," Mama said. I was surprised. It was the first time she'd spoken about Nannie that way, like she wanted to talk about her. It seemed like I should say something, but I didn't want to upset her. She turned to me, brushing her dark hair back and tilting her head slightly with a question on her face. She was wearing a white blouse and a thin red cardigan sweater over it with the sleeves pushed up to her elbows, and her lipstick was a perfect match. She was waiting for me to speak.

I knew by now to be very careful, though. After the Jeffrey Landry scare, Mama had tried to convince herself her dreams were more like coincidences and caused by stress. She explained to me that life events and changes triggered those dreams, like when she and Daddy lost their jobs and everything they owned, or when we moved into the new house and she was pregnant with Thomas. She could talk herself out of or into anything, Nannie would say.

So, instead of telling her that Nannie did know all about Thomas, I lost my courage and just said, "I wish she could've seen him, too."

208

"Genny, I want to tell you something." Mama reached out to me, and the way she paused, I thought maybe she was going to tell me about a dream she had, but at that moment, a newspaper clipping drifted to the floor between us. I picked it up and saw it was the tide schedule for October 24, 1965, and high tide was circled at three fifteen.

"Let me see that," she said and looked it over. I recognized it as one of many tide schedules Nannie used to keep taped on the front of the icebox. Aunt Alicia sure didn't track the tides; she never fished and didn't care one way or the other if it was low tide or high tide. "It's the tide schedule from that day," Mama said faintly.

"Where'd it come from?" I asked, and she shrugged.

"I don't know. Maybe Ruby came up on it when she was cleaning."

"Genny! You need to hurry," Rachel interrupted. "We don't have much time to practice for the show. Come on!" I didn't want to leave Mama, but we did have a show to put on, and they were depending on me.

"Aunt Louisa, we're done setting up outside. Uncle Jim says the hamburgers will be hockey pucks soon!" Ellie called behind her as we ran off, leaving Mama standing in the kitchen with a cake spatula in one hand and Nannie's tide chart in the other.

We weaved our way through the folding chairs and big pocketbooks and coolers and people sipping their drinks and smoking their cigarettes. I noticed James and Ryan and all the boy cousins gathered around the fire Daddy had started for roasting oysters, while Ryan entertained them by pulling a raw oyster tied to a string up and down his throat without gagging. As I yelled out to them to come practice for the show, I tripped and tumbled onto the ground, landing face down. I was getting ready to blame the twisted oak tree roots that were steadily working their way toward the porch steps, when I looked back and saw Porter Mitchell tucking his leg back under his folding chair, giving me his creepy smile.

"You know, Porter," I said loudly, not caring who heard me and brushing off the front of my shirt and shorts, "you're never going to have *any* friends if you keep being so mean. You're going to grow up to be a lonely, old man." His face turned beet red, and as I walked away, I heard Aunt Alicia's poodles barking loudly behind me. They sat in the red wagon next to Thomas, and there was Porter heading toward them. He reached down to take the wagon handle, but before he could, Ryan sped over from the group of cousins and jerked it out of his hand. The determined look on Ryan's face and the way he leaned the top of his body forward dared Porter to bully him or his brother. I smiled as I passed by Daduh, who was fanning herself underneath the tree and nodding her head in approval.

Even though I was in a hurry, something told me to stop and go back to Daduh. I ran over to her as she sat, stretched out in the lawn chair, taking a break from all the picnic preparations. She was watching the crowd with pride, like she was responsible for bringing everyone together. She was probably remembering many parties like this in the past, back when she was a little girl when her mama worked here for our family. She put her fan down on her lap and smoothed out her white cotton dress and the frilly purple apron from Nannie that she wore on special occasions.

"What's the matter with you, Genevieve?" she said in her warm, growly voice as she saw me running toward her.

"Nothing. I just wanted to say hi!" I said, and I hugged her. I think I must have surprised her because she didn't have time to hug me back.

As I began to let go of her, a soft blanket of warmth surrounded us, and the whooshing, whirring sound I got when Nannie was with me filled my head and ears. I paused, my cheek next to Daduh's, and felt her moist brown skin touching mine. Chills rushed across my shoulders and neck and down my arms, and I felt that I loved her so much I would never be able to talk about it. I smelled her — the familiar, comforting scent of sugar and cinnamon, and I memorized it so that I could have her with me forever. I was afraid to let her go. I knew Nannie was with us right then. But I did let go of Daduh, and I searched her eyes to see if she could feel Nannie, too. "Go get yer singin' voice ready, now," Daduh said, and she swatted me away with her fan.

Ellie rummaged through cardboard boxes of costumes we'd been collecting — ballet dance costumes and hats and coats and ties — and handed the clothes and props out to everyone. Rachel and I practiced our songs — especially "Downtown" because we knew that was everyone's favorite. Even as young as he was, Thomas was our biggest fan. He clapped his hands in appreciation, and I swear it sounded like he was joining in on the chorus when we sang, "You can always go — downtown!"

When we were done practicing, we started setting up for our show and trying to get people's attention. Drinks flowed, more foil-covered food was brought out from the kitchen, and voices rose up and bounced around in the air like bright balloons. Ruby shouted out at Thomas, who once again had dashed away from her. "Thomas Donovan! You come back here! Sweetman!" Ruby chased after him, ending up on her hands and knees under one of the long tables. She couldn't get herself up off the ground, and the harder she tried, the funnier it was. James ran over to help her, while Thomas came out the other end, and Ruby just sat there laughing. "Great day in the mornin'! He is tiring me out somethin' fierce. You'd think I'd be used to this by now, but no one can keep up with that child!" Ruby said.

Aunt Alicia shouted, "James! Ryan! Put the chairs in a circle, so people can see better," and held an empty glass, clasped by her three fingers, up to her brother, Uncle Donald, who was standing nearby with a bottle of bourbon. Uncle Donald was his usual odd self and roamed lost-like at the picnic, making jokes and offering bourbon as he went around from person to person. Aunt Theresa and Uncle Martin were showing Rachel a photo album they had brought with them, while Rachel gave me a "please help" look. Aunt Sis and Sister Mary Ignatius and Sister Mary Clare sat smack in the center of the circle of chairs, with their laden-down paper plates perched on their black-robed laps, while Father Cuddihy sat with the Mitchells, talking with them about their recent vacation to Ireland.

When I looked around for Mama, I noticed she and Aunt Marjorie were nowhere around, so I headed back to the house to tell them we were ready to start the show. Before I went up the steps near the kitchen, I paused and looked over at the wharf, empty and quiet. It invited me to come to it, its entrance darkly shaded by two slender oak trees, draped heavily with Spanish moss that moved slightly to the rhythm of the river. I wondered how it was I had never noticed these trees before—not in this way. They were different than Dora, my Dora that gave me such comfort. These trees were like tall, silver-armored goddesses that had special, almost intimidating powers and strength beyond anything I could understand. I didn't know how to take this all in— I felt suddenly very overwhelmed by their presence.

Even though I had tried, I still hadn't been able to go onto the wharf—not since that day with Nannie when we fished and crabbed and talked about the oyster shells. Seeing these trees now, noticing the way they were, I was even more convinced that I might never go back.

I went inside and saw Mama and Aunt Marjorie sitting together in the parlor. They were whispering as if they had sneaked away from the picnic and didn't want anyone to know they were there.

I backed away, and as I passed by the hall tree mirror and looked into it, I heard Nannie say, *"Genevieve — it's time to sing your song."* I twisted her ring on my finger and rushed back outside, my heart racing with excitement like it always did when Nannie spoke to me.

We opened up the variety show with Thomas and Ryan's comedy act, where we dressed Thomas up like a puppy dog with dog ears, a tail, and a leash, and Ryan had him doing smart dog tricks for candy. When Ellie came twirling out as a ballerina for her act, we all watched as she leaped into the air and turned in circles on her toes. I loved how her long, graceful arms and fingers floated out from her body. When she fell, she crumpled into a ball, and at first, everyone thought it was part of the act, but she didn't get up.

When Daddy and Aunt Marjorie got to her, Ellie said, "I'm fine now. I don't know what happened," and Daddy carried her over to a lawn chair and told her to wait there and drink lots of water. The magic act followed, and James and Curt brought out their card tricks and vanishing stuffed-rabbit trick, which were all big hits, and Curt seemed pretty pleased with himself. Thomas had fallen asleep on Ruby's lap, so she laid him down on the chaise longue chair in the shade, and Mama took off her red sweater and placed it on top of him.

At the end, Rachel and I sang our songs, and Daddy shouted out what he knew would be the big finale, "Sing 'Downtown'!" Of course, we had planned it just this way, and as we started singing the beginning, "When you're alone, and life is making you lonely, you can always go" — I instinctively looked over for Thomas, knowing this song would wake him up, and he would join us by singing loudly — "downtown!"

Only, Thomas wasn't there. Mama's eyes met mine; then she turned around and saw the empty chair and her red sweater on the ground. "Thomas!" My mother's wail came from the deepest part

213

of her. Daduh shouted out, "Lord, please!" and Ruby dropped the sheet cake on the ground. Daddy shot from his chair to Mama, who pulled away violently from him and tore through the crowd of family and friends.

I scanned the lawn for Porter but didn't see him, then threw the pretend microphone to the ground, and before anyone had a chance to even wonder what was happening, I met my mother's frantic gait—racing alongside her to the river. We both knew something at the same time.

"Thomas! Thomas! Thomas!" They all called out his name behind us, just realizing that he was missing. *Missing.*

I knew she saw what I saw—Thomas's red wagon lying on its side. It took a split second and forever to get to the wharf, and in that time, we became one person, no longer mother and daughter, Louisa and Genevieve, but someone else braver than those two. At the wharf's edge, fear and horror and heavy, desperate sadness slammed against our chests, knocking the air out of us. It was like that terrifying day when Jeffrey Landry was chasing us and we crashed through the smokehouse door, only this wasn't a simple door. For almost two years, Mama and I had tried to go back onto the wharf, but we could never do it. Never. We had lost the woman who connected us, the woman who understood both of us better than anyone in the world. We lost her off this wharf, in these waters.

It took both of us, but we pushed through it, past the silver-armored goddesses, down the long, skinny wharf with the dangerously wide railings, wide enough for a small body to fit through. Thomas was nowhere. We didn't know if we were touching the ground, but I think we were because I heard our feet thumping on top of the wobbly, wooden boards with their wide, splintered cracks. We ran past the hooks where Nannie would hang crab nets and fishing poles, past the built-in bench where she used to sit and lay out her tackle, past the very spot where she'd said, "I see her! A white dolphin! Genevieve, Ellie — look!"

We flew down the slanted planks perfectly spaced for tiny feet to slip through. We landed on the floating part of the wharf where it rested, rocking gently, on top of the river's new water, just in from high tide. *High tide.*

Mama fell to her knees. Thomas was sitting in the furthermost corner of the floating wharf, tucked out of view underneath the main wharf above it. The faded green, barnacled boat swayed and creaked on its chains above Thomas's head as he sat on the very edge, his chubby, strong legs kicking and splashing the water loudly.

As Mama reached her arms gently toward him so he wouldn't fall forward into the water, a streak of the afternoon sunlight hit the board beneath her, and there it was — the silver feather that had been tied to Nannie's fishing pole. That same streak of sunlight struck the face of her wristwatch. It was three fifteen, and Thomas turned his face from the river to us, calm and unafraid.

"Nannie," he said, and Mama started to cry.

Chapter Nineteen

September 2, 1967

WHEN THOMAS WAS LOST AT THE PICNIC, I thought the world was ending—and even afterward, I had trouble getting back to normal, but Ellie had helped me through it. What would we have done—what would Mama have done if he, too, had fallen into the river and gone missing? She would never have recovered. Our lives would be over for good. And Ruby and Daduh—especially after losing Rooster like they did? Ruby had felt like it was her fault because she'd left Thomas on the chair sleeping and started cleaning up. Of course, it wasn't her fault at all. We were all right there with him. He just got up without us noticing and slipped away—that was what Thomas did all the time.

Once we realized Thomas was safe, Mama picked him up and held him tight, still crying, as she made her way back up the wharf. I trailed behind, watching the two of them walk very slowly toward the Goddess Trees, whose limbs were not frightening at all like I'd thought earlier, but instead they were protective and welcoming. It had all been a misunderstanding.

Ellie was right there waiting for me when I stepped off the wharf. As people swarmed around Mama and Thomas, he giggled, unaware of the reason for all this attention as he got passed around from Daddy to James to Ryan to Ruby. Everyone moved away from the water, back toward the picnic area under the trees. But there was Ellie. Standing alone. Ellie ran to me, and she hugged me tightly and said, "Oh, Genny! I understand." We stayed there, sitting on the ground at the entrance of the wharf, until the party ended and everyone left. I waved to Rachel and Curt as they drove off with their family. Ellie and I didn't have to help clean up or do anything else the rest of the evening. They left us alone and let us sit there under the Goddess Trees.

Ellie said, "I still can't understand how Thomas got to the wharf so quickly and down to the floating dock without falling in the water." We talked and talked and then finally ran out of words, staring out at the river until the sun started slowly taking the tide out with it. The whole time, I kept Nannie's silver feather in my pocket.

"Do you ever have dreams about Nannie?" I whispered to Ellie late that night. We were under the covers with a flashlight, talking like we always did long after everyone else had gone to sleep.

"I guess so. I don't remember my dreams that much," Ellie said.

"What would you say if I told you she came to see me in my dreams?" I asked, watching her face for a reaction. I had her attention. "And what would you say if I told you they weren't really dreams?"

"You mean like a ghost?" That got Ellie's attention.

"Well, I guess you could say that, but I don't think of it that way. It's as if she never left. I can hear her, and I can see her sometimes. I think she's been telling me things I need to do or to notice. She repeats things she wants me to remember and sends me signals."

"I don't know, Genny. That sounds like dreaming. What kind of signals?" Ellie's face looked interested.

"The lights go on and off sometimes for no reason, and sometimes when I come back in my room, my ballerina music box is open and music is playing. Other times an object of hers will fall on the floor—like her bell or the tide chart—as if she's trying to get my attention." I paused because I felt like too much information was tumbling out of my mouth too fast. I'd been starved for someone to listen to me. But I also knew I had to be careful—this was a lot to handle if you weren't used to it.

Ellie didn't say anything for a minute but put her head on my shoulder, just like she used to do when we were little. I loved the way Ellie never tried to pretend she was something she wasn't. She let you see her real feelings. If she was scared or angry or if she liked something about you, she would just come out and say it. She used to say, "Genny, you're so lucky to live down here with Nannie and be around family and Gibson Island. I wish I could be you sometimes."

Now, in the dark, in Nannie's room, underneath the yellow bedspread, I could hear Ellie breathing softly and pausing as if there was something she wanted to say. "Genny, I do believe you. I know you're special that way," she said. I could feel her tears on my shoulder, and I pulled back to look at her.

"Ellie—what is it? Tell me, what's the matter?" Had I scared her with this talk about Nannie? No, not Ellie. She wasn't like that at all.

"Nothing. I just wish I lived here with you, and we could be sisters. Maybe one day." She smiled weakly and added, "I miss her."

I almost said, "Me, too," but then I realized I had Nannie with me all the time, that she was right here with us. I wished she would show herself to Ellie, that she would come right now, this minute.

"Ellie, I want to show you something. Look here," I said throwing the spread off of us and going over to the dresser mirror. The quote was still taped to the corner, thanks to me adding more tape to it when the edges started curling. "Nannie taped this to her mirror at some point—I don't know when—and neither does Mama, but I always thought it was interesting she chose this saying over all the sayings in the world to tape on her mirror. She never said anything about it to anyone. I found it right after the funeral."

I shined the flashlight on it, and Ellie read it out loud: "'They that go down to the sea in ships, that do business in great waters. These see the works of the Lord and his wonders in the deep. For he commandeth and raiseth up the stormy wind, which lifteth up the waves thereof. Then they cry unto the Lord in their trouble, and He bringeth them out of their distresses. He maketh the storm a calm, so that the waves thereof are still.' What does it mean?"

"I'm not all the way sure. I found out it's from the Bible, though. I think it has to do with fishermen and sailors. They do their work in the ocean, and sometimes God creates storms and big waves. When they're afraid, they call out to God for help, and then He hears them and makes the wind and the waves calm again. I think their work makes them feel closer to God, and so they love it." I paused to think about what this meant to Nannie. "Nannie loved the water, even though she didn't like to go in it, and she was a fisherman—or a fisherwoman," I laughed. "And we know she loved storms, even though they were scary to her, and she tracked them and warned us about them. It seems to me she loved the things she was most afraid of, and after a while she just came to an understanding with those things. Maybe they made her feel closer to God." As I said the words, I felt this was a truthful story Nannie would tell.

Ellie said, "Yeah. I think I can understand that—how you can love something and be afraid at the same time. I bet this quote helped her feel brave."

"Our great-great-grandmother Genevieve used to have pre-monitions—dreams about big white waves and storms, and she would warn the fishermen before a storm came. Nannie said she was always right, too," I said, wondering if Ellie ever heard that story. I started to tell her about Mama and how she had the same gift as our great-great-grandmother, but I knew that was off-limits until Mama was ready.

"Do you think Nannie knew she was going to die in the water?" Ellie asked, still looking up at the Bible verse on the mirror.

"Yes," I answered quickly.

And then we crawled back under the yellow bedspread, lying silently for a long time, and when I closed my eyes, I heard Nannie whisper in my ear, *"She needs you."* I looked over at Ellie, who was already asleep. I thought she must mean Ellie needed me, but I wasn't sure why.

The next morning, I got up before Ellie and peeked out through the little circular window above the water pitcher and bowl. Ellie was leaving today to go back to New York, and we were going back to our house at Bailey's Place. As much as I loved our house there and living next to Rachel, I was overcome by the feeling I should be here at Gibson Island all the time. I took my red journal out of the dresser drawer and tiptoed down the steps, running my hand along the polished banister, smooth and shiny but not quite with the same high gloss it used to have. I leaned toward the old clock on the wall and smiled—six a.m.—it had kept perfect time ever since that horrible night back in January when Jeffrey Landry chased Mama and me down and tried to kill us. After all those years of being broken, its clock hands moved steadily around now as if nothing had ever been wrong.

I curled up in the parlor on the love seat underneath the window that opened out to the front porch and began writing. I ran my finger across the words in the journal that Joe had written—"For your truthful stories"—and wished I could see him again. Joe had understood me from the moment we'd met. It was strange how after all this time, I still couldn't forget about him. The river breezes carried in the intoxicating smells of the pluff mud and the marsh and the salt water seasoned with fish and crabs and oysters.

I heard the whirring sound in my ears and felt the soft blanket around me. Nannie was here. I closed my eyes and listened to her.

"So, the truthful story is," she said now. *"Your great-great-grandmother Genevieve would sit on the porch right outside this very window and have her sweet tea in the afternoon. And Daduh's mama would sit here in the parlor on the other side, where you're sitting now by the same open window, and the two of them would talk and talk like the best of friends, each of them facing in opposite directions. Then tea would be over, and they would go back to being who they were."*

"So, they didn't sit together on the porch and talk?" I asked.

"No, never. It wasn't proper for the lady of the house and the maid to sit together like friends. White people and colored people weren't supposed to socialize like that. But they found their own way to have a friendship — one that didn't need any explaining or apology."

Nannie now sat across from me on an old gray tapestry chair with narrow, curvy arms and legs. Boy, was I happy to see her.

"Hi Nannie! Thomas saw you, too, didn't he?" I whispered to her, setting my journal down.

"Yes. He's always seen me since he was first born. He runs toward me every time he sees me. I take the credit for him walking so early," she laughed. *"You were the same way — you could see your great-great-grandmother after she was gone, but you just don't remember. Genevieve, I want you to know Thomas was always safe yesterday. I knew it was going to be all right. You and your mama did good going*

on the wharf like that." She was gone again, but not really. I could feel her here still, and I tucked my legs up underneath me and leaned back in the loveseat. I had to be the luckiest person in the world to be able to see and hear Nannie like I did. I kept thinking about all the signs Nannie tried to give Mama and me, and I was learning to pay better attention. Yesterday, Mama was trying to tell me something in the kitchen right before the tide chart fell on the floor in front of us, and I wondered now if she'd had another one of her dreams—maybe it had been about Thomas. I might not ever know. I opened up my journal and realized I only had a few pages left in it. I didn't want it to end. I rubbed the silver feather that lay between the pages.

In a moment, Mama and Aunt Marjorie walked quietly past me, carrying mugs of hot coffee, still in their robes and slippers, thinking they had the house to themselves and no one else was awake yet. They went out on the porch and sat in the white rattan chairs, setting their coffee on the little table between them and lighting up cigarettes at the same time. I could hear their voices, low and secretive, the voices of sisters.

"What are you going to do, M?" Mama asked.

"I don't know. It's not that easy," Aunt Marjorie said.

"Mama would never tolerate this. I wish you wouldn't, either," Mama said firmly.

"I guess I'm afraid. Where would we go?" Her voice quivered, and that was unusual for Aunt Marjorie, the strongest sister, the smartest sister, people said.

"Now, that's the stupidest question that's ever come out of your mouth. You will come here—here where you belong," Mama said. Aunt Marjorie got up and walked toward the porch railing, leaning forward, her face toward the river, tilting her head as if she was searching for her answer. Mama went to her side. "I know." She put her arm around her sister.

"Genny, can you help me in the kitchen?" Aunt Alicia walked into the parlor, ending my eavesdropping session, so I got up and followed her, tucking my red journal under the cushion of the love seat.

"Genny, I made some sandwiches for you to take to school today," Aunt Alicia said, pointing to a stack of white bread sandwiches wrapped in wax paper.

"We don't have school today, Aunt Alicia," I said, and she frowned. "But we can have them for lunch today. That'll be a big help to Mama." I didn't want to make her feel bad, so I put the sandwiches in the icebox for safekeeping and acted like what she'd done was normal.

Aunt Alicia was becoming more and more dependent on us, Daddy had said yesterday before the picnic. Instead of going back over to Bailey's Place yesterday, we'd decided to spend a couple of nights over here at Gibson Island, not only because we wanted more time with Aunt Marjorie and Ellie and Sam before they left, but because it was all too much for Aunt Alicia to handle by herself. We were still coming over every Sunday after Mass as usual, but now James and Ryan had regular work they needed to do around the island, and Mama brought meals for Aunt Alicia to have during the week. Ruby came every other Saturday to do the housekeeping, and she told Mama she was getting worried about Aunt Alicia's memory because last week she found the gas burner on the stove had been left on, and the milk and butter were on a shelf in the bathroom.

When Ellie came into the kitchen, we started carrying out plates to the breakfast room to set up, and I noticed the tide chart. "Ellie, this is what I was telling you about. The tide chart—see the date on it?" I said, pointing to the newspaper clipping that was now taped on the front center of the icebox.

"Fannie likes to keep the charts on the icebox so she can track those tides, so leave it there," Aunt Alicia chimed in, as if she was explaining this for the first time, her back to us as she stirred the big pot of grits with a wooden spoon. Ellie raised her eyebrows. We weren't sure what to make of Aunt Alicia's comment because it was hard to tell with Aunt Alicia these days what was real and what wasn't. The only thing is, Aunt Alicia had never spoken of Nannie in the present like that—in fact, she was like Mama in a way and rarely spoke of Nannie.

During breakfast, I couldn't help but notice that Aunt Marjorie and Ellie and Sam were moving in slow motion, and I thought to myself they don't want to leave Gibson Island, either. What Nannie said was true: *"Once it gets in your blood, you can't get it out — no matter how hard you try."* Having spent such a long time here this summer, it was going to be hard for them to drive all that way back to New York, but it was also more than that. After what I'd heard on the porch that morning, I knew they didn't want to go home at all.

"Ellie, is there something you want to tell me?" I asked, helping her pack up their car in the driveway. She'd grown more and more quiet as the morning went by. Ellie looked sad—so was I. We always hated saying good-bye, but this was the worst ever, and it was obvious something was definitely wrong.

"No. Why?" She lifted her suitcase into the trunk. As she did, she got real pale suddenly and fell up against the car, stumbling like she did during her dance yesterday at the party.

"Ellie, what is it?" I grabbed her arm to hold her up.

"I don't know," she said, leaning on me.

"Sit here for a minute. I'll get your mama."

When Aunt Marjorie came out, she looked very worried. "Ellie—this has happened too many times. As soon as we get home, we're going to get you an appointment and get this checked out."

"Mama, I don't want to go back home," Ellie said quickly, and we all just stood there for a minute not knowing what to say next.

"Ellie . . . ," Aunt Marjorie started. "It's been a fun vacation, but we have to go. And you need to get that checkup." Then she turned back to all of us, looking at Mama. "We need to get on the road. I'll call you when we get home."

"You'll think about what we said?" Mama asked.

"Marjorie, we can help," Daddy said.

"I know. I'll let you know," Aunt Marjorie said, opening the back door for Sam, who was talking to the boys. "Come on now, Sam, get in the car." He got in and nodded good-bye to James and Ryan. Aunt Alicia started her tractor in the background and drove by, waving.

"Oh Lord—I told her to stop driving that thing. Let me go get her before she kills somebody," Daddy said, "James, help me catch her!"

"M, please," Mama said, taking her hand.

"I'll call you," Aunt Marjorie said.

The sky was incredibly blue and clear. The hairs on my arms stood up as if Nannie was standing right next to me, and I wanted to take Ellie and pull her out of their old brown station wagon into the sunshine. Instead, I just stood there doing nothing. A group of squirrels darted nervously around the giant oak tree in the front, and Daddy and the boys disappeared into the dirt being kicked up by the tractor, yelling after Aunt Alicia. Ellie turned her eyes to mine. She was my sister just like Mama and Aunt Marjorie—the sister I always wanted—and it was so unnatural for us to say good-bye.

I saw Mama wipe the tears from her face and felt the tug of pain she was having at that moment. Ellie smoothed her light-brown hair back from her forehead, running her hand down to her shoulder, her face still pale and her eyes empty, and they drove off, blowing the horn and waving out the window.

* * *

That night back at Bailey's Place, I woke up and went into the kitchen, and there Mama was. "Genny, why are you up? It's after midnight," she whispered, wrapping her thin, pink robe with the roses on it around her. The crickets were chirping outside the open kitchen window, and the air was cool. Mama put a small saucepan on the stove, took the saltine crackers out of the cabinet, and got the milk out of the icebox. "Want some?"

I nodded. I crushed the crackers up while she poured the milk in the pan and stirred it so it wouldn't scald. We took our big mugs of saltine cracker milk out to the porch and sat for a while, not talking.

"Aunt Alicia is having a hard time," Mama said. "You and the boys have probably noticed how she forgets things more and seems confused. That happens sometimes when people get older. We want to make sure she is taken care of and safe, so Daddy and I've been talking with her about how we can help."

I stirred the cracker milk with my spoon. The stars were twinkling over the river, and we both leaned back in our chairs, their aluminum legs shifting lightly against the wooden floor.

Mama stared straight ahead to the river, and her face was turned away from the porch light, but I could tell she was smiling. "Genny, what would you say . . . if we moved back to Gibson Island for good?"

The very next weekend, we were packing up to move back where we belonged. Before the moving truck came Saturday morning, I watched Dora standing tall over the river, alongside the Edge, waiting patiently between our houses, wondering when I was going to come tell her good-bye. She knew the truth. "Something big has changed with Genevieve," she'd be thinking. I went straight to her, and I put my arms as far around her as I could—her old, sturdy body seeming smaller to me somehow. "Thank you, Dora,"

I said to her, my hands glancing across her rough bark skin as I walked away.

"Well, it's not like we're moving far away," I said to Rachel before I left. She looked like she was going to cry, but I knew that wouldn't happen because Rachel never cried. "We'll still see each other at school, plus you can ride home on the bus with me on Fridays, or I can come back here with you to Bailey's Place. It'll be fun. Why don't you come over tomorrow and help me set up my room?"

"Okay—and we can still sing together like always," she said, helping me drag a huge box of my clothes onto the porch.

The boys were loading books and lamps and kitchen items in the back of a big truck that Jackson had gotten for us on loan from the plant. Between him and Ruby and all the Robertsons, we were almost done with the move, stacking up the last bit in the final truckload and putting the finishing touches on cleaning the house. Ruby had been working at both houses—cleaning, packing, unpacking, and all the while keeping a sharp eye on Thomas. She never let him out of her sight. Jackson was going to continue bringing Ruby to work for us, only now it would be at Gibson Island. He said it was all for the best because Gibson Island was just down the road from Daduh and his mother, Lumpy, and he could check in on them every day.

"The wharf at Gibson Island is better than this one," Ryan said to the twins, carrying a box of comic books to the car. "This one still looks like a bunch of sticks in the water." The twins laughed and helped him with another box. Fella was lying in the middle of the road with Queenie, as if he knew this was the last day with her. "You can bring Queenie over to play, too," he added.

"Rachel, come give us a hand with the sweeping!" Mrs. Robertson called from the open door to the living room. I looked around me outside. So much had happened since we'd moved to Bailey's Place. I walked on the cool, green Carpet Grass in my bare feet and over to the Nuthouse, remembering how scared we'd been of Crazy Robby and how we'd thought someone was being held captive in there. I went around to the back and peeked into the window. Now that I was tall enough, I could see the half-filled burlap bags of pecans stacked against the walls. Pretty soon, pecans would cover every inch of the Orchard, and Robby would be at his busiest—storing and keeping close watch over them, making sure they didn't get wet.

"Genny." I turned to see Curt, surprised he'd followed me over here.

"Hi Curt." I smiled at him and realized I would miss being his neighbor.

"I was thinking Rachel and me could come over to Gibson Island soon and see how things are goin'," he said, looking down at his feet.

"What's wrong?" I asked.

"Nothin' really," he said

"Okay. But you seem different," I said.

"Just, you know, I like you, and . . ."

"I like you, too," I said. Then, I realized we were both looking at the ground instead of each other. We'd never had so much trouble having a conversation before.

We could hear car and truck doors slamming. He slipped his hands in the pockets of his blue jeans. "Genny, is it okay if I kiss you?" he asked.

"Yeah. I guess." I was a little surprised, but then, maybe I shouldn't have been. I realized that I did want to kiss him and to see what that was like, and I figured if we got it over with, we'd both feel a lot better.

Curt leaned toward me quickly and kissed me on the lips. I didn't close my eyes, and I didn't kiss him back because I wasn't all the way ready. "Let's try again. This time I'll be ready," I suggested.

Curt laughed. "Genny, you sure are interesting," he said, and then he leaned in slowly. I closed my eyes. It was a short, nice kiss. I liked it.

"Guess I better go," I said, starting to walk away. There was no doubt I was excited about moving back to Gibson Island, but for the first time, I felt a little pang of sadness to leave Bailey's Place, or maybe it wasn't Bailey's Place I'd be missing.

"I'll be seein' ya," Curt said, and I noticed for the first time that his eyes were grayish blue like the sky right before it starts to rain.

Chapter Twenty

October 20, 1967

THERE WAS A PARADE FOR HER FUNERAL. It was not like the one at Christmas. There was no fire engine or Santa Claus, no convertible with Miss Hollywood, no twirling batons or peppermint candies tossed into the street. But it was a parade like no other our town had ever seen. They came all the way from Toogoodoo Point past the old oyster factory on Yonges Island, past St. Anne's Catholic Church, past Gibson Island Road alongside the marshland, past Meggett Town Hall, and from the other end of Hollywood, stretching from the Hollywood General, Bear's Store, and the railroad tracks at Bailey's Place.

The line of shiny cars, still wet from car washes, gleamed as they moved in slow respect, and a long line of folks walked for miles in their Sunday best in the Lowcountry heat, still hard to take even in October. Most everyone started from Daduh's house just like she used to do with her family, and Mama let me join in their walk halfway. Ruby and Jackson chose not to ride in the family processional but to walk the entire way in her honor. I held Ruby's hand, and we sang Daduh's favorite, "Gonna put on my golden shoes down by the riverside, down by the riverside, down by the riverside."

We all ended up at the same place—Hope Baptist Church, its bell tolling every few seconds as we crunched up the dirt road packed down with oyster shell bits and gravel in our dusty patent leather shoes. Each time the bell struck, I felt it hit me inside, pounding on some deep place underneath my bones.

All of Daduh's friends came, and it seemed like hundreds. Lots of white people came, too. Mama and Daddy and Aunt Alicia drove up in the parking lot and waited for me at the entrance. Gloria, who'd come back from somewhere, and poor Lumpy, wearing a blouse and skirt that didn't even match, climbed out of the big funeral car. Mama said we shouldn't take up space in their church, but Ruby and Jackson insisted we come in, so we found a place in the back.

There were flower girls, just like for weddings, only they carried beautiful flowers up to the casket; there were women in white dresses sitting at the front with the families holding their hands; people telling their stories; prayers and singing and choir music; and lots of crying. Lumpy cried the most, yelling out for her mama and falling to the floor in front of the casket, until the ladies in white dresses helped her get back to her seat.

There was no holding back, no pretending it didn't happen, no denying the pain. It was raw and deep and jagged like the cut on my foot from the oyster shell. It was unbearable and beautiful. Daduh was loved.

After the funeral, we went over to Daduh's house, and lots of ladies from their church were there setting up food and helping with all the children. We almost didn't go, but Jackson insisted.

"My grandmother has been a part of your family since she was born, just like her mother and grandmother. It seems right that you come to her house," he said. And so we did. I'd always wanted to go into her house and was very curious.

"When Daduh's grandmother worked for the Gibsons, she lived on Gibson Island with her family," Nannie told me one day as we walked over to a little one-room cabin tucked away on the back of the island along the river. Instead of wallpaper, the walls were covered with old newspaper clippings. There were two windows, and the floors had holes in them. Nothing had been done to that little house in all those years, and it just stayed back there all by itself not getting used. "When my grandfather Ellis made all his money, he built Daduh's grandmother and her family their own big house within walkin' distance, and that's where Daduh grew up and where she and Lumpy still live today," she explained. "Same as her mama, Daduh has had only one job her whole life, and that was to take care of us Gibsons, so we make sure we take care of her. We take care of each other."

I looked around Daduh's house now. It was cozy, and the walls were covered with real pictures, not newspaper. One big picture was over the sofa, and it was a painting on a large piece of wood, cut into a perfect square, of two large ladies walking down that same road to Hope Baptist, wearing special church clothes and hats. I leaned over the sofa and saw that one of the ladies looked just like Daduh.

"That's right. One is Grandma Daduh, and the other one is her mama. That's them walkin' to church like they used to do," Jackson said from behind me "It's called acrylic paint," he added with a voice that sounded proud he knew it. I kept staring at it. It looked kind of like oil painting—similar to what I'd seen at Dr. Meg and Judith Moore's studio, but it was also very different.

The red and yellow in the painting were the brightest, richest colors that surely had ever existed. The ladies looked almost cartoonish but beautiful and joyful at the same time. The oak trees and the river were painted in a blurry, watery way, so that the women jumped out of the painting with their deep-brown skin and their floral-printed dresses and fine hats. The road they walked on, however, was not painted smoothly but seemed to have something mixed into the paint, like sand. I knelt on the sofa and got close to it, touched it, and I saw that the artist had mixed something into the paint to create the road. "What is it, Jackson?" I asked.

"Crushed oyster shells mixed into the paint," he said. "Kind of unusual, I know." He left me there so he could tend to the other visitors.

I backed away slowly, trying to take it all in, then turned to my right and saw a smaller painting on thick cardboard, framed crudely in what looked like bark and small branches glued together. It was of a little boy sleeping peacefully under an oak tree—curled up in its shade, his arms crossed high on his chest, his hands resting just beneath his chin. It was Rooster.

And then, I turned to my left, and on a wall in the dining room area, there was another painting on some type of cloth. I walked over and reached out to it—barely touching the handmade, white wooden frame that looked like it had once been part of a windowsill. It was a painting of a front porch with white rattan furniture and a red tin roof. Gibson Island. A window was open on the porch with filmy, white sheers slightly parted. On one side of the window, inside the shady interior of the house, there was a dark-brown face of a woman with a handkerchief tied on her head, her ear leaning to the open window. On the other side of the window, on the porch sitting in the white rattan chair, was a white lady, and I knew this was my great-great-grandmother,

Genevieve. *"Things are not always as they seem,"* I heard Nannie say over my shoulder. I turned, half-expecting to see her, but no one was there.

I realized I wasn't breathing. I looked around for an explanation, but people were talking and eating, and I was left alone. I took a paper cup of sweet tea from the dining room table and wandered to the back porch to get some air. "Nannie," I whispered. "Where are you?"

There was a chicken coop and a black-and-white dog in the backyard, and over to the far side of the porch was an old picnic-type table with small pails and tubes of paint and brushes carefully laid out. Jars of oyster shells and dirt and pebbles were lined up on the paint-spattered floor, and stacks of white cloths were draped over a wooden bench, and the smell was oddly strong and nice at the same time. There on a stool, sitting in front of a homemade easel bound tightly with cloth, was Lumpy, her elbow bent oddly into the air, painting with quick movements—purple flowers that draped down the front and along the sides like wisteria. I thought of Daduh and her favorite color, the purple apron Nannie had given her, and the new Christmas sweater she'd gotten with the purple flowers across the shoulders. Lumpy turned to look at me, her dark face tear-streaked with long, salty-white lines, pausing with a paintbrush in her hand, purple paint landing in little, sloppy drips onto her skirt. Then, she turned away and went back to painting.

Jackson and Ruby explained to me that day that Lumpy had been painting since she was a little girl, making her own colors and brushes out of anything she could find. Jackson and Ruby bought her real paint now, so she wouldn't have to make it anymore, but Lumpy still insisted on adding crushed oyster shells and rocks and flowers to it, and they figured that's what made it special. Jackson said that growing up, he never thought of Lumpy as his mother because she was always a little different and couldn't take good care of him and Gloria. Daduh was the one who really raised him, but he loved his mother and believed that God gave her a gift. He said now that Daduh was gone, he and Ruby were going to have to make some changes so they could look after her. I left Daduh's house with all kinds of questions and feelings in my head. This was not what I expected at all. When they learned about Lumpy's paintings, Mama and Daddy were almost speechless on the way back to Gibson Island.

"Who would have ever thought that about Lumpy?" Mama finally said. "And to see a painting of my great-grandmother in her house? That was just amazing. You know, Jim, we should tell Judith Moore about her. Somebody needs to see this artwork. This is really a gift."

It was strange to come back to Gibson Island after Daduh's funeral. It was like her second home, where she'd grown up and worked her whole life. Being at her house with her family was special for me. I liked seeing her dishes and pots and pans, seeing her prayer books by the sofa and the hooks on the wall by the back door with her cleaning aprons hanging on it. I wondered what it was like for Daduh to live in that house with her daughter who everyone knew was so slow and couldn't work, whom people called lazy and stupid, but who really was an artistic genius. It must have been the strangest kind of secret. Nannie was right again. Things are not as they seem. Not at all.

When we got back to the island, we found the boys working in the garden they had created out by the tractor shed, and Aunt Alicia rushed inside to change into her work clothes. She was teaching them how to build a fence to keep the critters out. It seemed to me it would be a lot easier to keep critters away if she didn't feed dog-food kibble to the possums and raccoons at night. We hardly left her alone anymore, and she was getting more and more forgetful, but Aunt Alicia seemed to be her old self when she was outside working. Just the other night, she had gotten up in the middle of the night and put on her clothes so she could drive her tractor and work in the yard, so Daddy had to hide the keys and keep the sheds locked up. Mama said we were going to have to put cowbells on the doors around the house so we'd know when she was coming and going.

We had not seen Aunt Alicia so happy for a very long time, and we knew, for many reasons, we'd made the right decision to come back. It had been about six weeks now since our move from Bailey's to Gibson Island, and we were settling in quickly, just like old times, only now we were rearranging the rooms with our own furniture and brightening up the space with new curtains. Nannie's room was now my room, and I got to keep her yellow bedspread and her dresser and washbasin. Cynthia Cook insisted that she help Mama with some "modern decorating" and make some new curtains again since most of the windows were odd shapes, so I ended up with some very cheerful yellow-and-blue-striped ones that tied back with long blue ribbon.

That afternoon after the funeral, we made a big dinner. While Aunt Alicia dredged the chicken in flour for frying, Mama started making her red rice, and I cut out the cheese biscuits. Mama said, "Before we serve up for dinner, Genny, let's go sit on the porch for a few minutes." She lifted the strips of bacon with a fork and laid them on the paper towels to drain. She would crumble that up into the red rice at the last minute when it was finished baking in the oven.

We took our iced tea out to the front porch, and she told me right away. "Honey, Ellie is sick, and Aunt Marjorie is bringing her here to get better," she said. "I don't want you to worry, but it is something that will need some attention."

"What's wrong with her?" I asked, wondering how I didn't know this. I should have sensed it. Was that why she almost fainted when she was here?

"It looks like she has what's called Hodgkin's disease, so Dr. Meg has arranged for her to see the best people here at St. Francis. Right now, Ellie gets really tired easily, and she gets fevers a lot, which makes it hard for her to go to school. So, they're coming down here at Thanksgiving, and then we'll figure all this out and help her get her strength back."

"Is that why she was falling down so much?" I asked, and Mama nodded. "I'm worried. Are you worried, Mama?"

"Not anymore—because we have the best medical help right here. Now that we have a plan, everything will be okay. It's always good to have a plan. There's something else you need to know, too," she said. "Aunt Marjorie and Ellie and Sam are coming, but they are moving here for good from New York. Aunt Marjorie and Uncle Peter are getting a divorce." She watched my face for a reaction. This was a lot of bad news for one family, and I wished I could talk to Ellie right that minute. I had to admit, though, I felt oddly happy. I would have my sister right here with me, and I could help her get better.

"Poor Ellie," I said.

"She needs you," Mama said. *She needs you.* That's what Nannie had told me that night that Ellie was so sad. Nannie was trying to prepare me for what was going to be happening with the divorce and Ellie being sick. I should have paid closer attention. "We're going to be all together, and we're going to help them get through this." Mama put her arm around me, and we sat on the porch until Aunt Alicia came to the door and rang Nannie's old dinner bell.

Chapter Twenty-One

October 22, 1967

MARYLOU GRIFFIN SQUIRMED IN HER PEW excitedly because we weren't sneaking out after Communion this time. Scraping the Communion host off the roof of my mouth with my tongue, I bent my head down as if deep in prayer, working my way back in line to the pew in front of her. Her black leather shoes knocked in gratitude against the seat beneath me. On the way out, Thomas ran his finger along the crack in the windowsill beneath the stained glass of Mary and Joseph, and Mama gave him a dime to put in it. At the rectory, I sat next to Marylou in her wheelchair and had our regular juice and cookies. Lately, when we didn't sneak out of Mass early, I just sat next to her like that and talked to her.

"So, Marylou, how're you liking that new book I found for you on the Seven Wonders of the World? I'd like to know more about that Great Pyramid myself," I said. "Mrs. Pratt says she can get some more books on each of the wonders if you're interested." She grinned widely, twisting and locking her hands tightly up under her chin to keep them from moving while rocking her bent-over body back and forth in her wheelchair. "Hey, maybe I can come back over to your house some time and look through your telescope." And I could tell by her reaction that Marylou wanted me to do that real soon.

Father announced that the local town hall meeting was coming up that week and that they'd be talking about rebuilding the oyster factory and cannery—again. People shook their heads with concerned looks on their faces. Not only was the factory still considered a threat to the local way of life, it was owned by a man who'd tried to kill his own father and our family.

"Jim, I think I'll pop into that town hall meeting this week. You know I don't usually go to those things, but I don't like the sound of this talk. I just wish they would tear the whole thing down. When I think about what he did . . ." Mama's voice trailed off as we all got into the car.

"Well, he's locked up, Louisa, so that's the good news." Daddy looked at Mama as he started the car. "And lucky he is locked up, too, because I don't think I could control myself. I have to say, though, old Mr. Landry is still having a lot of trouble adjusting to it all—can't say as I blame him. He still has trouble believing his own son really wanted to kill him," Daddy said, pulling out of the church driveway.

"I might not ever find out exactly what he did to Mama, but I know the truth, and that will have to be good enough for now," Mama said, staring out the window. "I just wish I could send him to prison for that, too." She sighed deeply. "So, who's managing the property since Jeffrey's not around? Someone must be carrying his torch."

"No idea. I know it still belongs to Jeffrey Landry, but his father doesn't have any dealings with it. Jackson heard Jeffrey has some new partner looking over the place, maybe someone he met in prison," Daddy said.

Mama still stared out the window. "Oh, just what we need," she said.

"Maybe we can both go to the town hall meeting together and learn what's going on," Daddy said. "Doesn't look like this subject is going away any time soon."

As soon as we got back, James and I changed out of our church clothes because Curt and Rachel were coming over for a visit. Moving away had not been that hard on our friendship, thank goodness. We still found ways to go back and forth to each other's houses and rode the same bus to school. Their father's pickup truck pulled up in front, and I watched from the kitchen window as Daddy greeted Mr. Robertson and helped Curt and Rachel take their bikes off the back of the truck.

Grabbing a bag with some sandwiches and chips that Aunt Alicia had put together, I headed out with James to join them. The plan, we told Daddy and Mr. Robertson, was to take our bikes around Gibson Island, collect old bottles and whatever else we might find, and have a picnic. I held the bag up for proof. What we didn't tell them was that we were going to go over to the old oyster factory and explore.

I knew that going over to the oyster factory was not a good idea, but it was something Curt and Rachel and James and I had talked about doing for a long time. We rode our bikes down bumpy paths until we got as close as we could. It was low tide, and the oyster factory was half hidden by the tall marsh and surrounded by oyster beds.

I still got the creeps remembering what Mama and I had gone through. I saw the dead tree where we hid and where she told me about her dream, and I was grateful Mama had brought us down here to create a new space for the baby oak tree. She wanted us to forget about the bad things that had happened here, but today, my mind flashed back to Jeffrey Landry running after us.

"Hey, you okay?" Curt asked when he saw me stop suddenly, while Rachel and James continued ahead.

"Yeah. I'm just remembering what happened. It was so scary," I said. "Let's go. I want to see the factory close-up."

"Have you ever actually been over there?" Curt asked.

"No. We were never allowed," I answered. We parked our bikes in the woods and walked carefully along the oyster bed, and as our feet trudged through the mud along the river's edge, I could feel it seeping into my tennis shoes.

The old oyster factory was such an eyesore, as Daddy called it. I couldn't imagine that place being renovated and expanded next to Gibson Island. James and Rachel were already climbing up the steps to the wide landing that surrounded the building, carrying our lunch bag and looking for a place to have a picnic. There was a long wharf that led from the building all the way out into the marshy waters, and it had a covered area in the middle of it.

The factory doors were like barn doors — wide and high — and they had padlocks on them. The building was a lot bigger than I thought it would be. The paint was peeling off in sheets, and there were holes in the slanted roof. There were wooden planks and shucking platforms underneath the building, and there were old barrels and thousands of oyster shells that had been piled off to the side. Remembering some of the stories Nannie used to tell me about the oyster factory in the old days, I asked Daduh once about her father working at the factory.

"He worked God-awful long hours, and I was barely awake when he'd come home," she told me. It was late in the afternoon back in early October, and we sat on the screened porch off the red breakfast room. Daduh had to put her feet up on a red chair because they were swelling up so bad. "Back then, the factory worked people real hard, Genevieve, and sometimes it wasn't right. My daddy would come home with oyster shell cuts all over his hands and arms. They'd cut right through the gloves. He'd soak his hands, and my mama would wrap 'em up good, but they never healed all the way."

"Did you ever go over there, Daduh?" I asked her.

"I did. When I was a young'un, I worked there a few times when we needed the money bad. I remember clear as day all the mothers and fathers and children workin' till way late, and sometimes they'd do some singin' to help the time pass more quickly. We just did what we had to do. My mama worked here for the Gibsons, though, and when they found out I did some work over at the factory, they made her promise that would stop and gave her a raise to help out," Daduh told me. That made me feel better when she told me that part.

As Curt and James and Rachel headed down on the factory's wharf, I walked along the landing, avoiding the rotting floorboards. The dead smell of oyster shells was everywhere. There were no windows on the back end, but there was one that was half boarded up on the side, so I tiptoed up to peek in. Through the filmy glass, I could make out a huge room with long tables and barrels and hoses. There was no ceiling—just lots of pipes running across the top under the roof. I got a sick feeling in my stomach as I tried to see as much as I could through the window. Something was wrong with this place and not just because of what we'd been through with Jeffrey Landry.

Right before I pulled away, I saw a dark figure—a man with overalls on and rags wrapped around his arms. I could tell he was from a long time ago, and I knew, when I felt a rush of chills cover my body and my ears were filled with a buzzing sound, he was Daduh's father. For a second, I thought I heard children and women's voices coming from inside. The dark figure moved quickly across the big room and disappeared right in front of me, and I jumped, falling backward onto the landing and hitting my head on a stack of wooden pallets.

"Watch it!" Curt yelled, coming back from the wharf.

"I saw something," I said, scrambling up off the filthy floor and brushing off my jeans.

"I don't doubt that one bit," Curt said. "There are probably rats and raccoons and possums livin' inside this dump. You okay?"

"Yeah. I'm fine, just lost my balance when I saw it," I said, rubbing the back of my head.

"What was it, Genny?" Rachel asked, running up the steps to me.

"It looked like a person running across the room," I told them. James eyed me from the bottom of the steps and immediately started walking in the opposite direction.

"I'm not stickin' around here," he said, turning around and shoving his hands in his pockets. "Might be gypsies! Or worse—Jeffrey Landry's new partner."

"Okay, let's go, Genny. Come on, Curt. This place is spooky," Rachel added and walked off with James. Their walk started turning into a run.

"Curt. I saw a person—a man," I said again.

"I believe you," he said, and I could tell that he did, but he didn't really know what I meant. "Let's go. We shouldn't be here."

And we left the oyster factory, moving fast along the river's edge, not caring about the mud and the fiddler crabs dashing around us, not caring about the tide moving in so quickly, not caring that our sandwiches still sat in a big paper bag at the bottom of the factory's steps. All I knew was that I could feel this was a sad place, and while leaving it now was a good idea, it wouldn't make that feeling go away.

"Maybe it was an animal, like Curt said." James was breathless as he grabbed his bike from under the tree where we left them.

"A big animal," Rachel said. "Or maybe it is a person, someone who doesn't have any place to live."

Since we couldn't solve it, we changed the subject but decided we wouldn't tell anyone about what happened. James and I knew for sure we couldn't tell Mama and Daddy—that would only make them worry about us being out by ourselves. After Curt and Rachel left that day, I couldn't stop thinking about the oyster factory and what I'd seen. I wished I could talk to Mama about it, but that wasn't really a choice. All I could hope for was that Nannie would come visit me—and soon.

After I put my bike away, I walked onto the wharf, running my hand along the railing, and sat on the floating dock under the old green boat. I drew my knees up to my chest, and the long day's leftover warmth settled on my face, even as the sun disappeared behind gathering clouds.

Something was bothering me—like a mystery with lots of missing pieces. There was only one thing I knew for certain— Nannie loved Gibson Island, and she wanted me to feel the same connection she had. She *was* Gibson Island. And I was Gibson Island, too. I remembered our walk the day she went missing, and even then, I could feel there were going to be a lot of changes coming our way. There'd been plenty, that's for sure, and Nannie was always there to help me through them.

Today, though, I had an unsettling feeling of being alone. Even with James and Curt and Rachel earlier, I'd felt alone. From my place on the wharf—where Nannie used to fish and crab and where she told me so many of her stories—I looked around, across the marsh with its stalky reeds and grasses waving lazily at me, then toward the first bend in the Toogoodoo River, winding quietly away. I gazed up at the Silver Goddess trees, their arms stretching up to the Lowcountry's somber sky as if they'd just finished an afternoon nap.

Where was Nannie today, and why hadn't she been coming to me as much lately? How was I going to figure out things by myself? I had so much to think about since coming back to Gibson Island. There was this sad feeling about the oyster factory and what might be ahead. And now I'd seen someone from the past—Daduh's father. Was *this* going to start happening to me more and more? I didn't want to see or hear others. I just wanted to see Nannie and no one else.

I thought about Ellie—she was moving here soon, but she was so sick, and we didn't know what was ahead for her. I had things to tell Nannie. I wanted her to know I'd been selected to write for the school newspaper and was going to publish my first article, but I really wasn't sure I was the best person for that job. I wanted to talk to her about Curt because he seemed to like me a lot more than just a friend. And I still had questions about Joe—I thought about him every day and wondered if I would ever see him again.

Most of all, Nannie had said I was supposed to help Mama see the truth about her gift, but I was very worried that the gift Mama and I shared was what was pushing us apart. I was scared. I couldn't do all this by myself. I began to panic thinking that I might not have Nannie forever. How could I do anything ever again without her?

That afternoon on the wharf, I waited and waited for her to come, but she didn't. I called her name. I pleaded for her to answer me. Maybe she was telling me I had to grow up now and be strong without her. I was grateful when the hard, angry rain started and the sharp pellets hit my face. That was much better than crying.

Chapter Twenty-Two

October 24, 1967

ON THE DAY — ON OCTOBER 24 — I woke up in her room at Gibson Island, and sitting on the side of the bed just as the sun was starting to rise, I asked out loud, "Where are you, Nannie?" Today, especially, I needed her.

I walked down the stairs and out to the wharf, and I saw her there — not Nannie, but Mama.

"I thought you might get up early today," she said. We sat together on the bench at the end of the wharf in our robes and slippers, like it was the most natural thing in the world for us to do. But it wasn't. We still had trouble talking together, especially on the wharf.

"I'm so sorry, Genevieve," she said quietly and walked over to the railing. I didn't understand what she meant, and I went to her, both of us standing there watching the October sun climb above the marsh and the glassy river. It was as still as it had ever been.

With both hands, she combed long, graceful fingers through her dark hair and then wrapped her arms around her body to comfort herself. "The dreams. I do know how it works."

"This is our time," I thought to myself. This is what I'd been waiting for! This was how it was going to happen. Time to talk—finally—about us, and Nannie. Then, Mama said with her head lowered, "I dreamed she was gone before it really happened. I couldn't find her in the water. And there was someone else in my dream who was there, who could have helped, but instead just watched her disappear into the waves. Of course, now I know that was Jeffrey Landry. None of us understand what really happened here to Nannie that day, but I know for sure he was there, too." I nodded in agreement.

"The truth is . . ." She stopped and raised her head. "I should have said something to her. I could have stopped it. I could have saved her. I keep trying to blame him, but I'm the one to blame. I'm the one who put her there," she said, her voice breaking at the end.

No. This wasn't the way it was supposed to be. Mama blamed herself? How could she? I thought she was going to say she understood her gift now and that she knew I had one, too—that we shared this special bond.

"Oh, Mama. Please don't say that. Please," I begged her. "You didn't understand your gift. You didn't know it would really happen that way. You have to forgive yourself."

"It's not about forgiving myself, Genny. It's her. I don't see how *she* can ever forgive *me*! I have done something unforgiveable." Her words shocked me.

"That's not true. That's not true at all," I said, looking up at her and touching her arm. She was still avoiding looking at me, and I walked to the other side of her, trying to get her attention. Now I understood what I was supposed to do. Nannie said the time would come. I felt the words pouring out. For so long, I'd wanted to tell her everything and for us to talk. "Mama, Nannie loves you! She tells me all the time she loves you. I can hear her. I can even see her sometimes. She tells me you're stubborn and need to pay attention because she's trying to tell you she loves you. It wasn't your fault. It was just supposed to happen that way. Nannie knew it before any of us . . . before you knew it, Mama. That's why she had that quote on her mirror. She dreamed it, too, and she knew it all along." I was talking so fast because I was afraid she would stop me. I fought back tears.

I wasn't sure Mama understood what I was trying to tell her—that I could actually see and hear Nannie—because she started talking right past me. "I keep seeing her in you—that's what makes it so hard," she said. Then she said it again, whispering, "I keep seeing her in you. I'm so sorry, Genevieve." Mama turned away from me and started walking.

There was nothing I could say to help her. She wasn't even going to try. The pain was just too deep. And I could feel it, too—I didn't want to feel what she was feeling, but I had no choice. This was how it was going to be. I would always feel her terrible sadness, and it was never going to get better for the two of us. I was always going to be the one who reminded her of her pain, who reminded her of her guilt. I knew for sure I couldn't do this by myself. Where was Nannie? Where was she? It was too much, and all I could do was stand there and watch Mama leave, willing her to come back.

Later, when I wrote on the last page of my red journal that night, I took my time. I wanted to remember every second on the wharf just as it really happened. The truthful story is that right at the very moment when her pain was too much for both of us and I thought she would leave me standing there, Mama paused, lifting her chin toward the water.

"Look, Genevieve," she said quietly, "a white wave. The river always makes that kind of wave when somethin's stirring it up from underneath."

A white wave. I turned quickly and saw the wave, and then I saw the dolphin. The dolphin, pure white like the crest of the wave it rode on — glistening and sleek, graceful and magical — as it cut through the glass and then dove beneath the water. I gasped and held my hand to my mouth to silence myself.

I saw it. I saw it.

I looked back to see if Mama saw it, too, but she was walking away from me again, down the wharf. I could feel the tears, hot and stinging, in my eyes.

But then, my mother slowly turned around and gave me the most beautiful, knowing smile I had ever seen. She held her hand out to me, and the three of us went inside.

THE END

Acknowledgements

ABOVE ALL, I THANK MY HUSBAND and best friend, Mike, who heard *The Truthful Story* for the first time many years ago when we were two English majors sharing our passion for writing and dreams for the future. He told me then that I had to write this book, and I finally did. He listened to and encouraged me through every chapter, supporting me with his enthusiasm, his feedback, and his great cooking. I am eternally grateful to my amazing children, Jessica and Daniel, for believing in me, for their patience, and for opening their hearts to powerful memories I've held so close and that I now pass on to them. To Luke and our sweet Michael and Thomas—how lucky I was to have those smiles and hugs throughout every step of this process. And thank you to Kourtney, who made me cry because she loved Genevieve like I did. I want to thank my three brothers, David, Chris, and Charles. They inspire me every day with how they live their lives and have shown that you can achieve anything you set your mind to, especially when it's the right thing to do. Thank you to my "sisters" for their endless support and for loving my brothers the way they do, and thank you to Debbie for noticing the cardinals and the white waves. To Laura, thank you for advising me in the early stages of the manuscript (when I was afraid to show it to anyone) and for giving me the courage to move forward. And a very special thanks to my brilliant editor, Lindsey Alexander, who truly understood what this book was about and whose gentle, honest guidance helped me get it across the finish line.

About the Author

HELEN STINE GREW UP NEAR CHARLESTON, in the heart of South Carolina's Lowcountry. After receiving an English degree from the College of Charleston, she raised a family, traveled extensively, and pursed a career in education, but she never lost touch with the powerful sense of place and family her childhood home imbued in her. *The Truthful Story* is a tribute to the land and the people that shaped her life. Today she lives in northern Virginia.